The
Brimstone
Chasm

B J MEARS

The Dream Loft

First published in Great Britain in 2013 by The Dream Loft
www.thedreamloft.co.uk

ISBN 13: 978-0-9574124-4-6

For Mum & Dad.

Special thanks:
To Joy for your support and for help with the blurb,
to Charlotte, for the *Tower of Doom*,
to my ever-diligent editor, Edward Field,
and to all the friends who have
helped along the way.

'And the beast was captured, and with it the false prophet who in its presence had done the signs by which he deceived those who had received the mark of the beast and those who worshiped its image. These two were thrown alive into the lake of fire that burns with sulphur.'

Revelation 19:20 (English Standard Version)

'If you're going through hell, keep going.'

Winston Churchill

Contents

THE CONTRAP

BACK

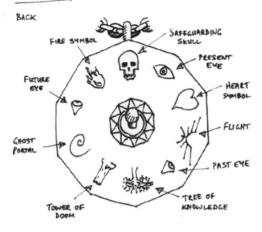

- FIRE SYMBOL
- SAFEGUARDING SKULL
- PRESENT EYE
- HEART SYMBOL
- FUTURE EYE
- FLIGHT
- GHOST PORTAL
- PAST EYE
- TOWER OF DOOM
- TREE OF KNOWLEDGE

SYMBOLS

- SAFEGUARDING SKULL — SAVES FROM DEATH
- PRESENT EYE — LOOK THROUGH WALLS, ETC (TELESCOPIC).
- HEART SYMBOL — ?
- FLIGHT — MAKES YOU FLY!
- PAST EYE — LOOK INTO THE PAST!
- TREE OF KNOWLEDGE — ASK IT A QUESTION & IT ANSWERS
- TOWER OF DOOM — ACHIEVEMENT INDICATOR
- GHOST PORTAL — IT'S A GHOST PORTAL!
- FUTURE EYE — LOOK INTO THE FUTURE
- FIRE SYMBOL — ?

FRONT

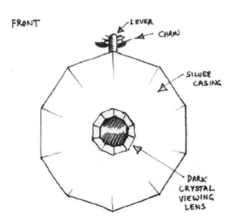

- LEVER
- CHAIN
- SILVER CASING
- DARK CRYSTAL VIEWING LENS

Prologue

Rain streaked glass. Tyler May edged into the room and crossed to the small window, breath fogging as she scanned the dark tempest. A noise behind her broke the near silence. She turned and levelled her Taser at a grey figure hunched in the shadows across the room.

"Albert?" She squinted, seeking details in the dark. A ghost youth; soot-stained, barefoot and wearing a shirt, waistcoat and shorts. Albert Goodwin, the chimney sweep. "Thank God!" She lowered the Taser.

Albert nodded and gave a half smile. He was still damaged but seemed a little improved, cradling one hand as though he'd broken a bone.

Can ghosts break bones? Surely they don't have *bones.* She wondered again about the way the ghosts appeared and disappeared. The stronger ones could make themselves visible to people. The strongest could even move physical objects. Tyler had seen Albert do this.

"'S'good t'see ya, Missy." Albert nodded towards the bay windows at the other end of the lounge and drew a finger to his lips. "Seems you got an admirer..." he whispered.

The dank figure outside the bay window looked in. Silvia Bates' pale, tortured face glistened in the rain, but the crazed, dark eyes that glared back at Tyler were those of the ghost, Violet Corpe. The storm had swept Bates' brunette glamour away and her usually lustrous, curling hair was now flattened, but the broad mouth that so easily twisted into a cynical smile and the imperial nose that brought a vulture readily to mind remained. An instant later the ghost-possessed woman was gone.

Tyler ran to the window to squint into the squalling night beyond the pitifully thin layers of glass. She turned at a heart-jolting thump from the front door, but caught sight of Bates dashing past the windows again.

What are you up to?

"She's trying to get in!" said Tyler, returning to the small side window.

"Can she?" asked Albert, his sooty, translucent face turning to her.

"If she really wants to. Plenty of glass. The kitchen window might even be open! I need to check the back door. It might have been left unlocked."

Chapman, where are you?

Tyler raced to the back of the house as Albert kept pace, slipping through furniture in his path.

"She knows you got that contrap," he said. "Does she know you could trap her ghosts inside?"

"Not sure what she knows. She's possessed by the ghost of a mad woman. Not that Bates was particularly sane to begin with..."

Tyler found the narrow kitchen window open, as her mother had left it, pulled it closed and latched it, a surge of nervous energy shaking her hands. No streetlights reached the back of the house. She worked in near darkness. Crept to the back door through the porch. Paused when she thought she heard something from outside.

"Albert, where is she?" she whispered.

"I'll go see, Missy. Wait there." Albert dashed away, dissipating through a wall, leaving Tyler alone in the dark porch. She didn't want to *wait there*. She edged closer to the door, listening intently, nerves jangling.

Rain and wind. Another sound, one too small to distinguish. *A human sound?* She couldn't be sure.

She eyed the doorknob with suspicion. Tentatively reached out. The key was still in the keyhole and she wondered if her parents had locked up before they'd left. A sound outside startled her. Someone *was* there. She bolted forwards to grasp the knob and turned the key to be sure it was locked. She tested the door: Secure! The door banged loudly. Her heart lurched. She involuntarily jumped away.

"Miss May?" a man called. "Miss May, are you alright?"

Tyler unlocked and opened the door to peer out at the stormy night and a man in a long black coat. He flashed a glossy MI5 badge as the wings of his coat flailed in the storm.

"Miss May?"

Tyler nodded.

"I'm Brown, Intelligence. Mr Chapman sent me. You're safe. We apprehended Bates a few moments ago."

You're safe...

The words meant nothing to Tyler May. She knew she would never feel *safe* again.

PART ONE

Orealia Stephensen

Two years had dragged, agonisingly, since Himmler's gloved ghost shrieked into the contrap and since the arrest, conviction and incarceration of Silvia Bates.

Two long years...

Tyler's parents, advised to move to a secure location for fear of targeted terrorist reprisals, had relocated to Brighton. Tyler also understood the need to get her own space. There had been arguments and much debate but, in the end, Tyler May, Melissa Watts and Lucy Denby had found a three bedroom apartment in Dulwich, London and had been allowed to move in together.

Tyler sat on the edge of her bed and turned the contrap in her hands. It was such a little thing, this silver contraption: a harmless-looking medallion with a large dark jewel set at the centre of one face. The whole thing fitted comfortably into the palm of her hand. Yet within this ghost machine resided numerous souls of the dead and not all of them were well-meaning. Along with an immeasurable number of Jewish ghosts was a seemingly random collection of ancient individuals, many of whom Tyler had already met. She did not know *how* they had all found their way in.

But there were also Nazi ghosts in the contrap.

"It's strange to think you put Adolf Hitler in there *and* Joseph Goebbels, the once Reich Minister of Propaganda in Nazi Germany," said Lucy, pulling on knee-high boots of supple, black leather to complete her goth outfit.

"And that you trapped Heinrich Himmler in there, too," Tyler replied. Himmler was Reichsführer during the Second World War and one of the most powerful leaders of Hitler's Nazi empire.

"Yeah, seems like a lifetime ago." Lucy checked her heavily-applied, black eyeliner and vampish lipstick in a vanity mirror. She rubbed blusher into gaunt cheeks. "Can I try the tree?"

"I guess. What you gonna ask?" Tyler passed across the contrap. Lucy set the switch to the *Tree of Knowledge* and peered into the crystal lens.

"I just want to see if it will tell me where the gloves are."

"Good luck with *that*."

"Where are the gloves right now?" Lucy asked the contrap and watched as the reply materialized like ink floating in mist.

In the hall, second drawer down, on the right

Tyler read the words.

"Thought so. What makes you think it's going to be any less annoying when you try?"

"I don't know. I just want to get on with things. You know?"

"Yeah. I know."

Lucy tried again.

"Where is the gloved ghost of Josef Mengele?"

Mengele is in the realm of the living

"I know that. Where about in the realm of the living?"

Mengele is in the realm of the living

Lucy tried with the other named ghosts: Adolf Eichmann, Reinhard Heydrich and, lastly, Adolf Hitler. She received the same answer to each in turn.

"Damn thing's like a scratched CD. She gave up, tossed the contrap back to Tyler and headed for the door. "Oh well. *Catch you later.*"

Tyler shuddered and called after Lucy.

"Don't say that! You know it freaks me out, Mojo." Lucy closed the door before Tyler had finished.

Tyler had trapped other Nazi ghosts in there too, and a handful of reveries and so this small, insignificant thing she now held had turned out to be not so insignificant after all. Quite the opposite. It had become *the most* significant thing in her life.

Of the six Nazi ghosts, *gloved* with missing kids and loosed upon the world, three remained at large. The last two years had been the most frustrating years of her life so far, because the gloves had gone to ground. Josef Mengele's tracer had either ceased to function or he had found and destroyed it. Neither her boss, Chapman, nor any of his security service agents had succeeded in finding as much as a glimmer of the gloves' unnatural, bluish skin.

Chapman phoned, rambling his way to the point. Finally he announced, "I'm sorry, Ghost. I've had to close investigations into the Urubici Castle." And with that bombshell detonated, he hung up.

Chapman had investigated the new-gothic castle in the mountains of Brazil where Lucy had *nailed* Himmler, but the initial probing had only proven the castle and its occupants to be a legitimate business, owned by a wealthy, international entrepreneur. Tyler was unsurprised to learn the place had become lawful and

3

devoid of Nazis overnight. She'd seen it happen before at the NVF headquarters in London.

She swore and looked again at the contrap in her hands, turned it to study the rear face with the ten incised symbols wondering for the hundredth time what the two symbols, that seemed to do nothing, were for. She set the central switch to the heart symbol and flipped the contrap to look into the crystal only to see nothing but dark, smoky glass. She pulled the little lever around the side of the silver casing but still nothing changed. Switching to the flame symbol she tried the same thing, but that, too, had no apparent effect on anything.

The flame and heart icons mocked her.

Whilst Tyler and her team were twiddling their thumbs at school, who could say what the remaining Nazi gloves were doing?

Tyler knew it could be nothing good.

She changed into running gear and left the apartment navigating streets of London at a jog until she hit the track on the service facility where, for the last year, Chapman had found them places on a course run by MI6 to continue their training in the Secret Service in a more official capacity. That was something, at least. She opened up, pumping legs and enjoying the sensation of her muscles stretching.

There had been a change in Tyler's physiology also. She'd become a woman in that time, filling out in places that had previously been less curvaceous and her face had become more streamlined so that, now, her friends told her she looked less like Sanya Richards-Ross and more like Beyoncé. Boys fled from her, threatened by her striking looks and confidence, except the ghost of Albert Goodwin, who spent every night faithfully watching over her as she slept.

She had kept up her gymnastics training and was as fit as she had ever been. Most Saturday mornings were spent on the training fields, enjoying her favourite disciplines: running, long jump, and hurdles. She could throw a javelin further and more accurately than most of the men she trained alongside. She frequently spent time on the punch bag in the gym, venting frustration - longing to get to work - to track down the three remaining gloves and rid the world of their presence.

Tyler pushed herself hard, feeling the burn.

She reached home, showered and dressed before taking out the old, creased, dog-eared list; something she did often.

Adolf Hitler	*gloved with Kylie Marsh (deceased)*
Heinrich Himmler	*gloved with Freddy Carter (alive) SAFE*
Josef Mengele	*gloved with Steven Lewis (alive)*
Reinhard Heydrich	*gloved with Susan Ellis (alive)*
Joseph Goebbels	*gloved with Emily Stanford (alive) SAFE*
Adolf Eichmann	*gloved with Harry McGrath (alive)*

Artefacts Acquired

Heinrich Himmler	√
Josef Mengele	√
Adolf Eichmann	√
Reinhard Heydrich	√
Joseph Goebbels	√

Find out what has become of Adolf Hitler

Begrudgingly, she added a question mark next to Hitler's name, no longer sure he was in the contrap. She thought for a while before adding another item to the list.

Find the missing chapter

The chapter of Zebedee's book, *Ghost Haunting*, was still missing, but Tyler wondered if it held a clue that might help her figure out what the last two symbols of the contrap were for. The problem was, she would have to find it first. She recalled the *Tree of Knowledge* telling her the missing pages were 'on the move'.

She set the contrap to the *Ghost Portal*, looked into the crystal and called for Zebedee, watching mist spiral. He soon stepped sprightly out of the ever-present miasma, tailcoat flapping, tapping his brass-handled cane and greeting her with a merry tip of his top hat.

"Good day to you, Miss May." Zebedee smiled at her through his extensive, grey beard and lit his long ghost pipe with a lucifer.

"Hi, Zebedee."

"How's young Albert?"

"He's fine, though I'm not sure his hand will ever fully recover. It's been two years now..."

"We ghosts are, in part, memory, you see? Albert needs time to forget his attack and remember how he used to be. As they say, time..." Zebedee looked away pensively.

"Heals all wounds?"

"Indeed. What they did to him in the castle was diabolical. Do you know, before that incident it was unheard of for ghosts to harm other ghosts in this way? Poor lad. It's madness."

"I guess that, before then, ghosts weren't really enemies with other ghosts. Seems a lot of things have changed."

"Yes, the balance has somehow shifted. Quite worrying, really."

"Zebedee, I wanted to ask some more about your old book, *Ghost Haunting*."

"Oh, yes? Ask away, dear girl. Ask away. Such a shame I never lived to see it published." He puffed enthusiastically on his pipe and adjusted his monocle to peer at Tyler. "Though, I can't guarantee I'll remember anything."

"It's about the chapter you called *The Dangers of Ghost Haunting*, the one that was missing from your book." Zebedee's eyes widened and he blew out an engulfing stream of smoke as he listened. "Do you remember much about that chapter?" asked Tyler. "It was torn out from the copy I had and a different page was taped in its place. On the page someone had scrawled 'Ghost Haunting is extremely hazardous. In no circumstances should anyone attempt to do it, ever.' Do you know who wrote that?"

"I'm sorry but I don't. I know nothing of the page that was added later. I did write the original chapter, certainly." He produced more smoke which plumed about to mix with the surrounding vapour.

"Right. Well, can you tell me what the original chapter said?"

Zebedee considered this while gazing up into the endless, dark expanse above him. He was so long before replying that Tyler spoke again.

"Zebedee? The missing chapter?"

"Yes, yes. Of course, the missing chapter. Er, no. Not really. I don't recall much of it. I know that at some point I became concerned that my book might lead folk into dark and dangerous places. I think *that* is when I had a pang of guilt and had the notion to write some manner of warning, but what the chapter actually included... Hmmm. Let me see..."

"Think, Zebedee! It could be really important. Somebody ripped out the pages. Why would someone do that?"

"My dear girl, I simply do not know."

"Do you remember anything at all about the chapter?"

"It was, as the title suggests, a passage on the dangers involved in ghost haunting. Like I said before, much of my book was codswallop. Utter nonsense."

"There must be *something*..."

"I recall writing something about demons and ghosts and the like, and that people should really think twice before endeavouring to communicate with entities of which they have no knowledge. After all, it *is* a very foolhardy thing to attempt. *That* part, I know for certain, is good, old-fashioned common sense, but beyond that I really don't recall." Zebedee puffed out an enormous cloud and, as she watched the smoke disperse, Tyler noticed he had taken out his pocket watch and was studying it keenly.

"My, my. Is that the time? I really must be going!" He made a hasty retreat into the depths of the portal. Tyler watched until she could no longer see his top hat bobbing away and then switched the contrap to the *Safeguarding Skull* setting.

Zebedee's watch had stopped ticking sometime in the late nineteenth century. She didn't know why, but her friend, Zebedee Lieberman, was hiding something. And this was *not* the first time she had sensed it.

*

It took Tyler two days of contemplation before feeling ready to tackle Zebedee again. She trawled through everything she could recall about the book and all that Zebedee had ever told her about the contrap. For several hours she racked her brain for the name of the contrap's next owner, the one following Zebedee, and eventually she remembered it. Zebedee had told her about the day he'd discovered the meaning of the *Tree of Knowledge* - that it answered questions - but that it was the ghosts within the portal who actually did the answering and, therefore, it could not be fully trusted. He'd also told her about Travis, the Norman knight, who had conned Zebedee into the contrap, but it was Zebedee's housecleaner who had let herself into his house to find his dead body hunched over his desk in his study, the contrap still in hand.

Orealia Stephensen.

Orealia had claimed the contrap as her own and had also kept the manuscript Zebedee had been working on. She'd had access to all his notes and probably learned, very quickly, everything Zebedee had ever known about the contrap. She even completed Zebedee's book by adding some notes of her own at the end, but had she printed a single copy of the book and then torn out a chapter? And if so, why?

Tyler began a friendly conversation with Zebedee, knowing that if she stood a chance at getting anything from him, she'd need to be a little sneaky. She asked about what life was like when he'd been alive and she talked about Albert, which always seemed to put Zebedee at ease. She slipped in a subtle question about Orealia.

"Do you remember Orealia well?" She did her best to make it sound like an innocent query and, to her delight, Zebedee didn't falter.

"Oh yes, I remember her, though she was only my housekeeper, you understand. I never knew her well."

"Oh, I see. And where did you live, back in those days?"

"Why, London, of course. Did I not say?"

Tyler shook her head.

"I lived in Knightsbridge. Number eleven, Raphael Street, to be precise."

"And Orealia? Where did she live?"

Zebedee took the pipe from his mouth and gave Tyler a long, appraising look.

"Now, why would you want to know *that*?"

I've been sussed.

Zebedee's reticence was instant. He forced a smile and quickly turned to leave, calling out over his shoulder.

"Must dash; things to do, people to see."

*

Melissa was glad to accommodate Tyler's request for help as always. The compulsory physical training had been good to Melissa over the last years. She had slimmed down and been left with sultry curves. Boys who had avoided her because of her frightening IQ now did so for a second reason. She was out of their class, a killer blonde. The only exception to this rule was Freddy Carter, a thin youth with an unruly mop of blond hair, who had never been intimidated by her powers, and was so used to being the fool that her superior intelligence left him unaffected. Freddy had other skills. His mind did not work like other peoples'. They had taken a shine to one another ever since he had been freed from the gloved ghost of Heinrich Himmler. As Tyler's best friend, Melissa brought added value to the team. Her IT abilities and knowledge were second to none and specialised training had helped her to hone the art. The laptop and extended PC system was already booted up and ready to go when the three girls sat down before it, Melissa and Tyler cradling mugs of hot chocolate. Lucy sipped strong, black coffee. No sugar.

"More research? *Excelente.* So, what's this all about?" Lucy asked.

"Family history stuff," said Tyler. She explained her theory about where Zebedee's book may have gone after his death. "The book survived - well, at least until it passed to me and was burned in the warehouse fire - so it must've been handed down from person to person. Between it being printed by Orealia and it passing to you and then me, several other people must have owned it. I need to know who. Then I need to find out which one of them tore out the pages. If I knew *that*, I could seriously start to look for them."

"You don't think that Zebedee has a good reason for holding something back about the pages?" Melissa asked. "That it might be in your best interests not to know? I mean, he *is* your friend. He's saved your life more than once."

"Good point, but I want to know anyway. He's a ghost. Maybe he doesn't quite understand. I sometimes wonder if he's all there..."

"He's not *all there*," said Lucy. "He's a ghost."

Tyler shrugged a mirthless smile.

"Okay. We'll start with Orealia."

"Right. She was his housekeeper and Zebedee lived at number eleven, Raphael Street in Knightsbridge. Orealia couldn't have lived far away. A housekeeper in the nineteenth century wouldn't have owned a car or a carriage."

Melissa called up ancestry.co.uk on her laptop and typed Orealia's name into the search window. She typed Knightsbridge, London in the 'place' window. When she hit 'search', the system displayed a list of surnames with only the initials of first and last names. Twelve pages of names. Tyler contemplated the many variables. Any one of them might have been the Orealia Stephensen she was looking for. She turned to Melissa.

"It's going to be a long night."

*

While Melissa was busy on an IT training day and Lucy was being tested to extremes on a logistical armed assault exercise, Tyler bought a small, black notebook with a soft, leather-like cover. Arriving home from the store she took it out and turned to the first blank page where she wrote 'History of the Contrap'. On the next page she scribbled fervently for the next few minutes, retelling Zebedee's initial account of how the contrap had come into his possession. She filled page after page with this part of the history, pausing every now and again to recall a name or a detail so that the account might be as complete as she could make it. She spent several minutes trying to remember the names on the letter Zebedee had found with the contrap in the small, secret drawer of the antique, walnut, Tuscan cabinet, but at length she was fairly sure she had recalled it all correctly. She reread her rendering of the note.

My dear Ramla,

Please keep this trinket safe until my return. If anybody comes looking for me, you must deny all knowledge of me for your own sake.

Eucrates Onuris IV

As far as she knew, that was pretty much what the note had said. She could not be sure how it had ended, whether it had said *with love*, or *yours truly*, or any such valediction because, to her recollection, Zebedee had never mentioned one, but she was left with the impression that Ramla and Eucrates were lovers, if not married. Apart from that, the note gave little away. Tyler continued her account and ended the section with everything she knew about Orealia Stephensen. It didn't take long. She looked over the few skimpy facts before turning to a fresh page and beginning a flowchart, which was little more than a list of names, notes and rough dates. She began with the Norman knight, Travis, because he seemed to know so much about the contrap that she assumed he may well have once owned it.

Past Owners of the Contrap

↓

Circa 1066   *Travis*
                           (from Normandy)?

↓

The Saxon who murdered Travis?

Here Tyler left a large gap to show an area of unknown lineage. She used her laptop to Google 'antique, walnut, Tuscany cabinet' and found a search result listing a piece matching Zebedee's cabinet with the hidden drawers. The cabinet was listed as seventeenth century, so Tyler continued with a new line.

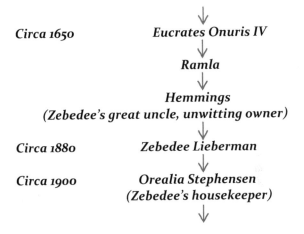

Circa 1650   ***Eucrates Onuris IV***

Ramla

Hemmings
(Zebedee's great uncle, unwitting owner)

Circa 1880   ***Zebedee Lieberman***

Circa 1900   ***Orealia Stephensen***
(Zebedee's housekeeper)

Here Tyler left another gap and considered the flowery pattern of Izabella's dress from memory. She decided it was like something she'd seen a woman wearing in a TV World War Two dramatization and so settled upon the rough date of the end of the war.

Circa 1945   ***Izabella***

Here Tyler left a third gap, not knowing who the contrap had passed to after Izabella.

Leopold Bagshot McGuire

Lucy Denby

Tyler May

When Tyler finished she was surprised by the number of names and dates already on the list, even though some of them were little more than guesswork. She closed the notebook and awaited Melissa's return.

The Heirloom

Tyler awoke, curled on the sofa, and watched as Melissa closed the door and crossed the room to dump her bags on the floor.

"Brain overload," Melissa sighed, collapsing into an armchair.

"Well, you can't relax yet. We've work to do. Did you find anything out for me?"

"Oh. Orealia Stephensen. Yes!"

Melissa's mobile rang and Tyler had to wait for what felt like an age while Melissa cooed to Freddy Carter.

"Orealia?" Tyler prompted when Melissa ended the call.

"Right. I did some digging on a certain Orealia Anna Stephensen who lived at the other end of Raphael Street, just a short walk from Zebedee's old house. I guess she must have rented a room. She was there around the end of the nineteenth century, died 27th March 1891. Thought she was a hot contender."

Tyler took out her notebook, turned to the timeline page and added the date below Orealia's name. She also jotted down her middle name in brackets.

"What ya' doin'?"

"I'm writing it down on my list of previous owners of the contrap."

"How do you know it's the right Orealia?"

"Why would you be telling me about the wrong Orealia?"

"Just checkin'."

Melissa was annoying when she'd been around Freddy. It was like someone had removed a vital synapse from her brain.

"*Is* it the right Orealia?" pressed Tyler.

"Oh, yes. It's the right one. I wasn't sure until I stumbled upon a few other relatives further down the family tree. Found a name that rang bells."

"Who?" Tyler asked, intrigued.

"We'll get to that in a minute." Melissa rose from her chair and switched the kettle on. "You're gonna like this. When Orealia died she had only one remaining close relative alive, a sister named Myah, whose surname became Dorf when she married, so anything Orealia owned must have passed to her."

Tyler made notes.

"Myah Dorf died soon after Orealia, without having any children. The closest family member I could trace who may've stood to inherit anything was the husband of a cousin. His name was Ivan Kremensky."

"Wait a minute. Slow down." Tyler tried to catch up with her notes.

"Kremensky was widowed at the age of thirty but, and this is where it gets interesting..." Melissa delved into her jeans' pocket and drew out a folded piece of notepaper. She unfolded it and checked some details. "...Ivan Kremensky had two children before his wife died. Both girls. One was named Valentina, the other, *Izabella*."

Tyler stopped writing to look up from her notebook.

"Izabella Kremensky.   A Russian woman named Izabella!"

"Yep."

"It's Izabella from the contrap. It has to be."

"That's what I thought, too."

"Okay, okay." Tyler added the two sisters' names to her timeline, which had filled out considerably in the last few minutes.

Circa 1650	*Eucrates Onuris IV*
	↓
	Ramla
	↓
	Hemmings
	(Zebedee's great uncle, unwitting owner)
	↓
Circa 1880	*Zebedee Lieberman*
	↓
~~*Circa 1900*~~	*Orealia Stephensen (Anna)*
DOD: 27th **March 1891**	↓
	Myah Dorf (Orealia's sister)
	↓
	Ivan Kremensky (father of)
	↓
Circa 1945	*Izabella*
	(& Valentina) Kremensky
	↓

Melissa made hot chocolate.   She stirred while carrying it back to her chair.

"Of course we could be wrong, but there's a very simple way you could find out..."

"Speak to Izabella," Tyler concluded. "All I'd need to do is ask for her surname."

Melissa nodded with a self-satisfied grin.

*

A deep fog had settled over the dark realm beyond the crystal. Izabella, eyes glazed by cataracts, peered distrustfully out at Tyler.

"What do you want?" Her Russian accent was strong.

"Nothing much," said Tyler, deciding to meet Izabella's bluntness measure for measure. "I just wanted to know your name."

"You already know my name. It is Izabella."

"Your surname?"

"Why would you want to know my surname?"

"Oh, I'm doing a little research into the previous owners of the contrap, compiling a list. You don't have to tell me. It won't really make any difference. You're already on the list, you see."

Izabella scowled and screwed up her lips, for a moment undecided. She shrugged, shifting her considerable girth.

"Alright then. I don't suppose it can hurt. My name is Izabella Kremensky."

"Thanks," said Tyler. "Did you tear out the pages of Zebedee's book?"

"No. It wasn't me. I only learned of Zebedee's ridiculous book after I died. May I go now?"

"Of course. Thanks for your help."

Tyler switched back to the skull symbol and turned to Melissa.

"She's a *real* charmer."

Lucy arrived home exhausted from training and, ten minutes later, fell asleep on a couch. Albert watched London from the one window in the apartment with a decent view.

"What will you do now?" he asked, shifting attention from the busy streets of lamp-lit rush-hour.

"I need to do more research on this particular Orealia Anna Stephensen. I want to know if she was the one who tore out the pages from the book. If she did, then maybe the pages were inherited along with the contrap." Tyler added some questions to her old list.

Who tore out the pages?
Why?

She tucked the list inside the notebook and closed it.

*

Tyler worked undisturbed in the lounge. The other girls had gone to bed and Albert was content to watch her as she surfed websites. She registered on a newspaper archive site and worked her way through page after page of archaic black and white print from late March, 1891. Her area of particular interest was obituaries and by midnight she had read so many that her eyes were starting to burn. She was about to call it a night when a name, highlighted in bold and in the old style font of *The Times*, dated 28th March, grabbed her attention.

Orealia Anna Stephensen of Pakenham Tavern, Raphael Street, daughter of the late Douglas Andrew Stephensen, died yesterday morning under suspicious circumstances. Miss Stephensen's body was found baring no outward trace of injury. It is thought Miss Stephensen died from a weak heart and it is the conclusion of Dr. Williams, the reliable physician, that she may have suffered considerable shock. A police investigation is ongoing due to the aforementioned questionable circumstances. Miss Stephensen, who spent her earlier years as a housekeeper but later in life experienced her own *rags to riches* story, leaves all her worldly possessions, including the tavern and a substantial library of books, to her sister, Myah Dorf.

Tyler rubbed her eyes and carefully reread the last line. *A substantial library of books...* She copied the obituary, pasted it into a new document and saved it on her laptop in a file named Research.

She then searched the archive website for Myah Dorf, all thoughts of sleep dispelled. By one a.m. she had found Myah Dorf's obituary and had copied that to the file.

Myah Helena Dorf of 43, Ham Lane, daughter of the late Douglas Andrew Stephensen, fell to her death today under strange circumstances, in the grounds of St Mary's. It is thought she was exploring the church bell tower and may have slipped whilst taking in the spectacular view from one of the tower's open arches. Just how Myah entered the tower, which is kept locked at all times and was, indeed, found thus after the discovery of Myah's body, remains a mystery. It is not known at this stage who is to inherit Myah's vast wealth, which includes several London residences and taverns, and a vast and highly valuable library of books.

Tyler checked her notebook and looked up Ivan Kremensky in the archives. It was gone two o'clock in the morning when she found his obituary.

Ivan Frederick Kremensky of 16 North Street, son of Olaf Kremensky, died today by drowning. His body was pulled from the Thames at approximately three o'clock in the afternoon by local policeman, John Richards. It is unknown whether Ivan took his own life or if his death results from a tragic accident. It is hoped that the on-going police investigation will extrapolate the matter. Ivan will be sorely missed by daughters, Izabella and Valentina, who stand to fully inherit his substantial wealth and his impressive library.

_____

Tyler copied this obituary and added it below the others in her file. She checked her watch.
Can't stop now! Sleep will have to wait.
She searched for Izabella Kremensky.

_____

Izabella Olga Kremensky, previously of Harrogate, daughter of the late Ivan Kremensky, died recently during a sightseeing tour of Germany. Izabella, who enjoyed the early years of her life in London, emigrated to her ancestral homeland of Russia some years ago, where she continued to prosper. The University of London wishes to express its belated thanks to Izabella for her generously bequeathed library of more than four thousand books. The executor of the will would hear from any claimants with ancestral relations to Izabella, who leaves no apparent heir to her significant remaining fortune.

_____

Tyler told Albert what she'd learnt and went to bed. In the morning she planned to visit the University of London's library and she would need all the help she could get.

*

Lucy was not pleased to learn that she was to spend her Saturday stuck in a library, searching for a few dull pages of an old book.

"Is this really going to get us anywhere even if we find it?" she asked, before hurling a third throwing knife into the dartboard on the other side of the apartment lounge.

"Why do you have to do that in here?" asked Melissa. "If you hit the wall you can fix it yourself."

"Haven't missed the board yet," said Lucy, collecting her blades.

"I don't know if it'll get us anywhere," said Tyler. "I just know we have to try. The missing pages could tell us something really important. And there's a chance they could be in that library. I want to take a look anyway. There's nothing else to try until a glove is located. If the pages aren't there, I haven't a clue where they might be."

"Didn't you say the *Tree of Knowledge* told you the pages were *on the move*?" asked Melissa.

"It did, but it might have been lying. It also told me Hitler was going to kill me and I'm not dead. Well, not yet, anyway."

"Right. Freddy's coming to help. He'll meet us there," said Melissa. "Chapman seems pleased with his training progress. Says he's a lateral thinker, a good man to have on a team."

"Let's hope he can think his way around a library. What about Weaver?" Tyler asked Lucy.

"He can't make it. He's on a stakeout."

"Okay. Just the four of us, then. That'll have to do."

*

When Tyler stepped out of the black cab to look up at Senate House, the University of London's massive library building, she knew that four people would be nowhere near enough. Gleaming in the morning light, its white, window-lined façade towered over her and would have been more at home in New York.

"Here comes Mojo on the Bat Bike."

Lucy arrived, reigning in her matt-black, supermoto, modified *Aprilia* motorbike to a halt, slick tyres biting tarmac. She slipped her matching helmet off and jutted her chin in greeting.

Tyler looked from the building to Melissa.

"Seriously? This is Senate House?" she asked, as Lucy secured her bike. "You're telling me this place is a library?"

Melissa gave a sober nod.

"All nineteen floors. A total of fourteen main collections."

"*Main* collections?"

"That's what the website said."

"So presumably there're other collections?"

"Presumably," Melissa agreed. "There's a head of *Special Collections* listed on the site."

"I'm thinking 'needle, haystack'," said Lucy, eyeing the nineteenth floor.

"My thoughts precisely. You didn't bring the knives?" Tyler checked with Lucy.

"No weapons. Just like you said." Lucy held out her hands as if to prove she wasn't armed, tugged off black leather gloves and shoved them in her crash helmet.

"Good. This place is likely to have..."

Lucy interrupted. "...metal detectors on the doors. I know. Where's Pratt, I mean Freddy?"

Melissa gave Lucy an icy look.

"He just texted. He's already inside."

Floor 17

Hours felt like days and Tyler was bored with books and documents. She found an entire section of the library that was not properly ordered and began obsessively sorting. Fifteen minutes later Melissa found her and reminded her why she'd wanted to visit the library in the first place. Tyler ditched her compulsion to organise and returned to her search. By ten a.m. the team had collected document wallets and files from the *Historic Archives* and *Printed Special Collections* and were gathered around a table in an otherwise deserted end of the *Historic Collections* reading room on the fourth floor, systematically sifting through every possible item in the hope of finding Zebedee's missing chapter.

"Orealia's library must have ended up here and been mixed in with thousands of other books," said Tyler. Around her, the room was wall-to-ceiling bookshelves.

"Yes, but *Ghost Haunting* didn't end up in the library. Bagshot had it, so maybe the missing chapter didn't end up here either," said Melissa. "I suppose Bagshot might have found it here."

"Chapman had Bagshot's old place searched after Bagshot went into the contrap," Tyler explained. "I checked. Bagshot didn't have the missing chapter. At least, not when he died. Thing is, we still don't know when the pages were torn from the book. It could have been four years ago or a hundred." Tyler finished the pile of documents she was checking through and slid another pile into her workspace.

"Do you think Chapman is going to keep this whole thing quiet for long?" asked Lucy. "I mean, ghosts turning up everywhere, and we can't be the only people who've seen these Nazis at work. There must be others, surely."

"Who knows," said Freddy. "The Nazis probably kill anyone who finds out about them. Is Chapman trying to keep it under wraps to stop worldwide panic, or does he need to keep it quite because he hasn't enough proof of what's been going on?"

"Good question," said Melissa. "It's because he can't prove it. Every time we find an NVF location, the NVF sanitise the site. They're operating in a very clever, extremely organised, way. It's as if they've banked on being discovered; every place they work has a documented cover story and they slip away into the night, along with all evidence. He knows who's behind the funding, of course, but he can't touch them for the same reason. Not enough proof. If he tried to oust them he'd only create an international incident that would lose him his job and risk some kind of retaliation."

"But couldn't someone else expose them?" asked Freddy. "Someone unconnected to Chapman? Seems to me the world needs to wake up to what the NVF is doing. People can't defend against an attacker they don't believe exists."

Melissa and Lucy put their documents down and looked at each other.

"*We* could do it," they said in unison.

"*We* could do it without anyone knowing it was us," said Melissa.

"All we need is an untraceable cell phone," Lucy stated. "We can start an MSM social network campaign. Text a few people we know who are likely to support it. Get the message out there."

"You're right. If it's not come from Chapman, he can't be blamed for it. And once the truth is out there, no one can be held accountable if they can't trace the source. The freedom of speech laws will protect everyone else, just as long as the texts cannot be interpreted as inciting racial hatred. Which they wouldn't."

Clipped footsteps alerted the girls to the librarian's approach.

"May I remind you, this is a library? We run a no talking policy. Thank you."

"Sorry," whispered Melissa, wincing.

Freddy scribbled on a piece of notepaper as the librarian left the room. He turned the page for the others to read.

T.A.A.N. – *The Activists Against Nazism*

Melissa and Lucy nodded their approval. Tyler regarded them wearily.

"Are you sure this is a good idea?" she asked. "I'm sure Chapman knows what he's doing."

"Right," said Melissa, collecting documents from the table. "Guess we'd best get back to work. I'm going to check the database again for references."

Tyler left her pile of documents and took a seat next to Melissa as she accessed the library's immense list of books and manuscripts on the library website, in turn, accessed via the library's wi-fi. Melissa had already logged on and browsed the multitude of categories, so she knew her way around the system well enough. Tyler read a list of collections and was drawn to the *Historic*

Collections subcategories of *Archives & Manuscripts*: *Printed Special Collections*, *Palaeography & Manuscript Studies & Book Studies*. She also thought the missing chapter might have ended up filed under several of the *Research Collections: English Studies*, *History*, *Manuscript & Print Studies*, *Philosophy*, *Psychology* and *Religious Studies*. The possibilities were overwhelming.

"What do you think?" she asked Melissa.

"It could be anywhere, but my favourites are *Religious Studies*, *Psychology*, *Printed Special Collections* and *Print Studies*. *Ghost Haunting* was an historic book because, as far as we know, there was only ever one copy printed. Maybe it was a proof copy and for some reason the print run was never fully commissioned."

"That's it!" whispered Tyler, realising it made perfect sense. "That's what happened! Orealia Stephensen finished Zebedee's book and was going to have it printed. She had a proof copy run off the press but, for some reason, never ordered the book to be properly printed. Maybe that's when she died."

"Or she realised it gave away a little too much information about her new toy. If that's what happened, then it probably wasn't Orealia who tore out the pages. That was most likely done by one of the people who inherited the book later on. So this one copy that you had would have been a complete one-off. No other book like it anywhere in the world. An old book like that is going to be worth a *lot* of money. And it would be a collector's piece. So would a single chapter from the book." Melissa stared pensively at the laptop screen. "*Print Studies*. It has to be *Print Studies*. It's almost a museum piece. I can't see them cataloguing it under anything else."

"*Print Studies* it is," said Tyler. "Let's take a look."

They checked through the database for *Ghost Haunting* and for *Zebedee Lieberman*, and were disappointed when neither yielded any results.

"It's no good. It's not here. This is a waste of time,"

said Tyler.

"Wait a minute. What was the title of the missing chapter?" asked Melissa.

"*The Dangers of Ghost Haunting*."

Melissa entered this into the search but again there were no hits on the system.

"Sorry," said Melissa. "I'm not sure what else to try."

Tyler had an idea, then.

"Try *Izabella Kremensky*," she suggested.

Melissa typed and a moment later they were looking at a hit in the search results window, amazed.

"Well, what d'ya know? There she is. Izabella Kremensky - under *Contributors' Files*."

"I guess she was a contributor. She did give them her book collection."

"Duh. Of course. It says those files are stored in the Stack; the upper tower. You have to put in a special request for someone to retrieve anything from up there."

Tyler headed out of the room to find a librarian. She didn't intend to wait a day while an email-submitted request sat in a queue and someone absently pottered around in the Stack. She wanted to go herself. She found an assistant librarian - Lisa Reynalds - the name clearly marked on her library lanyard. Tyler brandished her MI5 badge as Melissa caught up.

"Lisa, you're going to help me retrieve a file from the Stack. Right now, okay?"

Lisa collected narrow glasses from her décolletage, gawked at the badge and then at Tyler.

"You want a file from the Stack? You have to fill out a request form via email."

Tyler shook her head.

"Not today. We need the file immediately."

"Immediately?"

Tyler and Melissa nodded.

"I'll have to check the system. You'd better follow me." Lisa led the way to a booth where a PC was networked into the system.

"What's the file?"

"It's a contributor's file. The name's Izabella Kremensky."

Lisa typed and then peered at Tyler over her glasses.

"That file's on floor seventeen. It's in a restricted zone and is not accessible to the public unless there are unusual circumstances."

"We're *not* the public," stated Tyler, waving her badge in Lisa's face. Tyler decided she did not like libraries or librarians.

"Is that thing real?"

"Try me."

"Give me a minute," said Lisa, grabbing a phone from the desk to make a call. Tyler and Melissa waited with growing impatience as she explained the situation to her superiors. When she had finished, she replaced the receiver and stared at it for several moments before addressing the girls.

"You'd best follow me."

They took an elevator to floor seven and then ascended further floors in a cranky, old lift with a hinged door, as an awkward silence pervaded. The lift clacked and creaked as they rode. Lisa seemed uncomfortable about the arrangement and Tyler wondered what had been said at the other end of the phone. The lift eventually groaned to a halt at floor seventeen and Lisa took them through to a corridor, up a staircase and into a large, dusty, unlit storage room full of bookcases. Wind moaned against the outer walls of the Stack.

"This place is creepy," whispered Melissa. Lisa heard her.

"You're not the first to say that. The Stack is quite famous for its ghost stories. In fact, some of the staff refuse to come up here alone."

Motion-sensing lights blinked on as they walked, illuminating their immediate surroundings, but leaving the rest in shadows.

"The file you want will be in one of the boxes on the

top of the shelves," said Lisa. She scoured the room for the right bookcase and led the girls to a place between shelves where she checked reference numbers and pointed to a single brown box. Tyler fetched a set of steps and climbed up to reach it. She brought it down and lifted the lid, already knowing it was empty by its weightlessness. She met Lisa's eyes over the void.

"You sure this is the right box?" asked Melissa.

Lisa checked the file number on the box and nodded.

"This box is supposed to contain everything in the system relating to contributor Izabella Kremensky. It's supposed to hold the personal material. Sometimes that's diaries or letters, you know, stuff like that."

"Then where is it?" asked Tyler.

"If it's not here, I don't know why and I don't know where it is."

"I need you to find out. Can you do that?" asked Tyler, brimming with frustration.

Lisa nodded nervously.

"We'll need to go back downstairs. I need to access the offline system to double check that someone hasn't borrowed the file, privately."

"Let's go."

Back in the *Historic Collections* reading room on the fourth floor, Lisa accessed the database again and checked details, seated at a PC. She frowned as Lucy and Freddy joined the gathering in the corner of the room, to see what was going on. Lisa exited the system.

"I'm sorry. There's no record of anybody requesting or borrowing that file. I don't know what to tell you."

"There's no record?" said Melissa.

"It's like a ghost has taken the file," said Lisa. "It's just vanished from the system."

Tyler and Melissa exchanged looks.

"Okay," said Tyler. "Don't worry. I'm sure none of this is your fault. Can I speak to your superior? Is there a head librarian - someone in charge?"

Lisa blanched.

"I suppose I could fetch Mr Hatherow."

"Yes. Please do."

Lisa tried calling Mr Hatherow on the phone but soon gave up and, with increasing agitation, set off to find him on foot. When the staccato rhythm of her heels became a distant echo Tyler turned to Melissa.

"Can you hack this system? Get in behind the public database? I swear she knows more about this than she's letting on."

Melissa slipped into the seat before the PC and set to work.

"See what you can find out. I want to know who has that file and why." Tyler turned to Freddy and Lucy. "Keep a lookout for the librarian and Mr Hatherow from the door."

"What if a ghost really did take it?" asked Lucy.

"Knowing what we know, that's always a possibility."

Freddy and Lucy left to keep watch.

"They've a secondary database, one that's protected from internet access," said Melissa. "It's fairly well hidden. Think I can get in, though."

"Do it."

"Let's see now. There's a pretty hefty firewall." Melissa laboured with passwords and system software that Tyler did not understand. Minutes ticked by and Tyler thought the database was to remain a secret but finally Melissa broke into the hidden filing system and searched for Izabella's file. Lucy arrived at the desk to report, with Freddy close behind.

"She's coming back. She has a guy with her."

"Almost there," said Melissa, fingers traversing the keyboard at high speed. She stopped to read and then photograph the screen with her iPhone before exiting the system. She left the desk as Lisa and a tall, impeccably groomed man with a walking stick hobbled in.

"This is Mr Hatherow," said Lisa with a nervous flourish of her hand.

Tyler looked for a library lanyard but the handsome Mr Hatherow was not wearing one.

"Lisa tells me you wish to borrow a file that's not here." He flashed perfect teeth, laughing as though the notion was absurd. "I'm sure I can clear up this little mystery. If you'll give me a moment, I just need to consult the index system. And may I see your credentials, please? Miss..."

"Tyler May," said Tyler. She showed her badge. Hatherow gave a curt nod and took his place before the PC to access the system. "What was the file name again?"

"It's a contributor's file in the name of Izabella Kremensky."

A moment later Hatherow closed the system down and stood.

"It appears the file you require is on private loan to a friend of the library."

"And the name?"

"I'm afraid I'm not at liberty to divulge that information. As I say, the file is on *private* loan."

"You saw the badge. I need to..."

"You may return with a warrant but until then..."

Melissa cut in.

"That's okay. I don't think that will be necessary." She cast Tyler a knowing glance.

"Yes." Tyler looked from Melissa back to Hatherow, perplexed. "Alright. Don't worry about it."

"Well, if that's settled, I think it best you be on your way. Your little investigation here has left my poor assistant quite shaken. I'm afraid Ms Lypton has a rather nervous sensibility." Hatherow unrolled an unnervingly self-assured smile - teeth so white that Tyler wondered if they were false.

"Right. Sorry about that. We're leaving."

Hatherow and Lisa marched out of the reading room leaving the girls and Freddy to look at one another questioningly.

"What was all that about?" asked Lucy.

Tyler explained and paused when she reached the end of her story.

"So why did we let them walk?" Lucy asked.

"I found out who has the file from the system. I have his name and address," said Melissa.

"So who took it? Who has the file?" asked Lucy. Melissa looked at her knowingly.

"A certain Dr. Jonathan Hatherow."

Secrets

Bletchley Street was a broad road with a tall, gothic, spired church sitting curiously among brick-built flats and garages but, at ten o'clock on a Monday morning, the road looked little different than a hundred others in the small suburb of Hackney near London's centre. Tyler glanced over the kit in her bag: lock picking tools, iPhone, several pairs of latex gloves and a Maglite. She set her phone to mute.

She watched Hatherow leave flat number twenty-nine, stick in hand, and limp to one of four terraced garages. He swung open the black doors and entered. Moments later he drove out in a silver BMW and cruised down the road to turn into Wenlock Street, where she lost sight of him. That didn't matter. It was his flat she was interested in.

With Hatherow safely on his way to work, she moved in to get a better view of the block, surveying through solid wooden doors and brick walls with the contrap's *Present Eye*. She checked for other occupants and found none. Every window and door was locked. She pulled on latex gloves and studied the door lock, focusing the *Present Eye* with its small lever. Nothing unusual: a brass Yale. Child's play for a trained lock picker. Tyler allowed herself a quick glance around to be sure nobody was observing before she attempted to break in. In less time than it takes most people to find the right key, she was inside, closing the door behind her and looking around with interest. She smiled to herself. Were the missing pages really going to be found in a grimy flat at the south end of Hackney?

Tyler padded down a short hallway, dappled in tones of magnolia where light spilled from a room further in. She passed a closet annex housing two coats and racks for shoes, currently unoccupied except for a pair of brown, moccasin slippers. Hatherow obviously lived alone. No sign of child clutter or even a woman's homely touch. Entering his lounge she found the place almost barren; the décor of an academic. She viewed a coffee-coloured, two-piece suite and two broad, modern, pine bookshelves, crammed with various books.

Hatherow's phone rang, startling Tyler, and a woman - clearly familiar to Hatherow because she had no need to leave her name - left a message to say she'd call back later. Tyler sifted through books but the shelves contained no files or anything other than hardback and paperback volumes. Hatherow's dark taste in literature was evident throughout his shelves. Among his collection she found ghost stories, books on the occult and on the history of magic. A single picture graced the room, hanging in the centre of the wall over a small, modern, electric fire: *Dante's Inferno* by Botticelli, dated 1481. A print, Tyler presumed. She scrutinised a depiction of hell where devils with forks corralled and terrorised mankind in a sea of flame. Snakes overwhelmed, the hungry were taunted by a displayed banquet, demons devoured flesh and, at the centre, the Devil presided over all agonies. The picture gave her chills. She moved on quickly and resisted a glance back.

She searched other rooms, peering out of the bedroom window through net curtains onto the street below. After a good ten minutes spent unsuccessfully seeking the file, Tyler had a growing impression that Hatherow must have owned a second home somewhere else. This place didn't seem to fit with him; too empty, too unused for a middle-aged professional. Where was the evidence of the family she'd expected? Then she twigged. Hatherow probably had a house outside London, somewhere nice, somewhere comfortable with his wife and kids. She pictured a big Georgian house with a long drive. *This* was just somewhere to sleep while he worked in London. She slowly came to terms with the fact that she was unlikely to find anything here and turned her attention to a new search, one for Hatherow's main address.

Fifteen minutes later she was no wiser and growing frustrated by her lack of progress when she took a look around Hatherow's small kitchen. She wasted little time here and was leaving the room when she had second thoughts and doubled back to check what she'd presumed was a kitchen cupboard. She moved a coat that was hanging from a hook on the door and was perplexed to find a bolt and padlock. *Okay, Jonathan, what are we hiding in here?* Curiosity aroused, she picked the lock, removed it and opened the door.

The room inside was dark, the only window blacked-out with a heavy curtain, but she knew immediately that this room was different. Even in the gloom she could see there were strange markings on the floor and, against the far wall, she glimpsed the outline of something uncannily altar-like. Her pulse quickened and she put a hand to her shoulder holster, feeling the reassuring shape of her Taser gun. She entered, controlling her desire to switch on the light. Training had taught her to use her own light source to ensure no AC/DC incendiary booby-traps were triggered, and light switches were a good source of fingerprints unless they were prematurely erased by careless investigators. If she opened the curtains, others might be alerted to her presence and so she took out her small Maglite instead. Yes, she had the ear and the support of Chapman, and therefore the backing of MI5, but this mission was not strictly sanctioned and she would still be up to her chin in something smelly if caught.

Torchlight revealed a large pentagram with other strange markings and symbols around and inside it, all chalked upon bare floorboards. She swallowed and took out her iPhone to flash off several shots of the floor. What she saw spooked her.

In the glow of the camera flash she glimpsed shapes on the wall before her, not wallpaper or framed pictures, but a seemingly random scattering of clutter. Turning the Maglite on the area she revealed a covering of maps, diagrams and newspaper clippings. Watford was tagged with a map pin and a red cord leading to Whitechapel, London. Other locations were pinned and linked the same way. Among the clippings were articles on the Christmas Eve Incident and other strange reports of ghostly appearances. There were diagrams of strange instruments and devices, and a photograph of the GAUNT machine, its metal casing puckered and bent where an explosion had ruined it.

And then she found it: an old black and white photograph of the contrap, front and back. She took three steps back to fit the entire wall into the screen, set her camera app to wide-angle and flashed off several more photographs. Further study of this vast noticeboard would have to wait until later, but it was already clear to Tyler that Hatherow was hunting for the contrap. And she wasn't surprised. He was not the only one.

She turned her attention to the rest of the room, swept her light around to pause on the altar, which looked Stone Age to her, before taking a closer look at the incised spiral symbols and other unusual markings on its surface. She ran a hand over the darkly stained, excised cup at its apex and rubbed a grimy substance between a finger and thumb. She photographed the stone and moved on. On the wall facing the noticeboard stood several bookshelves end to end, the entire surface covered with dusty books. She rummaged her way across this expanse, stopping only when she located a wide, cream-coloured document file. She knew instantly what it was. She photographed the wall of books and completed her documentation with several more shots of the room before taking the cream file and replacing the padlock on the door. She took a quick look around to be sure she'd left everything else as she'd found it and when she was happy she had left no sign of her visit, except the missing file, she left the flat and locked the front door behind her.

Glad to be out of there.

*

That evening at the apartment, Tyler passed Melissa a memory stick containing the high resolution images she'd taken and soon they were up on the big screen of Melissa's computer system. The girls stared at the photographs, amazed.

"You weren't kidding," said Melissa, studying images of pentagrams and other occult symbols. "Hatherow's some kind of deviant."

"I've seen this kind of stuff before. He's a warlock," said Lucy. "Same as a witch, only male."

"Whatever he is, he's after the contrap," said Tyler. "Click forward a few images."

Melissa found photographs of the pin-board wall.

"See what you mean."

Tyler placed the cream file on the desk next to the keyboard and took out a thin wad of yellowed pages, still with their binding glue adhering to one edge.

"Izabella's file. And this is the missing chapter from Zebedee's book. I finally found it." Tyler couldn't supress a half-smile.

Melissa looked at the extracted pages, wide-eyed.

"Did you read it?"

"I did."

"Does it say anything that might help?"

Tyler turned to the second page and read aloud.

Ghost haunting is also dangerous to attempt because it could potentially, in certain circumstances, lead to a clashing of powers that [as far as one can discern] were not meant to be accessed by mankind. These powers, or realms of powers can, if controlled in the correct manner [at least, this in theory], bestow upon the *ghost haunter* abilities and reaches far beyond the natural state of existence. In short, it is possible to enter into other dominions where materials, that should not meet, collide. There exists a place where only the dead walk and inhabit and, beyond this, a second realm, even more terrifying, accessible through *fire*. This chasm should never be entered, for it is the resting place of great evil; the eternal prison from which there can be no return; a place of damnation, ruled only by the fallen and condemned.

Tyler put the pages down to find both Lucy and Melissa staring at her.

"He's talking about the *Ghost Portal*," said Melissa.

"And another realm beyond that, accessed by fire..." said Tyler.

"Let me see that," said Melissa, taking the pages and studying them. " 'And beyond this, a second realm, even more terrifying, accessible through *fire*.' The word 'fire' is in italics."

"I know," said Tyler, holding out the contrap to show them. "He doesn't mean fire. He means the symbol. He was talking about the flame symbol on the contrap. You see? I *knew* he was hiding something. I was right all along. There's another realm that can be accessed by the contrap and the fire symbol opens the gateway."

"Doesn't sound like a place I want to visit," said Lucy. "I'm not sure this helps us much."

"Uh-huh," agreed Melissa. "Sounds like *Hell*. Literally."

"Yeah, I know, but it might explain where Hitler has gone." Tyler heard the hope in her own voice and immediately doubted herself. "Perhaps someone put him in the chasm."

"Let's hope so," said Lucy. "If that's the case we can cross him off the list forever; *'the eternal prison from which there can be no return...'*"

"Exactly," said Tyler.

"There're still three gloves on the loose," said Lucy. "Maybe we should forget about Hitler and concentrate on them."

"No. I want to know for sure what's become of Hitler. I just have this feeling. Something's not right."

They looked quizzically at Tyler.

"I can't explain it. It's just a feeling."

"I say we move on," said Lucy. "This chasm thing answers a lot of questions, doesn't it? You put Hitler into the *Ghost Portal* and from there he went missing. There's no way we know of that he could've got out, and Albert searched the whole place inside. Hey, I'm no Einstein, right, but unless he found some way of hiding or escaped the contrap somehow, there's only one logical solution to the problem: someone put Hitler into the chasm. And who can blame them?"

"Okay," said Tyler. "But how did they do that?"

"I don't know. Maybe there's a way through from one place to the other. I mean, what do *we* know about it? What do we *really* know about the contrap? Not much."

Tyler remembered the tear she'd previously seen within the *Ghost Portal*; a shimmering view of something beyond its usual grey, misty elements. Zebedee had denied any knowledge of the tear, but had she glimpsed a way through to the chasm? Another thought occurred to her.

"Albert would have found out if someone had taken Hitler and put him into the chasm. Albert would have told me." Tyler felt betrayed. Zebedee had acted suspiciously every time she'd asked him about the tear or about the missing chapter. She was now certain he had withheld information from her.

Albert was there at her side, coalescing out of thin air.

"Albert, you would have told me, right?"

"Yes, course I would, Missy. I don't know nuffin' about no chasm."

Tyler left the desk and sank into a couch chair, feeling dejected.

"We should move on," Lucy repeated. "Track down the three gloves we do know *are* out there. While we're messing about here with this, they're planning world domination. We need to stop them. No one else even really knows what's going on!"

Tyler eyed the three bullet-like money capsules strung on the chain around Lucy's neck, knowing they contained summoning artefacts for the three remaining gloves. Lucy grasped the capsules and continued her tirade.

"I swore to myself I'd never take these off until those gloves are removed from our world. And I meant it!" She stalked off into her room, slamming the door behind her.

"She'll calm down. Eventually."

"It's not like we don't all feel like that," said Tyler. "But we've absolutely no leads and the gloves have disappeared. There's nothing else we can do to track them down right now, or we'd be doing it. Everything that can be done is being done. Doesn't she know that?"

"She knows. She's just frustrated, and when Lucy's frustrated, well..."

Tyler examined the small incised symbol on the contrap that looked like dancing flames, and wondered how it might give access to the chasm beyond. It was a gateway to another realm, but how did it open? She had tried everything she could think of already, yet nothing had worked and it seemed to her the only way forward was to once more approach Zebedee or Izabella.

She still fully intended to destroy the contrap, but the small voice in her head told her the time was not yet right, and she figured she still needed to capture the other gloves and put their ghosts into the portal first. Although now she thought the chasm sounded like a much better option. In fact, she wondered if putting the gloves' ghosts into the *Ghost Portal* had ever been a good idea. Doing so had set two children free but at what cost? And where were the ghosts of Heinrich Himmler and Joseph Goebbels now? Floating aimlessly around the *Ghost Portal*? Tyler doubted that. With an accumulation of Nazi ghosts in the contrap, she trusted the device less and less. *If only they'd all been put directly into the chasm*, she thought. No, destroying the contrap would have to wait. She needed to learn more about it before she could attempt such a thing. *What would happen to the ghosts if I did destroy it?* she wondered. *Where would they go? Would they also be destroyed? Can ghosts die twice?*

When Melissa and Lucy had gone to their beds and Tyler was left alone, she took out the contrap and switched to the *Ghost Portal*. She waited for what seemed an age before Zebedee showed himself.

"Why?" she demanded as he puffed smoke like a steam train.

"My dear girl, I'm sure I don't know *what* you're talking about."

"Don't play the innocent with me. You know very well what I'm talking about. The tear? The chasm? The other realm?" She held up the newly found chapter and read from it. "A second realm, even more terrifying, accessible through *fire*." Zebedee appeared to be uncomfortable, twitching and scratching his ear with the tip of his pipe.

"Ahhh. I see you found the missing pages. That's a shame..."

"Why? Why's it a shame?"

Zebedee did not respond but only watched her apprehensively.

"I'm waiting, Zebedee. I thought you were a friend."

"Oh, but I *am* your friend, Miss May." Zebedee took off his top hat and looked at her earnestly. "Let me explain. I was merely seeking to protect you."

"To protect me from what, exactly? Knowledge that might help me work out what on Earth is going on, like what's happened to Hitler? What else are you hiding from me?"

"Nothing. Nothing, really. The Brimstone Chasm is something that no one should ever have discovered."

"The *Brimstone Chasm*?"

Zebedee nodded, sheepishly.

"Knowledge of its existence won't aid you in any way, yet it could so very easily place you in extreme peril. Still, now you've discovered the truth, I'll explain. The tear you saw in the *Ghost Portal* was indeed a rip in the very fabric that separates the portal from the chasm - a benign, temporal failure of the plural curtain - in itself a harmless thing. It would be quite meaningless but for the unexplained disappearance of Hitler's ghost. Your supposition that the two occurrences were somehow connected was well founded. I too, have considered this."

"And are they connected?"

"The truth is I don't know, but I strongly advise you drop any thoughts of the chasm. The chasm can bring you only misery."

Tyler sat down on her bed, her anger at Zebedee subsiding.

"But I have to know for sure, no matter what the cost," she said. "It's too important."

Zebedee watched her intently while lighting his pipe. He took a long drag and exhaled smoke.

"I was afraid you'd say that."

Corpus Somnus

Albert came to Tyler's side to peer into the *Ghost Portal* at Zebedee.

"I'm with Tyler," he said. "We gotta know where that Hitler's gone. What if 'e's free - like the Tree told Tyler? What then?"

"Albert's right. It's too important for us to not worry about," said Tyler. "Albert searched the portal and couldn't find him anywhere. He's also searched for Hitler out here in the world too. He checked to see if Hitler was hanging around his grave site like a reverie, and Josef Mengele seems to be in charge of the Nazis now. It's like he's their new Führer and Albert hasn't found any sign of Hitler anywhere. Do you think the Jews put him into the chasm through the tear?"

Zebedee shook his head.

"No. I asked them. They say they put him in a room, a prison they constructed to hold him."

"And you believe them?"

"I've seen it - and why would they lie? They have

nothing to gain, or fear."

"Wait," said Albert. "There *is* one place in the portal I couldn't look, a place I couldn't go alone." He and Zebedee exchanged a look of mutual understanding through the portal's lens.

"The Shivering Pool," said Zebedee. "Of course. A very hazardous place to search. Especially if one is unaccompanied."

"Tha's right," said Albert.

"What exactly *is* the Shivering Pool?"

"As the name suggests, it's a pool that shivers, but there's more to it than that. It's a place where those who wish to forget go to lose themselves; a place where they, themselves, will be forgotten. Albert wouldn't have been able to search the pool alone. That would be far too dangerous. The waters there dampen the mind and erode the spirit until one is rendered as numb as a reverie. Ghosts who go into those waters tend never to come out."

"But it *is* possible to search the pool?" asked Tyler.

"Yes, in theory," said Zebedee. "Though that in itself could be treacherous. We'd need a team of ghosts. The more the better."

"Would three be enough?"

"Possibly, but who are the three you're thinking of?"

"You, Albert and me," said Tyler.

"Preposterous. Far too dangerous. I won't hear of it. And how on earth would you get into the portal without killing yourself?"

"I've done it before."

"Yes, but only for a couple of minutes and you nearly died."

"I fink's 'e's right, Missy. You'd 'ave t' become a ghost for that. Far too dangerous."

"I want to speak to Izabella. She knows all the spells. Maybe she knows something that'll help." Begrudgingly, Zebedee agreed to seek out Izabella and he returned a while later with her in tow.

"What *is* all this, girl? Zebedee tells me you've taken

45

leave of your senses. That you wish to enter the Shivering Pool. Take it from me - this is a very bad idea."

"I found the missing chapter from Zebedee's book," said Tyler. "I want you to tell me everything you can about the Brimstone Chasm and I want to know if there's a safe way for me to leave my body and enter the *Ghost Portal*."

"Pah! Always with the questions."

"Please help, Izabella. You're the only one who knows about this stuff."

"Oh, so Zebedee's little book did not enlighten?"

"Now, now, Izabella," said Zebedee. "I'm the first to admit not all my facts were entirely accurate."

Izabella chuckled derisively.

"With this I *do* agree. So, child, you wish to know about the Brimstone Chasm. There is a clue in the name. The chasm is a place of torture and misery where the very air is aflame with brimstone and sulphuric gases. A fire burns there that can never be extinguished. It is a godless place reserved for the damned. You would do well to forget you ever heard its mention."

"Can ghosts be put into the chasm? Is it true no one ever comes out? How can the chasm be opened?"

Izabella viewed Tyler with a measure of irritation and realised she was not going to give in until she had answers.

"You are aware of a certain saying, now, what is it? Ah, yes: *Curiosity killed the pussycat*."

Tyler nodded, but would not be put off.

"I know that the fire symbol on the contrap is the symbol for the chasm. It would surely be better for me to put the remaining gloves straight into the chasm, rather than leave them wandering the *Ghost Portal*."

"Hmmm. Well, don't say I didn't warn you," said Izabella, levelling heavy, whiskery brows at Tyler. "The chasm can only be opened with the correct command; a little precaution, installed by the contrap's creator, no doubt. The switch must be set to the fire symbol and the lever must be rotated until it has completed a full cycle, from twelve o'clock to twelve o'clock, you understand? You will find that, as the lever rotates to its original position, with a little applied pressure it will click back into place. Once this is initiated the command must then be given. You must remember this. The command to open the chasm is *Vorago expositus*. A second command will close it again: *Vorago termino*. Of course, to put a ghost into the chasm, one must use the other command, the one you already know, as I understand it; *Phasmatis licentia*."

"I see," said Tyler, scribbling down the commands in her notebook. "And the pool? Is there a way I can come into the *Ghost Portal* temporarily so I can help search the Shivering Pool? A way other than dying, I mean."

Izabella eyed Zebedee who was shaking his head in despair.

"You may as well tell her now," he said. "You've told her everything else." He clamped his teeth onto his pipe's tip.

"Very well," said Izabella, turning her attention back to Tyler. "There is a command that will release your spirit and put your body to sleep for seven days. Seven days and no more, you understand? And it may be used only once for any individual! This is a highly dangerous thing to do, though. If you do not return to your body before the seven days are up, the command will be irreversible and you will surely die. Your flesh will perish and you will be trapped as a ghost, permanently."

"The command?"

"*Corpus somnus* is the command that will put the body to sleep and draw out the spirit. It must be uttered whilst you are wearing the contrap. Upon return to the body, a second command must be uttered. *Corpus resurrectio* is the second command. This will enable your spirit to re-join your sleeping form and awaken flesh. Until this occurs, your body will be like the dead, but shall remain uncorrupted."

*

Melissa took it all in and was silent for a long time. She ate toast and tapped keys on her laptop.

"So what you are saying is that you want to leave your body, become a ghost and go into the contrap to take a dip in some weirdo pond, so you can check for the ghost of Hitler. Is that what you're saying? 'Cause it sounds like the ravings of a certified lunatic."

"I know," said Tyler. "It does, doesn't it."

"I say we call the men in white coats now," said Lucy, cradling a cup of freshly brewed, black coffee. "Save a whole lot of fuss later on."

"What's it going to take to stop you from doing this?" asked Melissa. "I'll pay you. Would that help? Name your price. I'll pay you not to go in. Just stay here and we'll hunt down the rest of the gloves like we always planned. You know, like a *team*."

"Just think about it. I've done it before. Not the Shivering Pool part, I admit, but I've been a ghost before and I even went into the portal. This time it will be different. We know the commands. It will be much safer. You won't need to keep my body alive and when it's done we'll know for sure what happened to Hitler."

"I still think you're completely nuts, but what's new?" said Melissa, typing some more. She studied a browser search result on her laptop screen. Anyway, what's with all these commands? I looked them up. They're all just Latin words."

"Who knows?" said Tyler. "Maybe they're triggers or something. There must be something special about them."

"They're magic," said Lucy. "They have to be. It's the only explanation."

"Well whatever they are, this whole thing's pretty freaky." Melissa checked her watch. "Sorry. I have to go. Due in at nine for an IT exam." She rose and collected her bag. "See you later. Promise me you won't do anything stupid. At least, not until I get back. Okay?"

*

At three in the afternoon the girls met up in Chapman's briefing room. He'd called a meeting to inform them of progress with the ongoing International Nazi Conspiracy Investigation, I.N.C.I. or *Incy Wincy*, as it had become known between the girls.

"The field work is slowly paying off," said Chapman, turning his chiselled face to study the fifteen agents gathered before him through his narrow, oblong spectacles. He ran a hand over his thinning, closely-cropped hair. "As you know, the incident at the castle was covered up by both sides. Seems nobody wanted exposure. Can't think why..." Some of the agents sniggered. "Worked out well for us this time but it could have turned out differently. The money trail is complex but it's naming new marks all the time and each new lead must be followed. You're all going to be kept busy on this one and I'm pulling in some fresh blood. However, I don't want any of you getting twitchy. They're all trusted; tried and tested individuals. Things will be a whole lot easier if we all just get on with the job in hand. So, help the new guys get up to speed and get alongside them. Okay?" The agents nodded. "Check your files for team info."

A hand went up at the back of the gathering. An agent named Pete.

"When is I.N.C.I. going to hit the media? Do we really need more evidence before we can warn other territories about what's really going on? As long as other countries are blind to it, surely they're more at risk of infiltration..."

Chapman cut the agent off in mid flow.

"Yes, I'm well aware of the way it all works. Our stats suggest a global infiltration, and it's increasing daily. The media will be informed as soon as we have something concrete and irrefutable. Until that day it's between you and me, alright? Obviously the CIA has been left enough clues to piece something together, but they won't trace it to this office. In the meantime we fight the good fight and keep it quiet. Understood?"

"Yes, Sir," muttered concerned agents.

"Right. Now, the castle in Brazil has proved very interesting, although the location itself is now officially out of bounds. I want all other leads shelved while we chase the remaining leads from the castle. I want all associated businesses quietly investigated. I want thorough reporting. Is that clear? I want names, facts and figures. The whole works. Chase the money. Can you do that?"

"Yes, Sir."

"Good. Get to it."

"Yes, Sir." The agents gathered belongings and filed from the room. Chapman called the three girls back and played with his glasses awkwardly.

"Sir?"

"In hindsight I have to say your jaunt in Brazil was a brave move. Possibly stupid, but brave. The network is proving to be huge. I think it's going to be the breakthrough we've been looking for and, if it is, it will all be thanks to you. How's training?"

"Fine, Sir," said Melissa.

"Alright," said Lucy.

"Tyler? You seem a little distracted."

"Er, yes. Fine, Sir. Just wish we could get on with it. You know, speed things up a bit."

"Yes, I think we're all feeling it. Well, hang in there. Maybe the Brazilian leads will see a way forward. I'd have you back in the field already if there was anything real to give you. I promise you'll be the first to know if something comes in."

"...appreciate that, Sir."

"You'll be aware by now of the level of infiltration within the police force. You've been following the court cases, I imagine. Your instincts to avoid them when you found the contrap were good. Tyler, follow your instincts. They've been good to you in the past."

"Yes, Sir."

"Okay. Off you go. I'm sure you'll be hearing from me soon."

*

Tyler looked up at her bedroom ceiling, her bed cool on the flat of her back, the soft duvet caressing her form. She tried to relax. Albert watched her with concern.

"I'm ready," she said. "I think I'm ready."

"I told you this is nuts," said Melissa. "What do you think you're doing? You're going to kill yourself!"

"I think it's quite a good idea," said Lucy.

"Thank you," said Tyler. "That's two out of three. You're out-voted, Mel."

"You *would* think it was a good idea," Melissa told Lucy. "You're a psycho."

"Sticks and stones," said Lucy.

"Ahhhh! You're both as mad as each other."

"Oh, come on, Mel," said Lucy. "We should try it too. Haven't you ever wondered what it would feel like to be dead? I do all the time."

"That's because you're sick and you need help."

"Now you're just being mean. Seriously, what could go wrong? If she gets scared and wants to head home she speaks to us from inside the portal and we bring her out. She goes back into her body and everyone's happy. We just have to keep an eye on her."

"For seven whole days?" asked Melissa.

"Seven days is your limit," Izabella reminded from within the contrap. Zebedee stood with her waiting beyond the crystal lens. "And one last thing: there's no day or night this side of the crystal. No clocks that work. Nothing to mark the passing of time. By its very nature this realm is disorienting. You will need to work hard to keep some measure of an awareness of time."

"I probably won't need more than half a day," said Tyler.

"See," said Lucy to Melissa. "You worry too much. That's your problem."

"And you don't worry enough. What if she gets lost in there? Have you thought about that? What if she never comes out? What if she disappears into the portal and we never see her again?"

"That's a lot of *what ifs*," said Lucy. "What if she doesn't?"

"What if the Nazi ghosts find her in there? Did you consider that? What if they find her and throw her into the Brimstone Chasm through a *benign, temporal failure of the plural curtain*?"

Lucy shrugged. "We won't let that happen, will we?"

"There might not be a lot we can do to stop it."

"Will you two stop bickering?" asked Tyler. "I'm trying to relax here. I've enough to worry about without you guys stressing me out."

"Sorry," the others said in unison.

"I'll be with ya'," said Albert. "And so will Mr Lieberman and Izabella. We'll look after ya'."

"Thanks, Albert. Right. Well, if you're finished with the *what ifs* and the *why nots*, can we get on with it, please? You'll have to take it in turns to watch for me at the portal lens. You don't even need to stop your training. Just wear the contrap and take it with you wherever you go. As long as one of you has it, I'll know I'm safe."

"Alright," said Lucy.

Melissa eyed Tyler with dismay.

"Are you really sure?"

"Sure as I'm ever going to be," said Tyler. "I know I'm placing my life in your hands, but if I can't trust you two, who can I trust?"

"You're going to put your life in Lucy's hands?" Melissa laughed and received a punch on the arm a second later. "Alright, alright. I'll go along with it, but for the record, I have a really bad feeling about this."

"Duly noted," said Tyler.

"Okay. Let me get this straight. You say the words while you're wearing the contrap and your ghost will leave your body. Your body goes into some kind of deathly suspended animation that can last no more than seven days, after which the condition is irreversible. We open the portal and say the command that puts you inside. You go in. When you're all done in there you'll come back to the portal and we set you free from it and put you back into your body."

"That's it, pretty much. All the commands are in my notebook here by my bed, just in case you forget any of them, but I should be able to remind you of them anyway. You'll still be able to talk to me through the portal."

"Right."

"Wait!" said Lucy. "Who gets the contrap if you die?"

Tyler rolled her eyes.

"You do."

"Why not me?" asked Melissa.

"I don't know. I think you'd be too scared to use it."

"Thanks a bunch."

Tyler looked her friends in the eyes.

"Wish me luck. I'll see you on the other side." She took one last look at the contrap in her hands, let her head rest on the bed, closed her eyes and gave the command. "Corpus Somnus."

The Room of Faces

Tyler experienced an all-consuming, inner tug and the next moment felt her consciousness wrench from her flesh and bones. She had the strangest feeling as she viewed her own body as though from another's perspective. She saw the contrap lying on her unmoving chest and instinctively reached out to Albert, who took her hand firmly in his. They touched for the very first time, ghost against ghost, and she sensed his presence in an entirely new way. His hands were larger than hers and more robust, strengthened by years of manual labour when he had lived. She glimpsed images, flashes of memory: Albert shovelling coal, climbing up into dark chimney vents, chiselling clinker from old, discoloured brick, deftly handling long-sectioned sweep's brushes, and then urgently scraping and clawing, fighting to escape a tight, claustrophobic chimney that would not let him go. She felt his desperation. His fear.

"Alright, Missy?" he asked.

"I'm alright." She nodded. "I feel you. I can actually

feel you here with me." She could not *feel* his skin against hers, exactly, but she had an awareness of him that *was* similar to touch. When their ghosts had met she'd experienced a perception of everything he was, and even his last living moments, as though their minds had kissed.

Albert grinned. Tyler smiled and turned to the girls.

"I'm out. I'm ready to go into the contrap, but one of you will need to make it happen." For the second time, Tyler found herself studying translucent hands and fingers, wondering at it all.

Melissa snatched up Tyler's notebook and turned to a fresh page to jot down the time and the date. Her phone chimed and she put the pad down to check a text message from Freddy.

"We'll watch over your body," Melissa said. "But return soon as you can. If this goes wrong there'll be no going back, so no unnecessary risks."

"Who, me?" asked Tyler.

"Who's going to do it?" Melissa asked Lucy.

"I will." Lucy carefully lifted the contrap from around the neck of Tyler's vacant body. She found the switch already set to the *Ghost Portal*. "Ready?"

Tyler and Albert nodded. Lucy held out the contrap with the crystal facing the two ghosts standing before her and pulled the lever clockwise around the edge. Tyler watched the crystal glow as the portal opened.

Lucy gave the command.

"Phasmatis licentia."

Tyler and Albert were swept up into a shimmering filament of blue essence as they were drawn into the gateway. Tyler felt again that icy chill as her morphing spirit passed through the crystal. Light dazzled as she and Albert coalesced into forms on the other side of the lens, inside the contrap.

Tyler looked around. Zebedee and Izabella stood close by. She heard Melissa and turned back to the lens.

"Remember what I said." Melissa was peering in, looking stressed.

"I will. Don't worry." Tyler glanced at those either side of her. "I'm in good company. Oh! I have an assignment that needs to be in tomorrow morning. If I'm not back by then can you hand it in for me? It's the pink file in my bag."

"I'll make sure it's in on time," said Melissa.

"Give me a couple of hours and then look for me again. With any luck I'll be ready to come out."

"Okay. Good luck," said Melissa.

"Good luck," Tyler heard Lucy echo.

"Thanks. See you soon."

Although she had been into the portal once before, that had been a very brief visit lasting only a few seconds and so this was the first time Tyler had really experienced the full draw of the contrap. She remembered tearing around the Nazi castle in Brazil at lightning speed when she was last a ghost, but now she became aware of a new gravity. It was heavy, a powerful pull on her spirit that kept her from leaving the place and slowed her progress wherever she tried to go. She attempted to break free of the frustrating feeling and dart away into the mist up ahead. She managed a turn of speed for a short distance, but the gravity was too strong for her to keep up the momentum for long. Albert called after her as she slowed with resignation.

"Hey, Missy, take it easy. You can't go racing around in 'ere or you'll wear yourself right out." He caught up with her. "Take it steady like. Don't forget the contrap uses the power of us ghosts what's inside it. It's draining. You can't fight it, so pace ya'self. Right? It's easier to walk."

"Alright." Tyler nodded as Zebedee and Izabella reached them. "Can you take me to the Shivering Pool? Is it far?"

"Good question," said Albert. "Like everyfin' else in 'ere, it ain't always in the same place. We'll 'ave to find it."

"May I suggest we first visit the city?" said Zebedee,

pointing with the long, curving stem of his pipe. Beyond the banks of drifting fog, the distant city shifted slowly like a mighty vessel on a tranquil, mist-veiled sea. "If we stumble upon the Shivering Pool along the way, so much the better, but I think Tyler may benefit from a trip to the city anyway. We really should show her the Room of Faces."

Izabella nodded slowly.

"I can see that could be beneficial," she said.

"Alright," said Albert. "We'll head for the city." They set off again, wading through fog up to their thighs.

Tyler's previous ghost experience had allowed little time to think. This time she had time to kill. It was vastly different from being in a physical body and yet, in many ways, remarkably similar. Her new kind of awareness was strange. It was not like feeling things with a sense of touch as a physical human does, but more like touching things with a sense of feel. She could still think and remember very well, but it wasn't like thinking with a brain, more like an inert awareness of knowledge. An ethereal, intangible perception. She wondered how she might explain the feeling to Melissa and Lucy when she returned, but realised there were no human words that could truly describe her ghost *sense*. It was as if all her physical senses of touch, taste, sight, smell and hearing had been removed and replaced with one infinitely simpler sense of consciousness. When she spoke she did not hear her voice as though through the ears of a body but, rather, it was like hearing herself thinking in her mind.

In the firmament above her, the vast, black, planet-like globe she had seen once before stretched from horizon to horizon and she wondered what it was. She studied it, found it featureless and doubted it was a planet.

She took a closer look at the misty substance that flowed beneath her feet and which seemed to pervade every part of the realm about her. She tried to scoop some up in the palm of her hand and watched as it trailed away like fine sand, slipping between fingers.

"What is this stuff?" she asked as they trudged.

"Oh, the mist. Yes, peculiar stuff," said Zebedee. "It's memory. Same as the city and just about everything else in here. It's unformed memory, a kind of building block that feeds everything around you. You'll see what I mean when we reach the city."

Tyler looked back expecting to see the crystal lens of the contrap but it had gone, or they had moved on so far from it that it was now too distant to see. She could not be sure which.

"Come on," chirped Zebedee. "This way. Seems we're in luck. I think the city is drifting towards us."

They walked for what seemed like miles and Tyler really had no way of gauging how far they'd travelled or how long it had taken them. Everything, including their destination, drifted constantly and the ground they traversed was not ground at all, but seemed to be, simply, a denser variety of the substance Zebedee had called memory. She looked down, hoping to glimpse the *land* between ebbing flows of mist, but saw only blackness beyond, as though beneath her feet was nothing, or an unoccupied, eternal expanse of night. In places this firmament was less dense and she sank lower as she moved. In other areas she climbed imperceptibly-shifting banks, and she had a notion that it was like dreaming about a hike through heath or moorland, only the land was alive and moving like a vast creature beneath her, and she was a flea upon its pelt. She found the entire place dreamlike and most surreal. She reached for Albert's hand again, feeling more secure when his fingers closed around hers.

"Not far now, Missy."

The city was clearer now. The grey, ghostly shapes of houses, high-rises and all manner of other buildings and cityscapes drew nearer out of the fog. She was almost at the nearest building, a farm cottage, neatly dressed with hanging baskets and well-kept gardens, when she realised it was a peculiar city for more than one reason. As she approached a low picket fence, buildings further in shifted slowly from place to place. New buildings arose and others diminished before vanishing altogether. She would not have been sure how this incredible thing was happening but then the cottage right before her drifted off to her left and, as though a strong wind had quickly arisen, fragments at its edge dissolved like dust into mist, or memory, or whatever it was, and then the whole place collapsed into a hazy sea of fog. Among the tumbling and rising buildings were others, seemingly solid, and Tyler noticed a bizarre mixing of styles. Here stood a Roman temple, a tower, the coliseum. There arose a modern block of flats and, next door, stood a Bronze Age roundhouse. She passed a cave with a fire burning at its entrance and, across the road, an Egyptian mud brick house stood shoulder to shoulder with a Saxon mead hall. And all around, ghosts walked, haunting once familiar streets and homes. Among those close enough to see more clearly, Tyler noticed Saxon warriors and maidens in flowing robes, Roman soldiers and slaves, Egyptian stone masons and royalty, Stone Age and Bronze Age tribesmen and women, medieval serfs and knights, both nobles and the poor, all manner of people and seemingly from all ages. It was the most peculiar thing she had ever experienced.

"Welcome to Memoria Gravitas," said Zebedee. "Though frankly, I'm the only one who calls it that. It is, without doubt, the strangest place you are ever likely to visit."

Izabella scowled at everything she saw, unimpressed.

"You mentioned a *Room of Faces*?" Tyler reminded Zebedee.

"Indeed," said Zebedee. "We'll take you there now. It is where Hitler's ghost was imprisoned, a place forged from memory for one purpose alone: to hold him captive."

"But how can any place in this city hold someone prisoner if everything is moving all the time?" asked Tyler. "Nothing here is constant. How can a room or a building be stable enough to hold somebody?"

"Another good question," said Zebedee, scratching his nose with the tip of his pipe. "When Hitler was brought here, his captives were of one mind. You must appreciate all that you see before you is a kind of projected memory, meaning that somewhere, someone, a *ghost*, is remembering. Not all memories are accurate and so it follows, not all of the places, here rendered, are accurate. When the ghost, or ghosts, who are remembering the place cease to recall, or begin to remember another place, that first location they were thinking of will dissipate on the ethereal breeze." Zebedee continued to explain as the four ghosts entered the city to walk temporal streets of recollection. "Now to Hitler's prison... Being of one mind, his captors forged a room from memories, a vast cell made entirely of the remembered faces of those for whose death he was responsible in life. They had in mind a place of confrontation, you understand, not a punishment as such, but a room where, wherever he turned, he would be met with the faces of those he had so persecuted. And so, such a room arose and Hitler was placed inside, to his torment."

"But he may have escaped when things shifted, when the room changed like these other buildings." To Tyler's right a tower block plummeted slowly into miasma and moments later was nothing but wisps of fog.

"No, that's not what happened," said Zebedee with certainty. "The committee that created the room were bound to maintain it, to keep it and to remember it in constancy."

"I see," said Tyler. She followed Zebedee across a street as it collapsed into a drift of cloud and she ran to escape the encroaching erosion but it moved faster and caught her. She wasn't aware she'd let go of Albert, but she realised she must have done at some point because she fell with the dwindling road and drifted away from her companions, screaming. Albert darted to her and grabbed her hand. Dragged her back onto the more stable surface. They ran for a more secure stretch where they rested in the shadow of an Elizabethan lighthouse that was oddly devoid of an ocean to oversee.

"Sorry," said Albert. "That 'appens sometimes. Best keep a hold o' me 'and."

Tyler regained her footing and watched the entire road at their backs dissolve like melting snow. They entered another street, this one lined with rows of cedars and paved with great slabs of ancient-looking, pale stone. A random mismatch of structures continued along its length. Castle walls merged into mud huts. A Romanesque villa backed onto a Polish ghetto. Tyler thought she recognised a figure and fought to name her. A simple, drab dress hung from the girl's slight form and mousey hair was held from her face by a thin band of leather. It was a ghost she'd spoken to once before; a Roman slave named Claudia, once murdered by her cruel master. Tyler had waved before she realised what she was doing. She stopped, unsure if she wanted to speak to Claudia again, but Claudia headed over.

Too late now.

"Oh. It's you," she said, peering at Tyler with her otherwise-pretty face screwed up, head tilted as though wondering what she was looking at.

"Hi, Claudia," said Tyler, thinking desperately how she might end the encounter and walk away but, uninspired, she resorted to "Nice to see you."

"Is it? I wish I could say the same, but you really are far too ugly for that."

"Gee, thanks."

"Well, what are you doing here? Sorry to see you're dead," Claudia said, brightening.

"Thanks, I'm hoping it won't be permanent."

"Really? That's a shame."

"Well, it's been nice catching up. Think I'll be going now." Tyler set off, hoping to leave Claudia behind but the girl followed and continued to ask ridiculous questions for a long time, such as 'Did you enjoy your last moments alive?' and 'Why *are* you so ugly, by the way?' When she finally ceased prying, she tagged along like a lost puppy, irritating Tyler continuously.

"We're getting close now," said Zebedee. "Just a few more streets and we'll be there."

"But how can you tell where you're going when everything's moving all the time?" For Tyler, who thrived on order and certainty, this place was a living hell.

"Oh, you get used to that. You'll know what I mean after you've been here for a while. You get a feel for it and then you just know you're close to where you're going. Am I making sense?"

"I'm not entirely sure," said Tyler, watching ghetto slums drift like a vast sliding-tile puzzle.

Zebedee led them up a winding road and through a sprawling expanse of dreary ghetto dwellings. This last path seemed to go on forever and Tyler was about to ask if Zebedee was sure he knew what he was doing when he stopped and turned to point at a door that looked no different from any other in the settlement.

"This is where they put him?" she asked. "How do you know?" But even as the words left her mouth she knew it was indeed the place. A deep sense of sorrow emanated from this drab building to permeate her being. It grew and settled over Tyler until she thought she might break down and weep.

"This is it," said Zebedee, opening the door for her – the door she honestly did not want to use. "It was sealed shut once they had him inside. It would've been impossible for Hitler to open it from within. Come. You'll see the faces are still here."

Tyler stepped inside with trepidation, trying to view what lay ahead of her but seeing only darkness. When she ventured further, a soft light flickered into being. As it swelled she was able to discern a multitude of candle flames dancing in a gentle breeze from the entrance.

"A flame for each individual," said Izabella, following Zebedee and Albert into the vault-like chamber. The light increased, brightening the walls. Tyler shuddered and recoiled. The walls, floors and ceilings were each made of faces; ghostly, grey faces of the dead, but they were not without life. The faces were looking back at her. Eyes followed her as she moved. The lights grew brighter still until a seemingly endless chamber was illuminated like a gallery corridor and the brightness from the millions of candles was almost overwhelming.

"You can see that Hitler would have been somewhat uncomfortable in such a room," said Zebedee. "Yet they truly treated him with mercy."

Tyler nodded. She was about as uncomfortable as she could get and yet the faces bore her no resentment, no judgement. She had done them no harm.

"There was a committee," she reminded Zebedee, wanting to exit the room as soon as possible. "Perhaps I might speak with them."

"Yes, of course," said Zebedee, sensing her discomfort and gesturing towards the door. "Let us go."

Once outside, Zebedee climbed a knoll at the roadside and called out a long list of individuals from the surrounding ghetto. A large gathering of ghosts, mostly comprising Jewish holocaust victims, gathered in a crowd around him.

"I have called you out to meet a very special visitor. We have in our midst the young woman responsible for the recent capture and incarceration of Adolf Hilter." Zebedee paused while the gathering shouted and applauded Tyler for her valour. "Our friend, Miss May, would like to talk with you, as you were responsible for the construction of the Room of Faces." Uneasy murmurs rumbled about the crowd. Zebedee turned to Tyler, beckoning her to take his place.

"My dear, I give you the *Council of the Wise*."

Tyler stepped forward onto the knoll and looked out at a sea of faces.

"I've come in search of Hitler," she announced. "To find out what has become of him and to learn where he might now be. We haven't seen him since he came here to the room you made. Do any of you know what has become of him? Did any of you move him from the room?" She watched many heads shake and heard the disgruntled muttering of many voices.

"No," said one of those gathered. "We are of one mind. We are in the full knowledge. Why would we do such a thing?"

"The full knowledge?" questioned Tyler. Zebedee explained.

"When you die you learn many things, many truths that are otherwise unknown. It's commonly referred to as the *full knowledge*."

"Ah, I see," said Tyler. "So nobody here took Hitler and put him into the Brimstone Chasm?"

There came a loud uproar from the council as ghosts shouted their abhorrence of such an idea. Tyler was unable to make much sense of any of it until the torrent of babble had subsided and the same spokesman as before summed up.

"No one who is in the full knowledge would ever do such a thing. It is not for us to use the chasm for our own ends. Such an idea is blasphemous to us. I beseech you; do not insult the Council of the Wise so!"

Tyler winced, not really understanding why her question had been received with such distain.

"If I have offended you, then I am sorry. It was not my intention. I simply wish to know how Hitler can have been held captive in your prison one minute and be gone the next?"

"We do not know how it happened, but it was as you have said. He was here one minute and gone the next. He was somehow taken from us. We do not know why, or by whom, but perhaps we were not meant to know.

You would understand this, if you were in the full knowledge."

Clearly...

"Thank you. I'm not in the full knowledge. Soon I'll return to my body and continue to hunt the Nazi ghosts who've entered my realm." This statement seemed to win over the crowd once more and there followed many shouts of encouragement and further applause for Tyler. "If any of you have any information that you think may help me, please find me. I thank you for your patience." Tyler made a simple bow of the head before stepping away, glad to be rid of the crowd's attention, but a Rabbi with a crazed look in his eyes caught her arm and pulled her close to hiss.

"Find them! For the sake of humanity, find them! And stop them before it's too late! You *must not* fail at any cost!"

The Shivering

For a while they rested in the ghetto, surrounded by ghostly holocaust victims. The effort of travelling within the contrap had exhausted Tyler and she sat on the firmament with her back against a hovel, hoping it would not dispel before she was recovered. Her weariness was like nothing she had known before. Not a thirst or hunger. Not a need to sleep, only an all-consuming heaviness that told her she could not go on. Her companions appeared to feel it also.

At length Zebedee rose, refilled his pipe, lit it and came to her.

"We should go now," he said between puffs. "We mustn't forget the clock is ticking." He checked his pocket watched. "Not mine, of course, but there we are..."

Tyler looked at her watch and saw without surprise that it was still showing the exact time her ghost had left her body on Monday night.

She wondered what the real time was and how much

of her allotted seven days she had already used. She knew that nobody this side of the portal lens had a clue about time passing and she wanted to return to the portal to talk with Melissa.

"I need to go back," she told Zebedee.

"You can't *go back*," said Claudia. "She can't go back, can she? Not now she's dead."

Zebedee frowned at Claudia and didn't answer.

"We'll take you back, but first we must search the Shivering Pool," he said to Tyler. "Come on, my girl. Let's be off."

Albert offered her a hand and helped Tyler to her feet. They set off, winding through the ghetto. Before her, a scattering of ghosts lined the edges of the road. As she and her companions walked, more and more ghosts joined the lines until the five of them were utterly hemmed-in on either side by ghosts bowing their heads.

"What are they doing?" she asked Zebedee with a whisper.

"It's a sign of respect. They are wishing you well on your journey. Do you not feel it?"

Tyler did not notice until Zebedee pointed it out, but she became aware of a rising feeling within. She was lighter and more capable of moving. As it grew, she felt more able and invigorated, as though a power had surged up inside her spirit. By the time they had marched out of the ghetto and the lines of ghosts could no longer be seen, Tyler felt strong. The ghetto was a deeply sad place and she realised she did not want to ever return to it, even though the ghosts there had somehow empowered her.

She watched the city move around her and wondered how long it would take them to locate the Shivering Pool. The metropolis seemed to go on endlessly and she had the feeling more than once as they travelled that it could well be extending itself in any direction they so chose to move, solely to frustrate her. The others didn't seem to share her fears and so she said nothing, but trudged on through obscure streets and surreal, shifting suburbs. She watched the ghost city with fascination and wondered at the hundreds and thousands of lives it represented - each with their own story in time - before her thoughts shifted to the Nazi ghosts she knew were also here, hiding among the many others. Himmler was somewhere in this realm and where was Goebbels? Was he sitting comfortably in a ghost Austrian villa beyond her view? Perhaps dipping his toes in a ghost Lake Grundel? Tyler shuddered.

She was glad to leave the city behind and re-enter the void-like firmament beyond. Something dug into her from the back pocket of her ghost jeans and she drew out a ghost pen and ghost sheet of notepaper. She did what she always did: She wrote a list - and then immediately ticked off the first item.

Check the Room of Faces   √
Search the Shivering Pool
Where is Hitler?
Where is Goebbels?
Where is Himmler?

The more she thought about it, the more she decided that putting any of the Nazis into the Room of Faces was a bad idea. She resolved to put them into the chasm if she found any of them. And then she knew why she was truly there. Multiple voices echoed in her mind.

'Only you, Tyler...'

'The task has been appointed to you...'

'When all you can do is what you can do, do what you can do...'

'Indeed, this task is yours to fulfil...'

'Use the knowledge you possess. Save yourselves.'

'And save untold masses from the oppressor. The oppressor must be defeated.'

She was *meant* to be hunting Hitler, Bagshot, Himmler and Goebbels, so she could put them into the

Brimstone Chasm. If she did this she would be able to leave the portal knowing they had been dealt with forever. She was pretty sure that no one ever escaped the chasm. She added a single item to her list of notes.

Put all Nazi ghosts into the chasm

She folded the list and tucked it back into her pocket along with the pen. She took Albert's hand again, saying nothing of her newfound quest. They hiked over undulating firmament until the city at their backs was once again a distant, enigmatic shape and Tyler wondered if they would ever actually find the Shivering Pool. It seemed that Zebedee simply followed his nose whenever he wished to find a place and that he kept moving until it presented itself at his feet. Whichever the case, she found a short while later that the mist ahead of them was dispersing and Zebedee let out a triumphant cry.

"We're nearly there!" He paused to place his monocle over one eye and scrutinise the haze ahead. "Up there, through the thinning fog." He pointed with his cane. "You can relax, Miss May. We've found it."

A further short walk brought them out of the featureless landscape onto the banks of what appeared to be a glistening pool of still water. The pool was edged with a smouldering, dense rise of the unformed memory-mist. It was like a small lake, the size of a large swimming pool, only roughly circular in shape and the water was not an inviting crystal blue but was colourless and dark. Releasing Albert's hand she went to the edge and, when nobody tried to stop her, bent to dip a hand in the water. It shivered at her touch and ran from her cupped hand like blackened mercury.

"Let me guess," she said, turning to Zebedee. "Some kind of unformed memory?"

"Very good, Miss May. Only, this unformed memory is quite the unhealthy sort. I would not recommend drinking this water, or spending too much time around it."

Tyler let the final drops of memory leave her fingers and backed away from the pool. A newcomer was closing on the opposite bank from out of the mist. Tyler instantly had a bad feeling and found Albert's hand.

"Who is it?" she whispered.

"Watch," said Albert. "You will see. Ghosts come here to forget; to be lost and to lose themselves."

As the ghost of an old man came nearer, his weathered, lined face became clear and Tyler saw, and felt, the shear hopelessness he carried. She didn't know why or how the man had ended up so dejected, but she knew with certainty that he had given up; given up on existing, given up everything. Even death.

The hopeless man slowed to enter the pool, which shivered in greeting as his toes, his feet and ankles sank beneath the black waters. Soon he was up to his knees, and wading in further and the entire surface shivered and trembled in response. It continued to shiver for a while after the man had gone to the depths and Tyler was saddened. The pool resumed its former tranquillity as though it had already forgotten the man.

"Some come of their own accord," said Zebedee. "Others are brought here through either malice or mercy."

"We must not tarry here long," said Izabella. "The pool emits a numbness that consumes all those who venture near. You do not need to enter its treacherous waters to succumb to the shivering."

"Izabella is correct," said Zebedee. "We must make our search and be gone. We must hurry. Watch over one another and be sure that no one becomes complacent. It is a sure sign that the pool is taking effect. We'll enter in pairs to be sure no one is left in there alone at any one time. Our dives must be short and our searches broad. We'll need a manner of marking the time." He looked lost at this juncture and turned to Izabella who offered no help, but he brightened with an idea. "I'll whistle a tune!

Each dive will last precisely four verses. If it takes longer someone will have to go in to fetch the divers out, lest they be consumed by the shivering."

Tyler questioned this logic, wondering what was to stop the rescuer from also succumbing to the shivering, but she agreed anyway. She was already sad and lonely, despite good company, and wanted to get on with it so that she could escape the place.

"Albert and I will go first," she said.

"Right you are," said Zebedee.

"Well, *I'm* not going in there," said Claudia. "Not now. Not ever. No way." She found a place to sit, far from the water, where she twirled her hair in her fingers and watched the others with unhealthy interest.

Tyler removed her boots and socks, dropping them on the bank.

"Are you sure you want to do this?" asked Zebedee.

Tyler nodded.

"Good luck," muttered Izabella.

"Good luck," mimicked Claudia.

Tyler tested the water with her toes. She watched it shiver into life and quieten when she withdrew. With a last glance at Albert, she walked into the pool and dived beneath the surface. She felt the shivering at once and fought against a growing shadow in her mind. It brought many things she only perceived on a deeply insular level: a coldness utterly devoid of love, a numbing resignation, a hopelessness and an ever deepening despair. These foes she battled as she swam, pushing dark waters to propel her ghost form deeper and on into the murk, checking periodically to see that Albert was still close by. The urge to surface and escape the pool was comparable to the need to breathe when diving in real water with a physical body.

The first figure she encountered was the man she'd watched enter. He did not swim but plodded slowly along the miry bottom of the pool. As she watched, he slowed until he stopped altogether and stood gazing at nothing, arms and hair buoyed by the surrounding water. As the shivering increased she became colder than when she'd passed through the crystal lens of the contrap. When she felt it becoming easier to stay there, she knew she should leave, but she wanted to complete the search so much that she carried on. She soon found more ghosts.

Hundreds of them.

They covered the depths of the pool like seaweed growing on an ocean floor. In places they had gathered and were clumped together. Elsewhere a solitary figure swayed almost imperceptibly in a submersed swell. Tyler checked faces but could see none resembling Hitler or any of the captured Nazi ghosts. She knew it was time to take a break from the pool when the idea to give it all up and simply let herself drift, entered her mind. She headed up. At her side, Albert did the same. She broke the surface and staggered numbly ashore, not affected to the point of depression but feeling lethargic. In fact she wanted to go home and forget about the entire idea.

If Hitler's down there, so much the better. He can stay there!

Zebedee helped her out of the water and she sat on the bank to rest as Albert sat beside her.

"Well done, both of you," said Zebedee. "Izabella and I will take a turn now. Don't forget to whistle and come for us if we're not back by the end of verse four." He placed his hat down on the bank and plopped his pipe into it.

"If we must," said Izabella, gingerly stepping into the water.

"Know any songs?" Tyler asked Albert, who now seemed distant, his eyes glazed. Her voice shook him from his thoughts and he turned.

"Songs? Yeah, I knows a few." He began to sing a soft, haunting melody as Zebedee and Izabella sank lower and the waters shivered. Tyler listened, mesmerised by the sound.

"Oh London town I see thee sleep
and sorrowfully mourn,
For winter's cruel and bitter chill
doth reach beyond the dawn,

Do you recall the day when once we met
and danced a merry step,
Upon the twelve days, feasting high,
when Solstice bells were born?

Come lamp-lighter with hasty tread
upon the cobbled street,
And on my doorway huddled so
I dance with icy feet,

For in my head and in my heart
I'm safely entered in,
And merry in good company
before a fire's heat."

Albert's voice was so gentle and the tune so calming that Tyler was falling asleep by the time he'd completed a fourth verse. He stopped singing and shook her awake.

"Where are they?" he asked. "They's supposed to be back by now." He rose to his feet and edged closer to the pool, squinting into the water. He waited there deliberating for several moments before turning.

"You wait 'ere, Missy. I'd best go in an' fetch 'em out." He dived neatly from the bank and plunged into the pool. Tyler crossed to the edge and peered after him but saw nothing but black, shivering water. She looked around, very alone despite Claudia's aloof presence. Tyler waited, hoping to see Albert come spluttering to the surface, but he didn't appear and the water stilled. She tried to remember Albert's song and began singing, thinking that he should at least be given the same four verses before she began to seriously worry, but she could not quite remember the words and the tune she sang just didn't sound right. She stopped singing to call softly.

"Albert? Albert, where are you." She'd never before felt quite so alone in all her life. After thirty seconds or so of unbearable silence she walked into the water and dived after him. Beneath the slick surface she realised something else strange about the pool. It was much larger below than its outer appearance suggested. She swam beyond the area she'd first explored, passing the languid forms of forgotten ghosts, and found new reaches of the pool where caverns and vast fields of the wretched *ghost weed* stretched out. Blank faces gazed into dark depths.

She caught movement at the edge of her field of view and turned away from a shaded cavern to investigate. Two ghosts were wrestling with another figure who seemed to be fixed to the pool's bed like the many others and, as she closed, she realised she had found Albert. He was with Zebedee, trying to heave Izabella from the ensnarement of the miasmic silt that had grabbed her and held her and all the weed ghosts fast. She swam to them with all speed and joined their struggle to free Izabella. Izabella was doing nothing to help. Her vacant expression and languorous stance suggested she had utterly succumbed to the mind numb. As Tyler fought alongside the others she noticed Zebedee, too, was showing signs of the *shivering*. She knew they would lose the battle if they didn't all escape the pool very soon. She battled the slick waters and the drag of Izabella's copious form with all her strength until the bond finally gave and they rose together as one body to the surface. Izabella was corpse-like as Albert and Tyler dragged her out. Zebedee made feeble attempts to help but could barely move himself, let alone take Izabella's weight. They stumbled ashore where they collapsed, exhausted.

"Oh, you're back," said Claudia, sounding disappointed. Tyler eyed her venomously.

No one spoke for a very long time and Tyler wondered if visiting the Shivering Pool had ever been a good idea. Even now, lying on the bank, she sensed its disheartening drag slowly eroding her mettle.

"Albert," she murmured. "I don't want to be here anymore."

Albert lifted his head from the smouldering bank and with great effort turned to look at her.

"We'll be alright, Missy. We'll be alright. You saved us all, you did." He let his head fall and didn't move again for a while.

Tyler recovered before any of the others and dragged them one at a time further from the water's edge. Slowly they each revived, first Albert, then Zebedee and finally Izabella, waking as though from a coma, and they sat up and were able to look around and talk.

"I'm sorry," said Izabella. "I know I am weak."

"It's understandable considering the circumstances," said Zebedee.

Albert gazed morosely at the ground.

"It ain't fair," he said, becoming angry as his vigour returned. "It just ain't fair."

"What?" asked Tyler, beginning to think she had missed something. "What's not fair? What are you talking about?"

Albert turned to Tyler. A deep, smouldering fury glowed in his eyes the like of which she had not seen before.

"Marcus. The pool has Marcus," he said.

Tyler only knew of one Marcus, dead or alive. He was a small boy ghost from the *Ghost Portal* who she'd met a long time ago. He had never said a word to her because he did not speak, but she had heard the sad story of his demise during the holocaust, via Albert.

The *silent fiddler*, Albert had called him.

"It was just too much for me," said Izabella. "I've always had a soft spot for that poor lad and to see him in there..."

Tyler had heard enough. She recalled Marcus's tale of separation from his parents and abuse at the hands of the Nazis, pictured his softly rounded, innocent, gentle face, and could stand it no longer. Albert saw the look in her eyes and shook his head.

"No, Missy. 'Tis too treacherous. We'd best leave him where his is. The longer they's down there the harder the pool's grip." He reached out to stop her as Tyler turned for the pool and launched headlong, back into the water.

The Mordecai Chain

Lucy parked the Aprilia, chained it up and entombed it behind the garage shutter, securing the chunky padlock. She took out her mobile when it chimed and entered the block leading to the apartment. Another text from frenetic Melissa, worrying herself to death about Tyler. Yes, it *was* true that two days had passed since Tyler had gone into the portal, but so what? She still had another five days before there was problem. Lucy tapped out a single word and hit *send*.

CHILL

Lucy didn't understand Melissa. Since Tyler had gone, she'd been half mad and completely unable to focus on anything. She knew they were close...
...but jeez, does she really have to be so co-dependent?
She was annoying and, since Tyler wasn't around for Melissa to pester, it was Lucy who was getting the grief. Melissa sat at Tyler's bedside for endless hours, watching

her body. The sooner Tyler returned the better, as far as Lucy was concerned, but she wasn't going to waste her time and energy worrying. That would be stupid. She had other things to focus on.

Important things.

She was doing well with her physical training and she was pleased with her progress on the shooting range. Chapman had given her an unexpected pat on the back several days earlier when she'd aced a shooting trial, outshining several older, more experienced male agents. All the same, Lucy's reports and assignments were not up to scratch and she knew it. It wasn't that she could not do the work or did not have the answers, but she found written work so uninspiring that she struggled to focus. It was always more tempting to throw some knives, head for the range, or take a ride on the Aprilia dream machine. Yes, Lucy had her own problems to worry about and she didn't need Melissa's to boot. And it wasn't like she was getting any help from anyone. Melissa didn't have a clue about Lucy's challenges and Lucy sure as heck wasn't going to share.

And then there was TAAN.

She headed up to the apartment, checking her reflection in the lift's mirrored walls and poking at her eyeliner.

When Lucy arrived, Melissa was waiting by the door, peering fanatically into the contrap's lens, hoping for a glimpse of Tyler. Lucy dumped her bag on the polished redwood flooring.

"Well?" asked Melissa.

"*Well* what?"

"Well, don't you think we should do something? She's been gone for days. I bet she doesn't even know how long she's been. She said she'd only be a couple of hours." Melissa tucked the contrap into her shirt.

"Like I said, *chill*." Lucy put the kettle on, craving caffeine. "She also said to hand in her assignment if she wasn't back."

"Oh no! The assignment..." Melissa sank into a chair, head in hands.

Lucy couldn't help but chuckle.

"You didn't..."

"I did," said Melissa. "It's still in her bag."

"Classic," said Lucy, chuckling. "You know what? You really need a distraction. Why don't you focus on something else for a while?"

"Like what?"

Lucy poured boiling water into a percolator and cast Melissa a sideways glance.

"Like TAAN. The Activists Against Nazism. Why don't you help me with it? It's not that easy creating a massive underground army of secret activists ready to move at the drop of a text."

Melissa considered this briefly before giving a nod.

"Alright. What do I do?"

Lucy paused and stared at Melissa.

"By the way, what time did she leave her body?"

"I don't know. I wrote it down, though. It's in the notebook by Tyler's bed." Melissa fetched the notebook and flipped through its pages. Light dawned. "I didn't write it down. I was going to but then I got a text from Freddy and... Hold on. I'll check the text for the time it came through. Oh, I can't. Deleted it. Oops."

"Why'd you delete the text?"

"I delete all my texts. Don't you?"

"No. So we don't know when it happened."

"Not exactly, no."

"Great. Wait. If Freddy hasn't deleted his text he'll be able to tell us the exact time he sent it."

*

Beneath the surface Tyler swam downwards seeking the place where Izabella had succumbed, knowing that Marcus could not be far away. She found him hanging limply in the depths, tethered to the bottom with an entangled knot of dense memory miasma. Taking a hold beneath his slight arms she pushed upwards trying to heft him to the surface but the pool's grasp upon him was solid and she wondered how long he'd been down there. She realised she hadn't seen him for years, so he could have been there for a very long time. Another wave of sorrow hit her.

Her exertions were getting her nowhere and the dark waters made every effort painstaking, but then and there, before the pool could dampen her resolve, she decided she would see Marcus freed, or the shivering could take her.

Forever.

Somebody somewhere has to care enough to help this boy and if I'm the only one, so be it!

She tried a different approach and drove herself lower to reach for the tendrils of grasping gloop at his ankles. She tore at them and found that they gave but clung to her instead and she became entangled as she fought, hands caked in syrupy, gripping fronds. She panicked, planted her feet on the pool's bed, thinking she could push off with her legs and free herself, but she sunk and the bed itself took a hold.

Uh-oh. Game over.

A hand found her in the murk and gave a sudden upward tug. She looked up to see Albert swimming away from the bed and dragging her free. She broke loose, overrun with a sense of relief, but stole away from Albert to return to Marcus, taking him under the arm and renewing her struggle. Albert swam to Marcus' other side and together they hauled, felt the ooze stretch, give and finally break and they took him up with them towards lighter reaches.

"You got guts, Missy. I give ya' that," said Albert as they recovered on the banks. "I ain't seen 'im for an age - didn't know 'e were in there, or I'd o'come for 'im. I swears!"

Tyler studied Marcus' motionless, glazed expression

and swept a swath of ghost hair from his brow.

"Will he be alright? How long's he been there?"

"Who knows?"

"Recovery may be possible," said Zebedee. "Time will tell. He must have been beyond despair to have gone in. Poor lad."

Tyler put her arms around Marcus and hugged him like she'd wanted to all that time ago when he'd first shared his story. She sensed the deep cold that had penetrated his form, but was also strongly aware of his presence. He *was* still there. Somewhere in the far reaches of his thinned essence, his spirit endured.

She didn't know how long she stayed at his side, feeling again that strange, unearthly need for rest. She closed her eyes and huddled against Marcus, wishing that some of her vitality would somehow pass to him.

Albert stirred her a while later with a hand on her shoulder.

"We'd best get on if we're going to search the whole pool."

Tyler shook herself. She'd almost forgotten about the reason she'd entered the *Ghost Portal*. She released Marcus and stood.

"You're right. And the longer we hang around here, the weaker we become." She took one look at Zebedee and Izabella and knew they were in no condition to exert themselves in the pool. "We'll have to do it. You and me. Though it will be dangerous. We'll take turns."

Albert nodded and headed for the water.

"I'll go first."

As he disappeared beneath the surface, Zebedee began to whistle. Four verses later, Albert returned, shaking his head.

"There's no sign of 'im, Missy." He pointed to the pool off to Tyler's right. "I've searched the big cavern over there. Nuffink."

Tyler submerged and found the cavern Albert had mentioned. She passed it and swam into a vast stretch that seemed to go on forever. She swam over the heads of a multitude of ghosts, checking for Hitler but not finding him. Albert took another turn and, between them, they slowly worked their way around the huge expanse of the pool until there was little remaining unsearched.

Tyler was looking forward to completing the search and getting far away from the pool. She figured she had one more dive to go, in which she hoped to cover the remaining area and she went in feeling drained. She searched many faces and swam as fast as she could to cover the expanse more quickly. Around her a low cave opened up and she baulked to find yet another mass of the deathly weed.

A faint shimmer drew her attention to an individual among the sea of faces. Swimming closer, she recognised him. He was different from the rest. She recoiled. Bagshot was lifeless and hanging in the soup like the others, but his arms were bound by a glimmering chain, a type which Tyler had never seen before. The chain appeared to have no beginning or end but coiled endlessly about his shoulders, clamping his arms flat against his body and continuing down to encase his legs, so that he was suspended like the cocooned larvae of a monstrous moth.

Swimming closer she was relieved to see he was just as zombified as the others. His mouth, however, was not gaping but tightly shut. Needing to speak with Albert, she turned and headed for the surface.

"Why's Bagshot in there? Did *you* put him in? And what's that chain holding him?"

Albert looked to Zebedee.

"I confess," said Zebedee. "I put him in the pool."

"What? How?"

"He's a trouble maker. I thought it best," said Zebedee. "I stumbled upon him a while ago and saw where he was staying in the city. I knew about the Mordecai chains and sought one out, though they're a devil to get hold of. I surprised him and bound him with the chain. Then I brought him here and shoved him in for safekeeping."

"The *Mordecai* chains?"

"Mordecai, meaning contrition, bruising or bitterness. They originate from the chasm, yet a few have found their way here, into this place. It is not known how. There aren't many."

"I found one other," said Zebedee. "I used it to bind Goebbels, who I also put in the pool."

"Anything else you've neglected to tell me?" asked Tyler, dumbfounded. She pictured Goebbels as she'd last seen him, his long, gaunt face morphing into blue light, shrieking into the portal.

Zebedee peered at his feet and then refilled his pipe.

"No, no. That's everything, I think," he said with inexplicable joviality.

"Right then. You'd best tell me everything you know about the chains. How do they work? Where can we get more of them?"

"You see, Izabella? I knew this would happen," said Zebedee.

"Can they be used outside, in my world?" asked Tyler. "Shame I can't go into the chasm and fetch them out. I can't go in, can I? Zebedee's book said no one ever returns..." As Tyler considered this, a new plan formed in her mind, but she needed answers before she could fix upon anything certain. She looked from Zebedee to Izabella, expectantly.

"The damage is done, Zebedee," said Izabella. "We might as well tell her all we know about the chains. Or she might go after the chains without knowing all that we know and that could be far worse."

Zebedee nodded and took a long draw on his pipe.

"We can but try, Izabella. Tell her."

"A Mordecai chain can be used to detain a ghost. It works within the *Ghost Portal*. To my knowledge, no one has ever taken one into the realm of the living, so whether or not one would work there, or indeed, whether one could even exist there, well, your guess is as good as mine. We kept this knowledge from you for fear that you would want to enter the chasm - something we'd strongly advise against - for it might very well be the end of you. The gateway to the chasm should never have been created. It is an unholy aberration. Quite unnatural."

"How do they work? What, exactly, do they do?"

"The chains can be used to bind any ghost. You simply throw the chain at the ghost in question and use the command *Mordecai obligo*. The chain will bind up and silence the ghost in a trice. Of course, the chains are incredibly heavy, so this task is not as easy as it sounds," said Izabella.

"To release the chain you use the command *Mordecai resolvo*," said Zebedee. "Anyone can use them. It just takes a free person to touch the chain and say the correct words. Those chained are unable to release themselves for they cannot speak. They are bound until released by another."

"So anyone could dive into the pool and release Bagshot and Goebbels?" Tyler asked.

"Yes," said Zebedee.

"But why would they?" asked Izabella.

"You are forgetting the other Nazis who're in here. Others who might want to free them."

"Yes, I see," said Izabella. "Well, it is said that nobody ever returns from the Brimstone Chasm. Perhaps it *would* be better to put the Nazis in there."

Tyler knew at once that this was what she had to do. Goebbels and Bagshot would have to be hauled out of the Shivering Pool and transported to the chasm. If she could locate Hitler and Himmler, then they could go into the chasm, too. It would be safer for all concerned, except for the Nazis. She turned to Albert.

"We have to finish searching the pool. Any Nazis come with us. Come on. Zebedee can watch for us. It will take both our efforts to drag up the Nazis." With Albert at her side she waded into the water again and dropped beneath the surface, heading towards the last unsearched area. Together, after an intense struggle, they pulled Bagshot's shivered and bound ghost free, dumped him on the bank and returned for Goebbels. They found him not far from where Bagshot had been and heaved him out. Tyler made one more descent into the pool to check the final reaches of the last submerged cavern. When she climbed out she settled by Albert and shrugged.

"He's not in there. Hitler is not in the pool. So where is he?"

"Who knows?" said Albert.

"He has to be somewhere. Are you sure you're not keeping anything else from me, Zebedee?"

"I swear on my... I swear. I am not withholding any information from you at all," said Zebedee. "I'm very sorry that I did, but I think you can see I had my reasons. I did it with your best interests at heart."

"Okay."

"Hitler has clearly escaped the portal somehow," said Izabella. She was sitting on the bank cradling Marcus in her arms. He looked small against her formidable girth. "If he is not here, he must be in the chasm or else in the world."

Tyler looked at her hapless group of friends and thought about all her struggles since discovering the contrap in Lucy's bag. It was crazy and only getting worse. She took out her list but found the hastily scrawled words were gone. She tried to remember exactly what she'd written but the words did not reappear on the ghost paper as she hoped. *Guess lists don't work this side of the lens.* She stubbornly rewrote the list as she remembered it before ticking two items off.

Check the Room of Faces √
Search the Shivering Pool √
Find Hitler
Find Goebbels √

Find Himmler
Put all Nazi ghosts into the chasm

She sat for a long time, thinking about what she should do before addressing Izabella.

"If only there was a way for us to fetch more chains from the chasm. We could bind all the Nazis and put them all into the chasm. Surely that would be the last anyone would ever see of them."

"And you'd be a big heroine," sniped Claudia, eavesdropping. "Save the world and everything. Yes that would be nice. Not going to happen though."

Izabella eyed Tyler, measuring.

"Are you asking me to find a way to do this? This is madness, girl."

Silence. Tyler brooded over the problem until Izabella spoke again.

"I suppose there may be one way," she said uncertainly. "There is an old summoning spell. I'll need to consult my book." She drew out a small brown notebook from a pocket in her flowery dress and skipped through its pages. She was a while searching and muttering to herself but, at length, she looked up to meet Tyler's awaiting gaze.

"Here it is. I've found it. It will only work for someone who has a body still living, but as long as that person is you, I don't see a problem. You will have the power to summon yourself out of the chasm. And you will have the power to summon others out also. In theory."

Tyler nodded to Marcus.

"Help him to mend. We're going into the chasm and we're going to need every pair of hands we can get."

Nine Ghosts

Melissa reread her notes and calculations.

"Freddy sent the text at eleven forty so that's our best guess for when Tyler left her body. Problem is sometimes texts get delayed."

"I didn't think it was that late," said Lucy. "But I guess it can't have been before then."

"Yeah and I thought it was even later."

"Okay. Let's go with eleven forty." Lucy shrugged and checked her mobile, the one she had modified with the help of a friend in the MI5 IT department. She had begun with a small circle of acquaintances; people she knew would be up for a bit of activism, but people who she was not too close to. She needed to keep it anonymous, and that was the tricky part. Her TAAN handle was Mojo, a deviation of Emo, which Melissa had nicknamed her until it had stuck. Lucy had messaged six individuals originally and had built that over the last few days to forty-three. After that, Melissa had really got on board and the number had multiplied as messages were passed around and word spread. The untraceable mobile in Lucy's hand now registered responses from over a hundred and fifteen respondents, all members of the newly formed TAAN. If they'd achieved that amount of growth in just a few days, thought Lucy, what could they do in a few weeks, or months?

I'm an uncelebrated visionary!

She intended to spread the word about the underworld of Nazi infiltration to as many as she could reach, with or without Chapman's consent. The world was soon going to know all about the NVF.

She watched Melissa checking the *Ghost Portal* and biting her lip in frustration.

"A watched pot never boils," said Lucy.

"Thanks for that. I just thought she'd be back by now. I wonder what's keeping her."

The entrance intercom buzzed, making Melissa jump.

"Relax," said Lucy. "You're *way* too uptight. You'll have a seizure if you're not careful."

"I'm okay." Melissa peered into the small video live-feed monitor and gasped.

"It's that guy from the library. It's Hatherow! He's here!"

Lucy joined her at the monitor and swore, squinting at the black and white, grainy image of the limping librarian. She pressed the speaker button on the console by the door.

"Yes?"

"Oh, hello. I'm here to see a Miss Tyler May."

Lucy and Melissa exchanged looks of concern.

"I'm sorry. Who?" said Lucy, feigning ignorance.

"Tyler May." Hatherow spelled out the name annunciating each sound with exaggerated care.

"I'm sorry. No one of that name lives here. You must have the wrong address."

"This is the correct address. I'm quite sure. I

double-checked."

Lucy released the button and backed away, watching to see what he would do.

"Don't let him in, whatever you do."

"I wasn't about to."

Melissa jumped again when the buzzer sounded a second time. On the screen, Hatherow hammered the button at his end and spat words they could not hear. Melissa gave a sigh of relief when he left the view.

"That's odd," said Lucy. "Our address is a state secret. How did he find us?"

"Who knows? Friends in high places?"

"Maybe. That's worrying."

"Okay, I'm severely creeped-out." Melissa took out her phone and called Chapman.

"Don't worry about it. What's he gonna do?" asked Lucy.

An explosion rocked the building and the entrance monitor filled with static. Melissa ran to the window. Smoke billowed up from the street below. Lucy had a gun at the ready and slipped out into the passageway.

"Does that answer your question?" Melissa swore and followed her as Chapman answered.

"Melissa. Everything alright?"

"Someone just bombed our front door. Gotta go." She killed the call and found Lucy battling to open the lift doors.

"Out of order."

"Due to bomb damage?"

Lucy headed down the stairs, her gun levelled. Melissa followed and they came out into the block entrance as smoke dispersed on the breeze. The battered door was in the lobby and a portion of the outer wall was little more than scattered shrapnel.

Hatherow was nowhere to be seen.

*

Tyler hesitated, peering ahead through a tumult of memory mist. Someone was there. She knew of the presence long before they walked into her view. The Polish twins, dark haired and dark eyed, approached and Tyler wasn't sure if she was pleased to see them or not.

"Hello, Danuta, Kinga."

The twins inclined their heads politely.

"We come to aid you, Tyler May," said Danuta. "Against the oppressor."

"The spirit of the oppressor is an ancient evil," said Kinga.

"Ancient? How ancient?"

"Throughout history he has plagued humanity," explained Danuta. "He has influenced many nations. He dwelt amongst the Egyptians when they enslaved Israel, and the Babylonians when they took Jerusalem in ancient times. He coerced the Syrian king, Antiochus Epiphanes, into the sacking of Jerusalem and the murder of her people. He led the Romans in their campaigns to enslave the nations. He inhabited the murderous emperor, Nero. He brought about the crusades."

"And he formed the Third Reich. We are at your service," explained Kinga, her robust features serious. "He must not prevail. What would you have us do?"

Tyler was astonished. She looked the twin ghosts over. They were young girls, once. Not tall. Not strong. They were shy and lacking confidence and yet they had somehow known she was in need of help and they had come. She wondered what use they might be on the other side of the *plural curtain* where brimstone fires never ceased.

"I can't promise you an easy ride," she said. "In fact, I think there's a good chance we may never return to this realm."

"Do not fear for us," said Danuta. "We are dead. There is little that can harm us now and we are in the full knowledge."

That again! Guess I'll learn what that is, one day.

Maybe sooner than I'd like!

"If you're sure. I'm planning to enter the Brimstone Chasm. I must warn you, nobody's expecting this to be much fun."

"We know," said Kinga. "We learned what you were planning before we came to seek you out."

Tyler pondered this.

"Alright then. You can come with me and help me in any way you can. Can you each carry a Mordecai chain? I need to bring back as many as I can from the chasm."

"Yes. We think we can carry the chains, though they will be a heavy burden to bear."

"We will try. If we cannot manage one each perhaps we can bring one between us."

"Good. You'd better follow me."

Tyler set off again, tramping the marshy, ethereal land as it rolled treacherously beneath her feet. Beside her, Albert marched stoically, followed by Zebedee, who carried Marcus next to Izabella. Behind them walked the twins and, lagging at the back and singing absently to herself, strolled Claudia. The Shivering Pool was far behind them, the city, nowhere to be seen and all that lay ahead, as far as Tyler could tell, was haze.

"You sure it's this way?" she asked Albert.

"It ain't far now, Missy. I promise."

"If you say so."

Tyler plodded on, feeling that otherworldly weariness weigh more heavily with every step. They walked for miles before she noticed a small gleaming shape in the distance and knew it was the *Ghost Portal*.

*

Chapman paced back and forth on the bomb-damaged street, his mobile clenched to his ear.

"I don't care. Pull them out. Find a team. Whatever it takes. I want every CCTV image in the vicinity collected and examined before five. Prioritise. Okay?"

He slipped his phone into a pocket and turned to Melissa.

"You're serious about this?"

She nodded.

Lucy glanced skyward with a *God help us* face.

"Well, you'd best lead the way," said Chapman.

Melissa headed back into the wounded building, ducking beneath police tape and avoiding a bomb disposal team, the damage assessment crew and police. She climbed the stairs.

"She's been gone for two days now. I'm getting kind of worried something's happened to her."

"Yes," said Chapman, close on her heels. Lucy followed.

In the apartment, Melissa led Chapman to Tyler's room and showed him Tyler's body, which might have been asleep except that she was not moving, not even to breathe. Chapman tentatively checked her forehead with concern.

"She's cold. And there's no pulse."

"She's not dead," said Lucy. "Her ghost's in the contrap. When it returns to her body she'll be alive again."

At the mention of the contrap, Melissa drew it from her shirt to check the portal and was amazed to see figures approaching out of the mist.

"She's back!" she said. "Tyler's come back!"

Lucy and Chapman huddled to see, although it was hard for more than one person to look into the contrap's lens at one time. Chapman took the contrap.

"Tyler, what were you thinking?"

Startled, Tyler was quiet for a moment.

"Sir, I have to find Hitler's ghost. He's not in here, which means he could be out there. I've assembled a team. We're going to enter the chasm to look for Hitler. Can you pass the contrap to Mel? We need to come out of here."

Melissa quickly explained to Chapman about the chasm and everything that they had learned from

Izabella. He read a new text message and surprised the girls by saying, "Alright. Do what you have to do, but do it quickly and get back to your training. I'm going to focus on Hatherow. I'm glad the blast didn't catch any of you." He left, looking paler than when he'd arrived.

"Well, that was unexpected," said Lucy. She told Tyler about Hatherow's appearance at their door and the bomb blast.

"I get the feeling we've not heard the last of him," said Tyler. "Mel, can you say the magic words and get me out of here?"

Melissa pulled the contrap lever anticlockwise.

"Phasmatis Licentia."

Tyler's ghost was drawn out the lens, spinning through air and back into her bedroom. Mel released the lever.

"No. Keep it open!" said Tyler, and Melissa repositioned the lever as the other nine ghosts streamed out to fill the room.

"That's everyone," said Tyler. Melissa released the lever, closing the portal.

"Good day to you," said Zebedee, tipping his top hat to Melissa and Lucy.

"Is that Goebbels? And Bagshot?" asked Lucy, gawping at the two chained spirits.

"They were in the Shivering Pool," explained Tyler, casting Zebedee a knowing glance. "I'm going to dump them in the chasm."

A girl's voice sounded distantly from inside the contrap.

"Hello? Are you there? Where did everybody go?"

Everyone looked at Tyler, who shrugged. Melissa peered into the lens.

"It's Kylie Marsh," she said. "The girl who was killed when Hitler's glove was blown up near the abbey."

"She must have been following us," said Tyler, taking the contrap and seeing the small, but erudite, school girl in a ghostly, purple coat. Kylie had straight, dark-brown hair and a narrow face with large eyes. "Kylie, are you alright?"

"Hi, Tyler. I'm okay."

"Were you following us?"

"Yes."

"What do you want?"

"I don't know. It's lonely in here. I guess I wanted to be with someone. I saw Zebedee and followed because he was kind to me."

Tyler hesitated, weighing options.

"You can come with us, if you like, but we're not going anywhere nice. Do you want to be part of my team? I need helpers. We're going into the Brimstone Chasm to look for Hitler. We're going to stop him, but it might be dangerous."

Kylie was quiet for a moment.

"You're going to stop him hurting other people?"

"Or die trying. Yes."

"Okay. I'll come with you."

"Wait there. Mel..."

Melissa pulled the lever. "Phasmatis licentia."

The ghost of Kylie Marsh joined them in the room and Melissa closed the portal. Tyler explained to Kylie what had happened in the contrap and all about the Mordecai chains. She introduced Kylie to the ghosts she hadn't met.

"I think we're ready now, Mel," said Tyler.

"Wait!" said Izabella. "We're *not* ready. *Not* ready at all!"

"Oh. Why?" asked Tyler.

"There are a few things you need to know about the chasm before you go hurling us all in. Firstly, you should know I haven't been there before, so what I am going to say is little more than theory, but, from what I have gathered, the chasm is not a place to be entered lightly. It's a place of perpetual torture, pain and death; a godless place. Once we are inside we may find it difficult to stay together. It is a shifting realm, by its very nature, disorienting, like the portal's city, only much more diabolical. If you get separated from our group, you must not despair. Despair is what the chasm realm was meant to induce. Your greatest weapon will, therefore, be hope. You must find hope in all circumstances. You are going to need it - mark my words! Fight despair with all the strength you can muster. Rally hope. And remember why we are doing this or we are all doomed. The chasm will do everything within its power to distract you and make you forget, but you must hold fast! Have faith in those you now see around you and the greater power. The chasm is likely to lie to you and try to deceive you, but remember the truth, that we are all in this together. And we are on the side of all things good!" She glowered at each of the ghosts in turn as if willing her words to sink in.

"Sounds like a *real* fun place," said Lucy.

"*Real* fun," echoed Claudia. "Why don't you tag along?"

Lucy sneered.

"There is one more thing I can add," said Izabella. "I think I have worked out a way to summon the ghost of Hitler once we are in. It may save us endless searching."

"You *think* you've worked out a way," said Tyler. "So if it doesn't work we won't know for sure if he's there or not."

"This is true, but it is worth a try. If it does work it will save us much time." Izabella added a new thought. "We may be able to test it with another ghost. Yes, we can test it and see if it works or not. I can use Zebedee or Albert to test my theory, but we'll have to collect the Mordecai chains first. If it works and if the oppressor is there, we will need a way to restrain him."

"Great. Can we go now?" asked Tyler. "I want to get this over with."

Izabella eyed her guardedly.

"We can go." She turned to Melissa. "Set the contrap to the fire symbol and take the lever clockwise full circle until it clicks back into place. Then say the words."

"You have less than five days left. Be quick," Melissa warned. Horrified at what she was doing, she followed Izabella's instructions. With all eyes on her, she drew the lever clockwise around the contrap and back to twelve o'clock, jumping when it clicked into place. She wiped her brow uneasily, glanced at Tyler and, with a nervous stutter, gave the command.

"Vvv... Vorago expositus!"

PART
TWO

The Chasm

The chasm portal opened. Melissa peered into the contrap's crystal and watched a dark veil of smoke disperse to its edges, revealing a vast, shimmering lake of fire. An otherworldly glow radiated from the lens to light the faces of the others as they gathered round and, strangely, it even reflected upon the ghosts.

Melissa smelt a sulphurous gas and nearly gagged.

"Oh, that stinks!" She recoiled.

Lucy smelt it too and grimaced.

"Uh-huh. I'm guessing that's brimstone."

Upon closer inspection the lake of fire proved to be something else. Tyler could see it clearly now. At the crystal's edges were the sides of a deep crevasse and, as this dropped away towards the centre, what had appeared to be a flaming lake was in fact a layer of broiling, churning fog. Here and there the fog burned with golden flames, but she could see beyond enough to know that the chasm continued its descent.

"The *lake of fire*," muttered Izabella. "It is as I

thought."

Melissa looked at Tyler and then Albert, at Zebedee and back at Tyler.

"Good luck."

Tyler nodded.

"Go ahead. Say the words and put us in."

Melissa pointed the contrap's crystal at Tyler.

"Phasmatis licentia!"

Tyler's ghost was gathered by an unseen force and hurled into the lens with an ear-splitting shriek. The room filled with a roaring maelstrom as wind tore at the ghosts and the living alike. Melissa battled to hold the contrap as it juddered in her grasp and when Tyler was gone she turned it upon Albert and then Zebedee. Izabella was next to be swallowed, closely followed by Marcus, Kylie, Kinga and Danuta, and the Nazis, and finally Claudia, who now appeared to want nothing to do with this quest.

"Close the portal!" bellowed Lucy over the din of the tearing storm.

Melissa wrestled with the contrap as it seemed to be seeking out other souls to consume. It fought her direction, turning towards the only other viable spirit in the room: Lucy.

"CLOSE THE PORTAL! CLOSE IT NOW!"

The rending air began to blur the edges of Lucy's form as Melissa fought.

"NO!" cried Lucy.

"VORAGO TERMINO!" screamed Melissa.

The torrent subsided, leaving the girls gasping and Melissa shaking. She collapsed as Lucy ran to help her into the lounge where she let her down into a chair.

"Sorry," said Melissa, dazed. "It was like... I swear, the contrap tried to take control of me! I couldn't stop it."

"Well I'm glad you *did* stop it. It nearly took me. And it would have killed me."

"Yes," said Melissa. Hands trembling, she put the

contrap's chain around her neck and tucked it into her shirt. She was surprised by a knock at the apartment door. Lucy opened it to let in a medical team carrying resuscitation gear. The head paramedic flashed Lucy a security services card.

"No need to panic. Mr Chapman sent us. I'm Doctor Adams." He offered his hand, which Lucy ignored.

"Nobody's panicking. Why did he send you?" asked Lucy. "He didn't say anything about this and nobody here is injured."

"Yes, well. We'll be the judge of that. We've come to examine Tyler May. Just following orders, you understand. It's all just precautionary."

"You're not needed. And this is a private residence. Please leave."

"I'm afraid I can't do that. Mr Chapman is expecting a report on the physical wellbeing of the girl in question. Please take me to Tyler."

Lucy shook her head.

"Mel?"

"On it." Melissa was busy calling Chapman.

Lucy blocked Adams but he brushed her aside and headed into the apartment to check bedrooms.

"Yes," said Melissa to Chapman. "They've just barged in. Please call them off. We don't need this hassle."

Adams found Tyler's body and issued instructions to his team. Various machines and monitors were swiftly carried in and hooked up to Tyler.

"She's not breathing," stated a female paramedic, listening to Tyler's chest with a stethoscope.

Another doctor was trying to take her pulse and watching a static line on a heart monitor.

"No pulse. She's dead. You want vasopressin?"

"She's not dead!" barked Lucy from the doorway. "Her ghost has been separated from her body temporarily. I don't expect you to understand but you must go. Please leave her alone!"

Melissa joined her in the doorway to see what was

happening.

"Chapman won't help. He wants a medical report. Prattled on about dealing with grieving parents and a looming court case. Sounded a bit weird."

Adams was shaving a patch of hair on Tyler's head.

"NO!" shouted Melissa. "DON'T!"

"No resuscitation just yet. I want to try something." Adams attached a probe to Tyler's scalp and switched on another machine. "That's odd. Very odd."

"What?" asked the female paramedic.

"Her EEG is good, quite strong, in fact. Somehow the brain is still living. Everything is still living."

"I told you SHE'S NOT DEAD," said Lucy. "PLEASE LEAVE!"

"Okay, we're going." Adams beckoned for a stretcher to be brought forward and unrolled.

"What are you doing now?" asked Melissa.

"We're taking her with us, of course. She needs to be monitored properly. I have some further tests to perform which can only be done in the proper environment. Alright?"

A metallic click answered Adam's question as Lucy switched the safety catch off her P99. Adams raised his hands as she levelled the gun at his head. Melissa left the doorway.

"You're making a big mistake, young lady."

"You're about to make a bigger one. Get out, before I shoot you, you patronising git." Lucy freed the probe from Tyler's head. "And take your stuff with you."

Another paramedic reached for something beneath his reflective, yellow coat. Lucy switched aim in a flash. Adams noticed and shook his head. *No, don't bother.*

"I'll not ask again," warned Lucy as Melissa returned, toting her gun. Melissa bent to check they had not harmed Tyler's body and the contrap swung free from her shirt. Adams eyed it, failing to conceal recognition.

"Okay. You win. We're leaving." He motioned for his crew to follow and they left. Lucy followed them to the door and locked it when she was sure they had gone.

"What is it with these people?"

"Guess they were trying to follow orders," said Melissa, bemused.

"Oh well, they're gone now." Lucy crossed the room.

"We better take shifts on guard. Chapman might send another team."

"Good call." Lucy viewed the street below from the lounge window. The police were talking with the medical crew. More officers were closing off the road with temporary barriers either side of their apartment block. "What are they doing? Why are they blocking off the street?"

Melissa joined her.

"Who knows?"

Lucy took out her mobile and dialled Weaver's number. She glared at Melissa.

"Call Freddy. Get him over here."

*

Tyler had felt the usual shiver as she passed through the crystal lens but a change occurred. She was more alive than in the *Ghost Portal*, more human. She was still a ghost but now with a deeper substance and aware of a certain vulnerability. She plummeted towards the churning flames of the fire fog, dreading what they might do to her, and prepared for pain. When she hit the fog she was amazed to find it did not hurt. She *was* aware of a searing heat, but one that did not appear to damage her. She wondered what the substance was as she passed through it and continued to fall into the darkening chasm. She glimpsed other figures following her and realised they were her ghost team. That was good to know at least.

She hit another raft of hot, shimmering cloud and tumbled through, watching the flaming substance cling to her form and dispel as she dropped. She noticed she was leaving a trail in the atmosphere like the tail of a burning satellite. Looking down she saw ground approaching and wondered how and why it moved. It was akin to the city in the *Ghost Portal*, except this was no city, rather it was an entire landscape that shifted and crawled and, as she closed on it, she heard its groan. Beings moved around. Some were large and she could not be sure what they were. Other small beings looked like thin ghosts. Buildings grew, wire fences broadened and she became lost in the view as she rushed closer. The fire fog was on everything, or everything was fire fog – she could not be sure. It drifted and flowed like vaporous mercury, like the memory mist, but always burning, always shimmering. Landing between two buildings, she sank beneath a layer of fire fog and was belched back out along with a plume of fine, dusty ash. Amazed the fall had not obliterated her altogether and there seemed no immediate threat, she stood on the surface of the broiling fog trying to gather her wits and awaited the arrival of her friends, wishing she could find shelter from the encompassing heat. Something fell like snow in the air. She caught some. Not snow, but ash. She looked up at a moon shining in a scorched firmament of reds and burnt orange.

Albert hit the building to her left, cleaving it like a bullet in jelly. The building rallied to vomit him out before reforming a few metres to the right of its original position. Albert righted himself and walked over to Tyler, brushing himself down and sweeping swathes of the dust into the hot air.

"Gor blimey! Am I on fire?" He looked at Tyler and seemed to forget about himself. "You alright, Missy?"

"Think so. As alright as you'd expect, I suppose. Where are the oth..."

Izabella arrived between them like an incendiary bomb and they were blown backwards with the resulting impact blast. A great cloud of ash filled the air and Tyler heard the others land before it cleared. She scanned the surrounding fiery landscape through haze. Her team were gathering. Kylie was looking around at the strange surroundings. Zebedee walked jauntily in from beyond the reaches of the two buildings as though taking a pleasant afternoon stroll. Marcus stood by the crater that Izabella had made, peering down into it as if in a dream.

"Will somebody get me out of here?" Izabella called from the hole. Tyler and Albert reached down and helped her up and, when Izabella was safely out of the crater, Tyler checked that everyone was there. The two chained Nazis were missing.

"Search the place for Goebbels and Bagshot. We need to know what's happened to them." The team searched and Zebedee soon gave a shout.

"I have Bagshot! Someone give me a hand to pull him out! I think the chains have made them heavier. They've sunk really deeply."

Tyler helped Zebedee to extract Bagshot from the fire fog and they dragged him out as Albert and the twins brought Goebbels.

"What we gonna do with'em now?" asked Albert.

Tyler did not yet know. She looked around and could see little but the two huts on either side. The huts were held above the fog by corner posts so that she could see a slim gap under them.

"Shove them under there for now." She pointed to the gap beneath the closest hut, and Albert and Zebedee maneuverer the bound ghosts in and pushed fog over them to hide them.

"That's good," said Tyler examining their work. "We'll come back for them soon when we have our bearings." She had a growing feeling that something was wrong and looked around nervously.

"Now," began Izabella. "We must firstly locate the Mordecai chains before we do anything else."

"I suppose we could free one of those two," said Zebedee, pointing to the gap beneath the hut. "That would give us one chain to use."

Tyler shook her head.

"Too risky," she said. "Where will we find more chains?" The little voice of her mind screamed a warning as a long shadow fell over her.

*

The sofa would barely fit through the door.

"Try hooking the arm through first," Melissa suggested. She didn't want to throw the sofa down the stairs but *needs must*. They readjusted positions.

"Okay, try again."

Lucy heaved. Melissa shoved as hard as she could and the sofa became wedged.

"Come on! They'll be trying to get back in any minute. If we don't block the stairway somehow there'll be nothing between us and them but a single, flimsy door."

"Okay, stand back." Melissa took a run up and shouldered the sofa further through.

"Nice! One more of those should do it," said Lucy, tugging unsuccessfully from her side. Melissa charged again and the sofa flew from the door frame to crash in the hallway. A brief moment of satisfaction passed as footfalls sounded from the stairs. The lift had been more easily disabled. Melissa had dismantled the control panel and snipped a few wires to be sure no one could fix the mechanism from below. It was now parked on their floor until someone fixed it from there.

On the count of three the girls launched the sofa down the stairwell where it lodged firmly halfway down the first flight.

"That should slow 'em down at least," said Lucy. "They won't be able to rush us."

"Good. Ammunition? We could be here for some time."

"Step this way," said Lucy. "I have some. Maybe not enough. I might need to sneak out somehow and fetch more. Have plenty of guns though."

"That's no good. We already have one each."

"Ah, but there's guns and then there's *guns*," explained Lucy, leading Melissa through the apartment to her bedroom and opening an innocent-looking pine wardrobe.

"Oh my gosh!" said Melissa gazing at Lucy's private armoury. "I'm living with a psycho!"

"Here," said Lucy, passing a tear gas grenade launcher. "A couple of shots from this will make them think twice."

"They'll come back wearing masks."

"I know but it will slow them down, right? Buy us some time. We have masks, too."

"Maybe we should just let them take Tyler. I'm sure they wouldn't hurt her."

"Over my dead body."

"That might be an option the way this is going."

"No way. Nazis have infiltrated every country we visited. Tyler has always suspected they've a presence in the police over here too. She's thought that from the start and Chapman confirmed it."

"But there's no proof to back the conspiracy theory up."

"And none to the contrary, either. Who's to say Hatherow isn't blackmailing Chapman. It could be him trying to get to Tyler. Perhaps he's *well connected*, if you know what I mean."

"Okay. I'm with you. I don't like the way your mind works but we'll ride this out."

"Good." Lucy pointed to parts on the weapon. "Safety's here. Pull this back to load. Make sure this is properly shut." She shoved tear gas canisters into Melissa's hands before heading back to the stairway. The footsteps sounded closer. Lucy gave Melissa a nod and she let fly two canisters. Gas flooded the stairway as Melissa's mobile chimed. She looked at the screen.

"Chapman."

Second Death

The shadow darkened and Tyler tremulously followed it to its source. At one end of the gap between buildings leered a huge, armoured, shaggy creature, twice the height of a man. The beast stood on two legs, human-like, but its long snout, face and tall, pointed animal ears were more like a jackal's. From the broad hackles of its neck rose a smouldering drift of smoke, which gave Tyler the impression that, somewhere, the creature was actually burning. Or perhaps it was just that it had been in the chasm for so long that it had imbibed some of the fire fog and ash that appeared to be the chasm's substance. On its bronze breastplate were engraved two S-shaped lightning bolts, side by side and it carried a machine gun at the ready and a lash, although it made no threat to use them, as yet. It watched the gathered ghosts with mild amusement as Tyler backed away. With a thunderous, growling voice, it spoke.

"Back to work, ghost scum! You can't hide from the Chasm Masters. We always find you."

The voice seemed to shake Kylie from a trance and she scrambled to make a fleeting bid for freedom, but was swiftly gathered, screaming, to the feet of the creature with one lash from its lengthy, smouldering whip.

"Get up, you filthy rats. Back to work." It extended one of its huge arms to point out beyond Tyler's view but as she rounded the side of the building she saw at last, in close quarters, where she was and understood the nature of the place. Smouldering wire fences surrounded as ash fell from the dark, hot sky and familiar large, black birds circled. Tall towers surrounded a prison complex and starved, ghost bodies swung slowly from gibbets, strung up by the neck. Other bony ghost bodies were piled in mountainous heaps and she noticed still more heaps were simply piles of ash. A short way off, ghost prisoners hacked at the broiling, stony surface of a quarry with picks and hammers while more of the jackal creatures loomed over them with guns and lashes, their brazen breastplates glinting in the heat. Tyler traced the trail of falling ash up into the endless void above her and then over to a massive chimney beyond the fenced complex from which the ash spewed. At the base of the furnace rose a mound but, as she gazed, Tyler saw that it was not a hill or a small mountain. It was yet another pile of the dead - those who had suffered a ghost death in the chasm? She could only guess.

Izabella already seemed resigned to their fate when she turned to Tyler.

"Welcome to Hell."

*

Melissa frowned. "That was odd. Chapman texted me a blank message. What does that mean?"

Lucy shrugged and checked her phone.

"Maybe he stuffed it up. Weaver's on a job but he's ditching it to help us. You heard from Freddy?"

"He's on his way but he won't be able to get in.

How's he going to pass the roadblock?"

"Good question. We're gonna need a way in and out. Oh! Get him to pick up some ammo on his way!"

Melissa nodded and sent a new text. She watched police getting organised in the street below and another ambulance pulled up beyond the barrier.

"Man, they're really making a meal of this." The area around the apartment looked every bit a full-on siege. "Anyone would think we're harbouring an escaped serial killer."

Lucy found the remote and switched the TV on, turned it off when she failed to find a news program.

"I'd like to know what they're thinking," she said.

"Maybe we should call Chapman again. Wait. Someone has a megaphone. They're going to try to talk us down."

Lucy joined Melissa at the window. Below, a policeman stepped through a small gap in the barrier and raised his megaphone to speak.

"Put down your weapons and exit the building with your hands on your heads. You'll be quite safe. There will be no use of firearms if you come out unarmed."

Melissa closed the window blinds.

"So why the police? I mean, we're the Security Service. Don't you think that's a bit odd? It should at least be our own people dealing with us, even if they thought we'd gone rogue."

"Told you something weird was happening. Try Chapman again. Maybe we can get some answers. Perhaps he's in trouble."

"Wait. I have an idea. I mean, how we can get Freddy in," said Melissa.

"Yeah?"

"Yeah, but we'll need some help from our new friends in TAAN..."

*

The creature cracked its whip and a spatter of smouldering debris dashed from its end each time, to sting its victim. Albert made a brave charge at the beast, nimbly dodging the lash and darting so quickly there was no time for it to turn its gun, but he was so easily overcome and cast to the ground that it only proved to watchers that such rebellion attempts were futile.

"We'll find another way," whispered Tyler as Albert re-joined the downtrodden work detail, nursing a bleeding temple and stinging flanks.

"We 'ave bodies!" he said. "I feels pain!"

"We are no longer living and no longer dead. We are neither human nor only ghost," explained Izabella, probing the density of her arm.

Other jackal creatures cast tools at them and barked commands.

"Work!"

"Get going, scum."

Tyler's ghost team took places alongside other dejected ghosts who were working the surface and collecting quarried rock in ramshackle carts. As it was in the *Ghost Portal*, the ghosts here were from all manner of times and places, adding to the dream-like impression the chasm gave, but they had some common features. They were each starved to the point of emaciation and they all had blackened, sunken eyes. Despite their evil appearance, Tyler found herself pitying the grim, unsmiling workforce.

"Who are they? What have they done to deserve this? Why are they all here?"

Izabella shook her head.

"This is a godless place. I'm forbidden to say any more. You will understand when you are in the full knowledge."

The quarry ground moved irritatingly. The heat was unbearable. Tyler set to work, glaring at the long shimmering lashes her overseers bore. Smouldering boulders and outcrops dispelled as she attempted to strike and she wondered if the fire fog itself actually had an awareness - some kind of intelligence or consciousness. It was as though the very substance of the chasm knew what she was thinking. She chose another spot and aimed her pick at the ground, swung but missed as the rock slid to the side.

"Faster!" bellowed one of the creatures, shoving its slavering muzzle in her face. Its breath hit her. Pure, recking brimstone. "Or you will be selected!"

Selected? Selected for what, exactly?

Across the quarry others worked with the same resigned weariness. Tyler saw an old maid with a bent back materialise in the midst of the others and join them in their work, and wondered what this meant.

Tyler left her place and chose another area to try working next to Izabella, who barely had the strength to swing her pick. Izabella let her pick rest for a moment to lean across.

"Before you say it, I'm well aware I shall be selected for special treatment before long. I can work no harder than I am already."

"But what *is* the special treatment?" Tyler asked.

Izabella took a feeble swing at the cliff face. The surface moved and a paltry few crumbs of rock rambled to her feet where they smoked. She gathered them and put them in the barrow at her side. She looked at Tyler before nodding towards the chimney that volleyed a constant stream of ash into the atmosphere.

"Take a guess."

Tyler stared at the industrial stack in confusion until a jackal creature lashed her and she hacked at the cliff with renewed vigour.

"They'll burn you? But that doesn't make sense. Will your spirit die? I thought ghosts were already dead."

Izabella nodded in understanding.

"This is the second death. Don't worry for me. It's not as permanent as the first."

"I don't understand."

"Have you ever died in a dream?" asked Izabella. "Or even feared you might die?"

"Yes."

"And was it any less frightening than if it had been for real?"

"It was terrifying. It felt real. At the time I thought it *was* really happening!"

"So it is within the chasm. The second death is just as real as the first and can be terrifying, horrific and painful. And yet it can happen over and over again. It does not affect a ghost mortally. Of course, a true ghost will return. It is but part of the torment. For a ghost this death is not real, but merely the chasm's illusion, but *you* are *not* a true ghost. Your body lives still."

"So for me the second death would be a real death?"

Izabella nodded and Tyler shuddered.

Great. That's all I need.

"I did warn you this place should not be entered and that it would likely be the end of you. But you never listen, do you?"

Tyler worked the rock with little progress, brooding over Izabella's words as weariness crept over her again. And hunger. That was new. Hunger was something she had not experienced before as a ghost. She eyed the overseers.

"Wish the jackals would back off," she said. "They give me the creeps."

"They're meant to," said Izabella.

"*Contrapassi*," a ghost girl working on Izabella's other side, who looked like she might have lived in ancient Greece, corrected.

"What?" asked Tyler, turning to the girl.

"We call them *contrapassi*, not jackals. *Contrapasso* if it's just one."

"Contrapassi? What are they? Why are they here?"

"Who knows? They're here to torment us. That's as much as I know."

A contrapasso approached and squatted to the girls'

level.

"Silence! Work harder! Work faster! Quarry the rock!" He sent an almighty lash across all three workers' backs with one stroke. A jolt of searing pain seemed real enough to Tyler. She focused on her work while worrying about Izabella. The lash had nearly finished the old woman. As she watched, Izabella dropped to her knees and the pick slid from her hands. A moment later, two contrapassi lifted her by the arms and dragged her away.

"NO!" cried Tyler. "DON'T TAKE HER! LEAVE HER ALONE!"

Her answer came in the form of a lash that flayed her to the ground, gasping and sobbing.

What am I going to do without Izabella? She's the only one who knows what's going on around here!

"Izabella!" she called as they took the old woman away.

Izabella managed to lift her head enough to meet Tyler's gaze.

"Don't worry child. I will return," and with those muttered words, Izabella became limp, like a ragdoll in giants' hands.

With Izabella gone, Tyler turned her attention to Marcus, who was still weak from the shivering. He was faring little better than Izabella, swinging his pick in a languid arc and Tyler guessed it was only a matter of time before the contrapassi noticed. She lowered her pick and, when the overseers were not watching, slipped across to his side to resume work.

"Marcus. Try to look like you're working harder or they'll take you away!" she urged, but when Marcus turned slowly to her. His eyes were dull and vacant and she wondered if he had even heard or understood what she had said. She sought out Albert and beckoned him over, thinking that between them they might shelter Marcus a little from view and buy a measure of respite while he healed. A second death for Marcus now would surely weaken him further. When he found the opportunity, Albert did as Tyler indicated and they worked closely, hedging Marcus.

Tyler set her mind to work on an escape plan as she hacked. The other ghosts on her team seemed able enough for the time being to avoid the attentions of the contrapassi but she couldn't be sure how long this would last. She planned to have them all out of the complex as soon as possible, even if that meant waiting for Izabella's promised return.

On the other side of the complex, movement drew her attention. Contrapassi were gathering around a roughly hewn gallows where a solitary noose dangled. With mounting distress she watched a rounded figure being coaxed and cajoled to the place of execution and, in horror, recognised Izabella. Others had noticed also and lowered tools to watch, grim-faced. Soon the entire workforce was static and even the contrapassi turned to observe the execution.

Izabella slowly climbed the steps to the gallows and Tyler could watch no more.

*

Tyler eyed Zebedee with concern. Izabella was dead. Marcus was protected to a certain degree as long as she and Albert sheltered him, but Zebedee was tiring and it was becoming obvious.

"Albert, how are we ever going to get out of here if we're constantly being picked off by the contrapassi? I don't think Zebedee will last much longer. Look at him. He can barely lift a pick."

Albert looked across at Zebedee with a nod.

"We can't shelter everyone, Missy. More's the pity."

"Izabella said she would return. How long do you think it will take?"

"Lord knows," said Albert. "You got a plan yet? Ain't gonna be easy, trying t'a get out of 'ere."

"I'm working on it," said Tyler, but in truth she

didn't have a clue. The whole situation seemed hopeless and she was so tired she could barely think.

If only I could stop working for a while and rest.

Ash blew in rifts around the complex and the quarry, like autumn leaves. Across the camp, contrapassi piled bodies into a cart and, when it was full, they cajoled ghost labourers into hefting it up a track and out of the tall gates to the towering furnace. Tyler turned away from the harrowing sight and saw in the distance, far beyond the camp's reaches, a lone tower breaching from the rolling, foggy landscape. She thought nothing of it at first, but glanced a second time. It was familiar. Squinting, she recognised it as the *Tower of Doom* from the contrap, only now it wasn't a small image in a glass lens but was a real tower, complete with huge birds circling. Around it dark, gnarled trees twisted inwards with clawing limbs.

That's odd...

She noticed something else. Out in the mid-distance ran a series of low, grey buildings. She counted six of them and saw movement close by. A large crowd of ghosts were approaching the units from further down the road, driven by a handful of lash-wielding contrapassi. As they reached the buildings, the ghosts were jostled into lines, each ending at a door, awaiting entry. Tyler turned to the ghost of an old man who was scraping lethargically at the quarry side with a blunt pick.

"What's happening over there?" She pointed.

"Oh, they're being taken for purification," said the wizened man in a croaky voice.

"Purification?"

"Yes. Once all are inside, the contrapassi will close and seal the doors. Then they will be purified."

When Tyler looked at him quizzically he ran a finger across his throat by way of explanation.

"*Killed?* They are all going to be killed?"

The man nodded and continued his scraping with a wary eye on the contrapassi punctuating the quarry edge.

"It happens from time to time. Whenever the contrapassi feel the need..."

"But why?" asked Tyler.

"*Why* what?"

"Why do they do all this? Why do they punish and kill and persecute the ghosts? Us?"

"Don't you know?" he asked. "They do it because we are different to them. They do it because they hate us."

Hours passed and Tyler watched Zebedee work slower and slower. When she was convinced he had been spotted and was about to be selected and dragged away, a loud blast sounded from the top of the quarry where a contrapasso blew a huge ram's horn. Workers around her dropped tools and groaned their relief.

"He's made it!" she said to Albert with surprise. She noticed the day was darkening and wondered if there was night in the chasm.

"Back to the huts!" bellowed the contrapasso with the horn, and the workers gradually filtered out of the quarry to stream into the hut compound where Tyler and her friends had first landed. She headed over to Zebedee and helped him back as Albert guided Marcus, but the boy had been spotted by a particularly malicious looking contrapasso who had his gun hoisted across his back so that he could wield a lash in each hand. He lowered a lash briskly to separate Albert from Marcus.

"Not you!" the contrapasso said, shoving Albert away. He studied Marcus with interest and took his violin and bow. "Here's another for special treatment. Take him away." He prodded Marcus towards two awaiting contrapassi who grabbed him and dragged him away.

"NO!" screamed Tyler before thinking. "YOU CAN'T TAKE HIM!"

The three contrapassi turned to her as the entire place fell silent.

"We can't?" asked Two Whips, dropping the fiddle and bow. "And how do you propose to stop us?"

Albert stepped forward to put himself between Tyler and the three.

"You can't take him 'cause I'm gonna to stop ya!" he shouted, and Tyler knew at once what he was doing - taking the heat off her and putting himself in danger instead - protecting her, as always.

"No, Albert!" she whispered.

"Is that right?" said Two Whips towering over Albert so that smatterings of smouldering drool rained on him.

"Urgh! You got a serious hygiene problem there, mate. Anyway, why all the questions, you big, dumb dogs? Didn't you hear me?" asked Albert, fronting up to the beasts as best he could. "I said *I'm* gonna stop ya!" He hooked his ankle around the fiddle with its bow still clamped beneath strings and slid it back towards Tyler, hoping the contrapassi wouldn't notice. Tyler grabbed it and tucked it behind her back.

"Why you little..." Two Whips withdrew the lash from Marcus' shoulder and brought it round on Albert with full force so that its length snaked about him with an almighty, agonizing crack. Albert blacked out and Two Whips hauled on the lash, casting him away in a uncontrolled spin to crash in a heap at the other contrapassi's feet.

"Leave the runt for later. Take this one instead," Two Whips commanded. Albert was collected and dragged to the gallows. As he looked back at Tyler, she saw his expression and wondered at it.

Is he smiling at me?

The Plan

Zebedee stuffed ghost tobacco into the bowl of his pipe and lit it.

"Jolly rotten luck we landed in this place, I'll say."

The seven remaining ghosts were gathered in one of the many Spartan huts, some sitting on bunks, others cross-legged on the bare floorboards. Tyler leant her back against the wall and tried not to sob.

"They *will* come back to us, won't they, Zebedee?"

"Of course they will, my girl. We must remember what Izabella told us all before we came in. Fight despair with all the strength you can muster. Rally hope!"

"Hope? What is *that*? I think I've already forgotten."

"Then you must remember!" said Kinga. "Izabella said it would be our best weapon here and she was right."

"If we do not find hope then we will surely give in," said Danuta. "And the oppressor will prevail. All will be lost."

Tyler considered this and nodded slowly.

"You're right."

"How's the escape plan coming? Anyone any ideas?" asked Zebedee.

Tyler shook her head. The others looked disappointed and did the same.

"I'm sure I could think better if I wasn't so tired and hungry."

"Will they feed us?" asked Claudia. "I've never been so hungry before. Not even when I was alive and eating the leftovers from my master's table." Tyler studied Claudia who seemed drained and like a different person to her prior cocky self. Even she had no energy for the usual attitude.

"I'm starving," said Kylie. "It's weird to feel hungry again."

"They will feed us," said the ghost of a native African boy with big, wild hair and stripes of white face paint, sitting close by. "They will feed us rotten bread whilst they feast richly before us. You will see. It will happen soon. There is never enough bread for us all, but you can eat a little if you pick out the rot. Don't eat the rot. It will make you sickly and then you will be selected."

Claudia looked disgusted.

"I'm Taji."

"It's good to meet you, Taji," said Zebedee offering his hand. Taji shook it warily.

"And what are we supposed to drink? I'm so thirsty," said Claudia.

"They give us water, but that tastes bad too. Don't drink too much or it'll make you sick."

Nobody spoke for a while.

"I saw a ghost appear in the quarry earlier," Tyler said to Taji. "I've noticed we can't just come and go in here. We must walk everywhere, like in the portal and like the living do. So what did I see in the quarry?"

"Oh, you probably saw a return. Once someone has been killed, they come back after a while. You must have seen someone returning," Taji explained.

"So why did the ghost I saw return to the quarry?

Why not elsewhere? If I was returning I'd rather come back outside the fence."

Taji laughed and Tyler wondered what was so funny.

"Wouldn't we all! You don't get to choose where you return. You return to the place where you died."

"Oh, I see." Tyler felt foolish. "One of our friends was killed today. Can you tell when she'll return? How long does it take?"

"Nobody knows. Sometimes it happens quickly. Sometimes it takes a while. I don't know why. Nobody knows."

"Thanks, Taji." Tyler pulled an old tattered blanket more tightly about her. The evening was cooling rapidly.

"Nice blanket, by the way. I can get you things. Fancy a trade?"

"Really? What kind of things?"

"What is it you require?" asked Tanji.

*

Marcus was statue-like and Tyler hadn't heard him play since she'd seen him in the contrap a long time age. She wondered if playing might help him recover and grow stronger.

"Can you play for us?" she asked him. "Some music might help us think."

Marcus slowly reached down to collect his violin and bow. He looked at them for a long time before eventually nuzzling the fiddle beneath his chin and drawing out a single, long, sorrowful note. The sound sent a shiver through Tyler and it was as if that note had imbibed every sad thought in Marcus' mind. It did, however, appear to do the boy good. Upon hearing it, he looked up and seemed to recognise the others for the first time since before entering the Shivering Pool. A moment later he began a sorrowful melody that Tyler found strangely soothing. It was like the song of her heart, a soft cry in the darkness, a gentle expression of grief. They quietened for a time, listening, even Taji and the other ghosts around the hut, lulled by the sound.

Tyler thought about escaping. Her first notion was that escape was possible but only if you were dead by the second death. Those ghosts murdered during the day had been piled on a cart and born out of the camp. Yes, they were bound for the furnace, but that was beyond the fence, at least, and so she began working on a plan in which they would all somehow manage to get on that cart, playing dead until they'd passed the gates. The accompanying contrapasso would still need to be dealt with, and that was the hardest part. They were huge and very strong. They had guns and lashes. On top of this problem, Tyler considered the Nazi ghosts she'd brought with her. Presumably they were still under the hut, unless the fire fog ground had shifted and revealed them. If they were still there she would need to bring them along too. She considered leaving them here in the camp but the thought of the contrapassi finding them was unsettling. Would they torment the Nazi ghosts or would they set them free of the chains? She really had no idea and so that was not an option. Goebbels and Bagshot would have to come with her and the team until a good place could be found to leave them, preferably somewhere they would never be discovered.

It wasn't much of a plan but it was a start, and that in itself was more hopeful than no start at all. She took out the list from her back pocket and was unsurprised to find it was a blank sheet of paper again. She rewrote and stared in frustration at the page.

Check the Room of Faces √
Search the Shivering Pool √
Find Hitler
Find Goebbels √
Find Himmler
Leave all Nazi ghosts in the chasm

She wanted with all her heart to tick off some items, but could not. Nor could she see *that* happening any time soon. For something to do, she added more lines at the bottom.

Find somewhere safe to leave Goebbels and Bagshot in the chasm
Locate and secure Mordecai chains

She refolded the paper and tucked it away as another horn sounded and out in the complex a contrapasso bellowed a command.

"Eat!"

Ghosts streamed out of the huts to scrabble for crusts as contrapassi cast rotten bread on the ground. Tyler collected a few pieces and picked through them for good bits to give to Marcus. The rest of her team shared what they scavenged making sure each had something to eat, all except Claudia, who kept everything she grabbed for herself. Zebedee noticed that by the time Tyler had fed Marcus there was little left for herself, and he gave most of his food to her.

"You have it. I'm not really hungry in any case," Zebedee said, but he looked famished and exhausted.

Tyler settled in her bunk to sleep, sharing one thin mattress with Claudia, which was a painful experience not because of the extreme confines so much as the constant whining. The heat of the day was gone, now replaced with a biting cold that the hut did little to allay. She lay in discomfort, hunger gnawing at her belly, her mind reeling with thoughts of what was to happen at first light, when Albert was to be publically executed as a deterrent to further rebellion. Through a crack in the hut's wall she watched a blood-red sky darken to shades of black and all the while, the large, pallid moon glowed with cold indifference.

*

Melissa's phone chimed and she read a text. Lucy returned to report.

"It will work. You'll see."

"Freddy's here. He's outside somewhere down there," said Melissa.

"Great. He'll be up soon."

Melissa and Lucy watched from the window. Below on the street a TAAN public demonstration was crashing the party, overturning police barriers and brawling with outnumbered, armed officers. Placards read 'The Activists Against Nazism', 'Wake Up World', 'Oust the Nazis', 'Nazis Out!' and 'For a Nazi Free Britain'.

"There he is!" Melissa pointed to a slight figure forging his way towards the damaged doorway on street level. Two minutes later Freddy was with them.

"That's an odd place to leave a sofa. Is that some kind of new-fangled feng shui? What on Earth did you girls do?"

"Nothing. They think Tyler's dead. They want to take her away. How did you get in here so easily?"

"I have my ways." Freddy tapped his nose. "So she's *not* dead?" He peered through the open doorway at Tyler's static body.

"No. She's alive. Her ghost's in the Brimstone Chasm, in the contrap."

"Right. 'Cause that makes sense..."

"Forget it. Did you bring the ammo?"

"Here you go." Freddy dumped a rucksack on the coffee table with a clunk. "Should keep us armed for a while." He drew his p99 and checked it over, clipped a full magazine back in.

Scuffling sounds reached them from further down the building.

"Just in time. They're coming for us," announced Lucy. She slipped out into the hall and took a quick glance down the stairwell.

"We're armed," she shouted. "Keep out or someone's gonna die." To prove it she fired two warning shots into the wall at the base of the first flight. She gave Melissa the nod. Melissa pumped two more tear gas canisters into the well and retreated. They heard more scuffling and someone approaching. A voice, strangled by a gas mask, reached them.

"We just want to talk terms. You can't keep this up forever."

Lucy glanced at Melissa, who shrugged.

"We'll talk terms with Chapman. No one else."

Windows in two bedrooms smashed and a mist crept into the apartment at their backs.

"Tear gas," said Lucy. "Masks on.

"We'll talk to Chapman. Find Chapman and bring him to us."

"We'll get back to you," came the distorted reply. Footfalls retreated down the stairs.

"What now?" Melissa went to the window to watch police exit the building into the street.

"We wait for Chapman, or for Tyler to come back," said Lucy. "Whichever comes first."

*

Tyler awoke, hungry and shivering in the dishevelled hut.

A cold day in Hell? Well, an extremely cold night anyway...

She wondered how long it would be before she was herded out with the other prisoners to watch Albert hang. Her gut lurched and she wished she was still asleep. She heard gunshots from beyond the thin wooden walls, followed by screams, and sobs spoke of grieving fellows. Someone else had muttered the wrong word, looked the wrong way or fallen behind in their chores. She wanted to get out as soon as possible, to get far away from this horrible place and the monsters that ran it. She checked around for Izabella and was disappointed not to find her. Through a crack in the wall where an evil wind whistled, she spied Albert still clamped to the post by the Mordecai chain the contrapassi had set in place the night before, and she wondered for the hundredth time if there was any way to rescue him, but the post was in the centre of the open ground between the huts and the quarry and was surrounded by nine tall watchtowers, each of which sheltered a pair of contrapassi with mounted guns. The situation seemed without hope.

Hope... That word again...

A horn blast sounded and contrapassi rattled doors.

"Out, ghost scum! Get out!"

Ghosts left the partial shelter of the huts, filtering into the yard which soon became crowded. Contrapassi paced beneath the gallows as Albert was released from the chain and harried towards the noose. Tyler recognised an admirable strength in him as he strode to his death, showing no fear before the massive creatures and she wondered how he did it. She was terrified for him. They prodded him up steps and Tyler watched until the noose was around his neck. With her eyes closed she heard his voice, defiant even now.

"Don't worry, Missy. It's gonna be alright!"

She felt her throat tighten. He was reassuring *her*, even as he went to his death! She heard the steps being hauled out from beneath his feet and a silence overcame the crowd.

"Tell me when they've taken him away," she said to Zebedee.

"It's all over," said Zebedee a few minutes later. "He will return to us soon."

"But that doesn't make it right."

"I know, my girl. I know."

"Zebedee, we've got to get out of this place as soon as possible. I have the beginnings of a plan. I intend to have it finished by the time Izabella and Albert are back. Then we're leaving."

"Right you are. Care to share?"

Tyler told Zebedee her plan to have all the team add themselves to the cart of the dead and wait until they were carried out of the camp. As she explained, Two Whips led out the cart again, heading for the furnace.

"The problem is Two Whips. He seems to be in charge of the furnace so he'll probably be with the cart. We'll have to overpower him somehow. It won't be easy."

Zebedee sucked on his pipe and spoke through tobacco smoke.

"Well how about that chain they used on poor Albert? They must store it somewhere, and they probably have more of them. If we can learn where they are, we might be able to steal them. They're what we came for, after all."

"Will the chains work on contrapassi?"

"I don't see why not."

"If we could take one at least, we could maybe hide it in the cart under the bodies. Once we're outside we could use the chain on Two Whips. We'd be free to escape. It would buy us some time to find a hiding place at least."

"Exactly!" Zebedee smiled.

"Zebedee, I could kiss you."

"Oh, that won't be necessary, Miss May. Your gratitude is reward enough."

Another voice reached Tyler above the now murmuring crowd, one with a robust Russian edge.

"Well, child, what are we still doing here? I thought we were planning a break-out..."

The Storehouse

Izabella stepped closer.

"Izabella!" Tyler ran to hug her before she knew what she was doing and sobbed on her shoulder.

"Yes, yes. I'm back, just as I said I would be. Now, pull yourself together. That's quite enough of that."

Tyler released Izabella from her embrace and took a step back wiping tears on her sleeve.

"Yes!" Tyler whispered, drawing Izabella and Zebedee away from the rest of the crowd. "They just murdered Albert, but when he's back we'll launch our plan as soon as we can. We just need to make sure no one else gets killed or we'll be waiting forever."

"Indeed."

Tyler and Zebedee explained the plan so far and, with Izabella's approval, the rest of the team were gathered and informed before the day's work shift began.

Marcus was stronger today. His own music had gone some way towards his healing and Tyler was relieved because it meant he could work more ably and ward off the unwelcome attentions of the contrapassi. Once again her main concerns were Izabella and Zebedee who were not great with a pick or hammer at the best of times. She instructed Kinga and Danuta to work either side of Izabella while she and Kylie shielded Zebedee as the day warmed to a sweltering heat. There was no bread in the mornings, no water. No rest. Only work in the heat with a painfully empty stomach, a ravaging thirst and a tiredness that made it hard to stand.

Tyler knew she was slowly learning the true power of the chasm. It was a wretched place that made you wish you did not exist. To begin with she had thought the second death was a respite, something to hang on to. At least the ghosts knew they would not be erased outright, but now she realised that this was all part of the torture inflicted by the chasm. The imprisoned ghosts wished they could be erased and the torment was knowing they would repeatedly return to suffer.

All day she watched over her team while looking for Albert's reappearance, but it did not come. She was relieved Zebedee and Izabella had made it through the work shift without being selected, but constantly feared the contrapassi might take an interest in them, even after the ram's horn had sounded. She ate bad bread ravenously when the sky darkened and the temperature fell and for a brief few seconds enjoyed the coolness before it became an unbearable freeze. Izabella passed her another old blanket, smouldering with fire fog, which Tyler gratefully wrapped around her shoulders, clinging to the edges with numb fingers. They gathered in their hut.

"We need to learn where they keep that Mordecai chain," said Tyler. "Did anyone see where it came from when they used it on Albert?"

Heads shook.

"Right, then we'll need to search. Whenever you get a chance, search for the chain. Maybe the contrapassi have a store for stuff like that, stuff they don't want us to get hold of. We need that chain."

The others agreed and they left the hut to mill around the complex amidst other prisoners. Along with the many huts there were other buildings in the camp. The contrapassi had a vast banqueting hall at one end on higher ground, with numerous long windows through which the prisoners could watch them feasting on fresh bread, colourful, ripe fruit, cakes, pies, meats and stews. Carafes of red wine punctuated the spread of delights. The smell emanating from the hall was mouth-watering. They feasted now as the team spread out across the grounds looking for other hiding places. To one side of the long hall stood a scattering of well-built structures that, to Tyler, appeared to serve no purpose. She strolled casually in their direction to take a look but met Kylie heading back towards her

"It's in there," she pointed to a squat, stone building no longer than the huts.

"Good work," said Tyler.

They walked closer. Prison bars lined the storehouse's windows and a solid-looking door was furnished with an iron bolt and lock. Tyler looked through the bars to be sure the chain was inside. At least two other chains dangled on hooks along the far wall. She looked at Kylie.

"You and me. Tonight."

*

The chasm night smouldered in deep dusk and the bitter wind harassed them as they slipped from the hut door, leaving behind other tortured souls attempting sleep in the claustrophobic gloom. Tyler peered across the compound from the end of their hut to see searchlights roving, casting long shadows wherever they struck buildings or fences. She gave Kylie a nod and they sped over open ground to flatten themselves against the neighbouring hut. They dashed from hut to hut, always watchful of the searchlights, dreading what might happen if they were caught. Up ahead, Tyler saw the long shape of the feasting hall and the other buildings beyond. Lights were on in the hall, candles peppering long tables still laden with food and wine. Several contrapassi were still inside, drinking to excess.

They shouldn't be a problem.

Crouching low, Tyler led the way across to the hall and skirted its flank, making sure to duck below the line of windows. She came to the end and froze on the spot as a contrapasso staggered from the door and dropped his machine gun. Another contrapasso joined him as he tried unsuccessfully to reclaim the weapon. The first contrapasso laughed at his own incapacity. A deep, booming laugh. The second stooped for the gun and passed it to his fellow.

"Here. You'll need this tomorrow."

"Yeah, I'm gonna kill me some more of the filthy, ghost scum." More throaty laughter. They moved on as Tyler and Kylie stood, backs to the wall. When the contrapassi were no longer in sight and the sound of their immense feet scratching the fire fog ground had abated, the girls left the wall and toed over more exposed ground to the other buildings where the storehouse was nestled, and sheltered in its doorway. Tyler fished around in her pocket for the two lengths of wire she'd traded with Taji in exchange for a blanket. She thought again about the conversation she'd had with the rest of the team.

"You can't go."

"You mustn't go. Albert wouldn't want you to go."

"Albert's not here right now."

"If you get caught they'll kill you and you'll die for real. You'll be stuck as a ghost forever."

"Yeah, send one of us. At least if we get killed we'll come back."

But Tyler had decided long before she'd shared the news of the chain's whereabouts. She was the best thief of the bunch. Ghost or not, she was a trained lock-picker and a seasoned cat-burglar. There was nothing to debate.

"I'm in charge. And I'm going," she'd concluded.

"Stubborn child..."

Tyler applied her mind to the lock that secured the hefty bolt on the storehouse door.

"Keep watch while I work," she whispered to Kylie as she eased the two wires into the keyhole. Moments later the lock clicked open and Tyler carefully lifted it away from the bolt.

"Someone's coming!" Kylie whispered. "They've seen me. It's Two Whips!"

"Run!" whispered Tyler, desperately thinking what to do. "Hide!"

But Kylie didn't move.

"No. He's not seen you yet and we need that chain. He doesn't know you're here. You go in! I'll keep him busy for a while. If he kills me, I'll see you later."

Tyler slid the bolt back, opened the door and slipped into the store. She closed the door behind her and ran to the chains hanging from their hooks against the side wall. She noted a rack of machine guns against the end wall and a line of the huge contrapasso's whips against another. Around the room were piled other supplies, boxes, ammunition, cans, rope and long, metal spikes. The chains were large and closely coiled side by side like a curtain. She slid behind them and hid as voices rose outside. A voluminous roar and a shrill scream shook her. Kylie's voice.

"NO!"

Tyler heard a sickening sound, the cracking of two lethal whips and something thudded against the storeroom door. She heard something being dragged away and, finally, silence. The door burst open and Two Whips' massive head appeared in the gap, checking the room for other wayward prisoners and leaving spatters of drool on the floor. Tyler glimpsed him between chain links and tried not to shiver for fear it would give her away. For a terrifying moment she thought he saw her, but Two Whips left and closed the door. She heard the bolt being fastened and the door relocked.

What now? I'm trapped!

*

Melissa shivered at the darkness outside and called the others away from the window. She watched the BBC News at Ten, images of Bates, mug shots from the front and sides. Lucy and Freddy left their posts to join her in the lounge. The reporter gave a recap on Bates' history. Her suspected involvement with the *Christmas Eve Incident*. A trail of murders spanning several years. They glimpsed shots of bodies and a bloodied hotel in Tel Aviv. Chalk sketches of a trial in progress. And finally video of Bates hiding under a coat as she was transported to Holloway.

"She's escaped," explained Melissa, having caught the introductory headline that the others missed.

"That's *all* we need," said Lucy. "One more nutter on the loose."

The report cut to shots of Holloway. Tall, red brick blocks. Doors and gates. And then a still of Bates behind the presenter, top right.

"Officers remain at the scene where investigations continue. Exactly *how* the escape was orchestrated is still an unanswered question. What *is* known is the extent of violence used by Bates during the breakout. The families of the four officers killed have been informed of the tragedy. Police have once again issued a plea for public to..."

Melissa's mobile rang.

"It's Chapman."

"Yes?"

"Have you heard? Bates is out."

"Just now, yes."

"She killed four guards at the facility. Hanged two of them using their own belts. We're still not sure how she broke free from her confines. We're investigating. Better keep a look out. She's targeted Tyler before. She could be heading your way."

"Mr Chapman, can you call off the police? This siege thing is getting out of hand. And it's pointless. Right now Bates would have to have an army with her just to get down the street, so there's no chance she'll get to us here."

The line went dead. Melissa looked at Lucy.

"Well that was strange."

Lucy shrugged.

"What's new?"

"Not like Chapman to avoid the subject," Freddy commented. "Do you think he's alright?"

"I think he was trying to tell us something," said Melissa, looking concerned.

"But what?" asked Lucy.

They looked at each other, wondering.

"He's in trouble. It's the only explanation. Where's Weaver?" Melissa asked Lucy.

"I'm expecting him any minute."

"Text him. Get him to visit Chapman before coming in. Warn him something's not right."

Lucy tapped out a message and hit send. Moments later she had Weaver's reply.

WILL DO

They waited as the night deepened. It was nearing midnight when Weaver phoned.

"Everyone alright?" he asked Lucy.

"Fine." Lucy put him on speakerphone.

"Did he find Chapman?" asked Melissa. "Is he okay?"

"Chapman's definitely not okay. Wouldn't talk, but something's amiss. I'm going to check on his family. Make sure they're alright. Not sure what else it could be.

Anyone want to join me?"

Silence.

"I'm gonna stay with the girls," said Freddy. "They need some backup and it looks like this siege is going to run another night."

"Right. Probably for the best if I go alone anyway. Easier to work covertly. I'll get back to you."

*

Tyler skirted the wall to the barred window to peer out. Two Whips had gone. She searched for a weakness in the fabric of the building, tested the door, the bars on the window. All were good and solid, as were the walls. She didn't need to try passing through the wall or the door. She already knew her ghost had taken on a new constitution since entering the chasm, one solid enough to be trapped, one human enough to feel hunger, discomfort and pain. With no way out, she made herself as comfortable as possible and waited.

Some while later, a voice shook her from her dozing.

"Psssst!"

Morning had come and the heat was already rising, a hot glow cascading in stripes through the window bars. A pale face appeared there, making Tyler jump.

"Albert!"

"'Ello, Missy."

"Albert, are you okay?"

"I'm fine. You?"

"I'm alright. Just need to get out."

"Use the chains. We can't get the key. We don't even know which of 'em 'as it. When the next one opens the door... Got to go!" Albert left the window and Tyler was left alone again, pondering his words and wishing he'd waited long enough for her to tell him that Two Whips had a key.

Use the chains? Of course! Use the chains on the next contrapasso who opens the door.

There were three chains. That meant she could afford to use two to bind any contrapassi who came into the storehouse. She had considered using a machine gun, but the din would alert every contrapasso in the camp.

A pair of contrapassi passed the window and Tyler understood why Albert had bolted. She readied herself, hoisting one of the heavy Mordecai chains down from its hook and taking position behind the door, where she waited.

The shift horn sounded and she heard prisoners and contrapassi making for the quarry. She wondered how long she might be waiting, but was shaken from her thoughts by shouting and gunfire. Someone had stepped out of line, but still she did not know if the selected was to be shot, hanged or chained. Perhaps they had already been killed. She had no way of knowing. The commotion outside settled, and Tyler let the chain rest on the floor. It was heavy and she couldn't stand there all day carrying it. She decided a gun might be useful too, and fetched one from the rack, checking it was loaded and throwing the strap over her head.

No harm in a backup plan.

She returned to her place behind the door as heavy footfalls approached from the other side. Metallic sounds startled her as somebody turned a key in the lock. The bolt slid and the door swung open.

Hope

Tyler backed into the wall, grasping the chain to her chest. The hulking, shaggy shape of a contrapasso filled the room. It sniffed the air and turned.

"Mordecai bind!" she blurted, so nervous that she almost forgot to release the chain. Once encouraged in the right direction, it left her hands to sail of its own accord. She had worried she would not be strong enough to hurl the thing, but needlessly. The chain took on a life of its own as if knowing what was required of it, targeting the huge jackal creature, and growing in size so that enough of its length could enfold its prey. With a metallic crashing of links it seized the beast and brought it smashing to the floor where it remained in silence, eyes bulging with fury.

Tyler stood gasping for a moment before checking around to be sure there were no others. She poked her head out of the doorway and glanced about the compound. Everyone was in the quarry and her way was clear. She quickly dragged ropes and other gear over the chained body to hide it. Hardly believing her good fortune, she hoisted a second chain onto her shoulders and slipped out of the storehouse, struggling with the weight, closed the door quietly behind her, secured the bolt and turned the key in the lock. She pocketed the key and fled to the edge of the hut where Goebbels and Bagshot were concealed beneath floorboards. Here she dug in the fire fog to bury the chain and the gun in a shallow pit alongside the Nazis. She considered returning for another chain but ditched the idea when a contrappassi approached the store area.

She ducked and rested for a moment, thinking. She couldn't join the work detail in the quarry. Somebody would notice and ask where she'd been. *Too many questions.* Instead, she returned to her hut and hid beneath her bed, awaiting the return of her friends. She was sure Kylie was dead and so they would have to delay their plan but, even so, a new hope had kindled in her - a slow-burning excitement about what they were about to do – and it smouldered like a fuse. Lying there, she realised everything Izabella had said was true. Hope really was the most powerful weapon anyone could wield in the chasm.

She wriggled on the floorboards. Something was digging into her back and she shuddered as she recognised movement beneath her body. Panic made her skitter out urgently from her hiding place. *Am I lying on creatures? Bugs? Rats! What new torment is this? No. Not rats. Something else is happening.*

The movement was coming from her.

She staggered to her feet, all the while trying to feel her back with her hands, but she stilled when she understood. Strong limbs were growing from between her shoulders, unfolding, pushing outward and strengthening as her confidence in the escape plan deepened, as hope swelled. She could feel them, elongating, muscles stretching, tendons tightening. She lurched to the middle of the hut and planted her feet, subconsciously knowing she needed space. And then it happened: she flexed her shoulders and unfurled, into full glory, a pair of blazing, fire fog wings.

*

Lucy shook Melissa rudely awake.

"Your shift, sleepy head. There's a pot of coffee on the side. Not heard from Weaver. Our friends are still outside and the news just broadcast a story saying we're holding an injured girl hostage but they're not clear on our demands. Nought from Chapman either."

Melissa looked up blearily.

"Can't they just leave us alone?"

"Would be nice."

Melissa dressed and poured herself a coffee. She checked the contrap for any sign of Tyler and saw only the smouldering fire of the chasm.

Come on Tyler! Deal with Hitler. Come back to us and we can all get on with our lives!

Melissa checked her facts and recalculated for the hundredth time. She stared at the countdown clock she'd set going on her laptop, watched seconds retreat.

69 Hours : 47 Minutes : 38 Seconds

Tyler had less than three days left to reunite her ghost with her body.

Melissa had reopened the chasm so that Tyler and the team would be able to call themselves out when they were ready, but it emitted such a stink that she stopped wearing it. She put it back on Tyler's unmoving chest, checking it periodically.

Lucy was already asleep in her bedroom. Freddy made toast. Lucy's mobile rang. Melissa read the display and answered it.

"Hi, Weaver. Any news?"

"Mel?"

"Yep. Lucy's sleeping."

"You might want to wake her. She'll want to hear this."

"Wait a minute." Melissa switched speakerphone on for Freddy's benefit. "Go on."

"Chapman's heading over to call off the police. It's over. I spent the night with a hostage team tracking his family. A certain Jonathan Hatherow had them abducted. He was forcing Chapman's hand, threatening to top his wife and kids if he didn't get the contrap, though I think he would have settled for Tyler's body. Nasty piece of work, that Hatherow."

"Yeah. He nearly got it, too."

"Well anyway, Chapman's very pleased you girls did what you did."

Melissa allowed herself to collapse into a lounge chair.

"Where is he now? I mean Hatherow?"

"On the run. He'll know we're onto him by now but we couldn't locate him so he's still loose. Suppose he might come your way. He'll be pretty narked."

"Thanks, Weaver. I'll tell Lucy."

"Great. I'm coming over so I'll see you soon."

*

Tyler's wings vanished as quickly as they had appeared. She folded them away and a moment later, they had gone. Albert was the first to arrive in the hut after the work shift. His frown eased when she slid out from under the bed.

"Where you been, Missy?"

Tyler explained and asked, "Kylie?" Albert looked blank.

"We thought she was with you."

"She *was* until a contrapasso found her outside the storehouse. If she's not been with you I guess they killed her." Tyler was disappointed and angry with herself. "It's my fault. I shouldn't have let her..."

"No, no. You did well, but we 'ave to wait. She'll return and then we can escape."

"Are they looking for me?"

"No. Don't think they can keep a track of who they's killed and who they 'aven't. They took six today. They know somefing's wrong though, 'cause a contrapasso's a'missin'."

Tyler produced the storehouse key and smiled.

"Guess we proved they're not infallible, if nothing else. Albert, something really freaky happened. I have wings! I grew a massive pair of flaming wings! They're folded away now but I think I might be able to bring them back."

"Well I'll be... You 'ad wings? How?"

"I don't really know. I was as surprised as you are and it completely freaked me out. I was feeling like giving up, but then I had this new kind of hope and the next minute they were there."

"Maybe it's 'cause you're the owner of the contrap."

"Perhaps. I think if I hope strongly enough they'll return."

"I'd like to be around to see that!"

Tyler tried to conceal a smile and desperately wanted to talk more and experiment with her wings, but voices outside stopped her.

"That's the others. Don't say anything, please, Albert. I'll tell them when I've got my head around it."

Later that evening, after their unfulfilling meal of rotten bread and foul water, Tyler unfurled her wings for the first time consciously. Despite their incredulous stares and endless questions, Tyler had no explanation other than her theory that hope made things better, sometimes in unexpected ways. She tried to sleep throughout the cold night and managed a couple of hours' reasonable rest. She figured Kylie would reappear during the next day or perhaps that night, but when the hideous work shift had ended and Kylie had still to return, her worry resurfaced and her concealed wings evaporated.

"Perhaps we'd best get on with it without her," she whispered to Albert as they waited for the evening's allotment of mangy bread. "I'm not really sure how long I've been out of my body. I could be running out of time. Do you know if a day in here is the same as a real day?"

Albert shrugged.

"I ain't a clue. Better ask Izabella."

Izabella knew no more than Albert. Tyler decided to set the escape plan in motion at dawn. If she was correct, and the chasm days were the same as normal days, she figured she would still have two days remaining. She told the team.

"We'll have to get the Nazis and the chain in the cart first before the contrapassi are up and about. That won't be too difficult, but we'll need to cover them with bodies once they're in the cart or they'll be too obvious."

"If three of us are lying on top we should pretty much be able to cover them up," said Zebedee. "If we're careful. The contrapassi don't really check the cart. They're too used to it. They just keep dumping the bodies in all day long."

"Right," said Tyler. She picked those she thought would be at the greatest risk of selection during the day. "Izabella, Zebedee and Marcus, you must lay on top of the Nazis and the chain, cover them up. Albert and I will get them in first. As soon as you see we've done it, you'll have to make your way over and hop in when no one's looking. You could be lying there all day."

"We can do it," said Izabella. Zebedee and Marcus nodded. "Don't worry."

"Okay. Then we need to get everyone else in the cart but we need to do it in a way that won't attract attention. One at a time, alright? Albert and I will distract the contrapassi on the way back from the quarry. Kinga and Danuta, you go ahead as fast as you can while we keep them occupied. Get in the cart. Claudia, can you sneak in while they're throwing out the evening bread? If we need to, we can always create another distraction. Then it's just Albert and me. We'll find a way in. Work something out."

"Just don't do anything to get yourselves killed," said Zebedee.

"And Kylie?" asked Izabella.

"I won't leave the chasm without her," said Tyler. "But if she's not back by the time we're all in the cart I'll have to come back for her and break her out. Our mission is too important to postpone."

Everybody looked at Tyler expectantly.

"Right then, that's the plan basically. We get on the cart and play dead until they wheel us out of the compound. Then we jump the contrapasso. Use the chain, and we run."

They each nodded.

"What if they take the cart out during the day when only half of us are on it?" asked Izabella.

"If that happens it's down to whoever is on the cart to use the chain and free themselves. Get away and hide. Whoever remains will have to find another way out. Alright? Any more questions?" They shook heads. "Like Zebedee said, just don't do anything to get yourselves killed."

Tyler spent a very restless night playing out scenarios in her mind, testing what might go wrong with the plan. She slipped into a semi-dreaming state in which she was trying to get on the cart and was selected for special treatment before reaching it. Another time, she was on the cart and heading for the gates when Two Whips noticed she wasn't really dead, plucked her out by the leg and gunned her down. She spent her unsleeping hours unravelling the thread from the replacement blanket Izabella had found for her and by the morning she had a ball of yarn bigger than her fist.

As the light dawned and the temperature rose, her stomach tied itself in knots as nerves jangled, but she rose and readied herself for the work ahead. She knew she would need every ounce of her wits this day. Flattening the ball of yarn as much as possible she crammed it into her pocket hoping the contrapassi would not notice it.

She left the hut with Albert and went to retrieve Goebbels, Bagshot, the gun and the chain. The contrapassi were feasting in the hall, as was their usual routine and this morning they were making merry with a boisterous din. Tyler took it as a good sign they were not giving the complex much attention and she shoved Bagshot across the open ground while glancing periodically at the watchtowers to be sure the contrapassi there were not taking an overt interest. They didn't seem to notice anything out of the usual and, with relief, Tyler and Albert reached the cart and hoisted the two bodies in, followed by the chain and the gun. Zebedee, Izabella and Marcus were there the next moment as Tyler and Albert left the scene. Nobody noticed them climb in to lie across the others and the chain, playing dead. Tyler risked a glance across the grounds and was impressed by the stillness of her friends. They looked every bit like a small heap of corpses, albeit less emaciated than the usual pile.

Tyler worked at Albert's side. She had planned a small distraction and worked all day filling barrows and carefully positioning them near the quarry edge that overhung the path back to the huts. She gathered full barrows from the others also, and added them to her collection. The barrow nearest the top was precariously propped up on a rock and she had bound the yarn around the barrow's wheel axle and trailed the yarn back to her work place, scuffing fire fog over it to hide it.

After an incredibly long day's toil, the horn sounded and Tyler watched Claudia sneaking to the head of the returning party, heading back to the huts with Kinga and Danuta.

"It's now or never," she whispered to Albert as contrapassi lashed at stragglers and the entire workforce filtered their way back to the huts, and she tugged the yarn. Claudia glanced up at the barrows as they began to topple and sped away from the others. Kinga and Danuta glanced back at Tyler. This was not the plan.

There was a great roar as fire fog and smouldering rock avalanched down the quarry side, racing towards the returning party. Tyler allowed herself a half smile and joined the line. It seemed to be working. Fire fog, barrows and debris crashed around the pathway engulfing all in a great cloud of dust. Contrapassi were half buried and knocked to the ground. Ghosts grabbed one another to help free themselves, but Claudia wasn't at the cart yet and a contrapasso nearby grabbed Tyler and hoisted her clear of the ground, growling amid the growing commotion as dust and fog filled the air.

"I have her! Here's the culprit! Special treatment for you, girl!"

Tyler screamed and flailed trying to break free but the contrapasso's grip on her leg was unyielding. Another contrapasso shoved away fallen rock that was trapping him and tried to clamber out. Ghosts remained stuck, along with other contrapassi and the path was blocked, but her captor mounted the smouldering rubble easily and carried Tyler to the gallows in front of the feasting hall. Several of his comrades were able to join him and Tyler knew she stood no chance against them. They bound her hands and forced her up the set of stairs to the hanging rope to draw the noose tight around her neck. The coarse rope burned her skin as she searched the scene for Albert. Away to her right she glimpsed the *dead* cart being wheeled away towards the gate as it was opened to let the cart pass. She wondered if her friends, already on the cart, would escape or not, but understood she would not live long enough to see. She noticed Claudia was one of the ghosts who had been sequestered into hauling the cart and that Two Whips was lashing her to pull harder.

A hulking contrapasso approached the gallows and

aimed a kick at the steps to drop her to her death. She closed her eyes and sobbed as she felt herself plummet.

Machine Gun

At the last moment she remembered.

Wings! I need the wings! They had folded, concealed themselves and vanished as quickly as they had first appeared, but she hoped she could bring them back. Hope rose in her chest, bubbling like a mountain spring to unfurl the burning wings. They burst out from her skin, through her clothes, the fire fog substance rendering as she fell. Contrapassi gasped at the phenomenon. Tyler was no ordinary ghost.

She swept the huge wings back and, gathering a great draft of air, brought them down with a powerful sweep to slacken the rope about her neck.

Not dead yet...

A girl ghost materialised near the storehouse as Tyler struggled to free her hands. With the noose still about her neck she was tethered to the gallows and could fly nowhere. Contrapassi closed and those in the nearest watchtowers turned their guns and fired. The girl ran towards Tyler, and Tyler recognised her with a jolt.

"Kylie!"

Kylie flitted from the shadows of the storehouse cradling a machine gun in her arms and Tyler didn't understand why or where she had found it. Kylie opened fire at the contrapassi and Albert dashed forward from the gathering crowd that was forming from the straggle of returning workers. He shoved the steps closer to Tyler, skipped up them and lifted the rope from her. She flew as contrapassi dropped, riddled with bullets. Kylie wheeled her gun upon the guards in the towers, spraying smoke and metal. Tyler sped out from the camp to the gates where the cart was passing. Two Whips was returning, aware of her escape yet unsure of how best to catch her. She beat her wings, cleared him easily to dive for the cart where she snatched out the Mordecai chain. She turned and hurled it with a vast sweep of her wings. Two Whips fell to the ground like a tumbled monolith, bound and silenced by the chain, sending a vast billow of dust and fog into the air. She grabbed the gun from the cart as Kinga, Danuta, Albert and Kylie fled the camp and passed the gate, heaving it shut.

"Go!" screamed Albert, securing the gate lock so the contrapassi could not follow. Kylie joined the others at the cart. The dead-pretenders were rising, aware something new was happening. Zebedee clambered out and helped tow the cart as the boy ghost, who had been put to work hauling, bolted.

Ahead of the team and to their right, beyond the billowing haze of the gate, lay a forest. To the left the land dropped gently into a plain where a rough, dirt road snaked out, in the open. Tyler headed for the smouldering trees, dreading what was beyond its fringe yet knowing this was their only hope. Below her, the others had climbed from the cart and were pushing from the rear to speed their passage away from the camp. Nobody voiced it, but all knew it would not be long before a party of armed contrapassi gave chase.

Tyler flew ahead, ducking branches and dodging tall

trunks. The trees were massive, making her feel even smaller and more insignificant than she did already. After covering some two hundred metres or so, she returned to the rambling cart and her breathless friends, alighting on a soft fog, deep with pine needles.

"This way. It's all clear."

"We must find the Mordecai chains," said Izabella, breathlessly. "If we get separated, seek the chains."

Tyler knew where she wanted to go. There was one place she'd seen in the chasm so far that was familiar and she was drawn to it, was intrigued by it.

The *Tower of Doom.*

But the tower was not in this direction. The woods spread out before her and without needing to fly up above the treetops she knew they would need to change tack before long or she would be leading them further away from her objective. They went deeper into the otherworldly forest, slowing periodically to listen and peer around, scanning the woods at their backs for traces of following contrapassi. They took turns to pull the cart carrying the two bound Nazis.

"Where did you get the machine gun?" Tyler asked Kylie as they heaved the cart together.

"I didn't know, but when you come back from the second death, you bring with you whatever you were holding at the time you died."

"You were holding a machine gun?"

Kylie nodded.

"I snatched it from the contrapasso at the door to the storehouse just before he lashed me to death. Forget the gun. Where the heck did you get the wings?"

"I'm not sure. I'm not sure why I have them. They just appeared when I... When I found some hope. Guess Izabella was right." The wings had folded away and disappeared into Tyler's back as soon as she'd begun to walk with the cart. She wondered if they were still there or if they came and went as they pleased. Her gut told her they would probably vanish, never to return, if she lost all hope. *Just one more peculiarity of this strange chasm-realm.*

When the level ground fell away to their right into a valley, they gathered to rest and talk. Trees drifted around them and the forest floor undulated as though alive.

"Which way should we go?" Kylie asked. Tyler didn't know.

"If we go up, we might be spotted more easily," stated Zebedee.

"Agreed," said Izabella.

"But in the lowland we might be more easily attacked," said Kinga.

"True," said Tyler.

"We 'ave to move somewhere," said Albert.

"The boy's right," said Zebedee. "The worst thing we can do is stop moving."

Tyler took them to the right, planning to veer left as soon as the ground permitted, so that they would be heading roughly towards the tower. The cart trundled down the slope as the party was hemmed either side by banks, a tall one to their left, a lesser incline to their right. A short way down Tyler stopped. The little voice in her head was warning her again.

They're coming!

"I don't like it. We're in danger."

"Really? You don't say," muttered Claudia.

A heavy scuffling sound reached them through the trees.

"RUN!" shouted Tyler, as hulking shapes broke the ridge. Armed contrapassi thundered out along the high ground snarling and lashing whips, brazen armour and teeth flashing between trees. The ghosts scattered in terror, abandoning the cart and overturning its cargo. Tyler unfurled her wings, took to the air and loosed a hail of bullets at her enemies. The returning fire overwhelming and she swooped away, wings rushing wildly amidst bullets. Sheltering behind a screen of trees she watched through branches, guiltily, feeling as though she was abandoning her friends. Below, Zebedee scuttled along alone in blind panic and Izabella, Marcus and the twins circled in the pit of the valley as contrapassi closed on them in an ever-tightening ring. The huge monsters bayed and fired into the air with delight, their shaggy arms raised in anticipated victory. Their wolfish jowls drooled as they paced closer, through leaf litter and the sparse scattering of trees that stood between them and their prey.

Tyler had to do something, though she knew it could be lethal. She broke cover and dived at the beasts, swooping in a great arc to fire at them. Pain stung her as several bullets tore into her wings. She lost height and spiralled, a wounded bird. A huge net filled her vision and rough cord singed her skin, dragging her from the air. Crashing through trees, she hit the leafy ground in a dizzy heap of bruised limbs, not knowing what was happening to the rest of her team. A contrapasso gathered her in the net and bundled her away on its back as she desperately tried to catch a glimpse of her friends. Her vision waned.

Where is Albert? Did anyone escape? Did anyone survive? What have I done to us all?

Over the next hour or so she glimpsed fleeting images of her surroundings, the mighty trees, now the open expanse of fire fog sky, then the darkness of a tunnel, or was it a cave? She wondered where the contrapassi were taking her and blacked out several times only to be woken by a shock of pain from her throbbing wounds. She tasted blood. Wiped sweat, blood and tears from stinging eyes. Tried to shift her body into a more comfortable position. Failed.

"Albert..." She heard her own voice murmuring distantly. *Where am I?*

Beyond her net, chasm-light flashed hotly. They were outside again. She scanned blearily for the *Tower of Doom*. Saw nothing but dappled fog. The net sapped her strength and she longed to be free of it. When relief finally came she was in near darkness, tumbling down an endless, stony slope that bruised her further. She came to a sprawling stop and lay struggling for consciousness for an age before sleep overcame her.

*

Bars. At first that was all she saw. Her eyes stung and refused to focus, disobedient and sluggish. She hurt all over and the bullet wounds in her bedraggled wings were agony. She swore under breath and felt the cold, vice-like grip of a Mordecai chain binding her and realised she could not move from the shoulders down. But the chain did not appear to affect her in the same way it had the other ghosts. She found she could move her head and hadn't she just sworn aloud? If she could speak then she could still command the chain. *Like Izabella said, I'm not a true ghost and the usual laws don't necessarily apply.*

She whispered.

"Mordecai resolvo."

The chain fell to the ground.

She crawled up the hard slope towards the bars to find they were set in a sturdy, locked door. *Great. Another prison. What is it with the chasm and prisons?*

She hauled her aching body closer and saw beyond, where a cave broadened. Feasting contrapassi edged a lengthy table piled high with food. She feared she was back in the camp, but couldn't recall a cave there. Where then? She recoiled into the shadows of her sloping prison, hoping to go unnoticed, needing time to think, time to heal and to plan. The contrapassi continued troughing like pigs, oblivious. *Good.* A detail drew her attention. They had swords strung at their waists. This was new and she tried to recall seeing any contrapassi with swords in the camp and could not.

Not the camp, then. Definitely not the camp.

Light spilled from an entrance way beyond the feasting table. She tried to swallow, mouth parched, as she watched them tear meat from the browned roasts, and listened to them guzzle drink from goblets. Her stomach groaned painfully at the enticing aromas of fresh food and she feared she might faint. Jackal drool pooled on the table. She edged closer again, repulsed by the creatures, trying to see beyond the long cave, but it was useless. Too many delicacies and creatures blocked her view. She hid in the deep shadows to think, to gather her wits. At least for now they were leaving her alone. She examined her wounds and counted three bullet holes, each congealing with blood. Stretching her wings brought pain. She cleaned them as best she could and folded them away and, as she did so, her hand brushed against cold metal on the ground. She sought the object, her fingers alighting upon the machine gun she'd taken from the camp.

The idiot creatures didn't even search me when they threw me in here!

She couldn't believe it. She checked the weapon quietly and could find no real damage. Figuring it should still work, she considered mowing down the contrapassi where they sat, but decided that was a bad idea. She would remain trapped and what if she ran out of bullets before killing them all? What if she couldn't escape before the second death returned them all to the cave.

Do contrapassi die for real in the chasm, or do they come back like others? Tyler had no way of knowing.

Her eyes had become accustomed to the dark. She explored the slope and found it was not endless but was enclosed by cave walls that rose steeply to a craggy low roof above her. Her study of the cave was interrupted by voices. The contrapassi were talking. Tyler crept closer.

"If they come this way again they'll feel the edge of my sword, I swear. I'll chop them into pieces."

"What right do the others think they have, anyway? Blasted menace. Kill 'em. Kill 'em all, I say!"

"We should lay traps for 'em. That's what we should do! Go up there and lay big traps where we know they go."

"More wine!"

"Yeah. That'll teach 'em."

Many contrapassi roared and jeered.

"Trap 'em! Kill 'em!"

"Kill the others!"

"Death to the others!"

"Wait! We cannot go up to the cave. We're forbidden. It is beyond our bounds."

"This is true. The Cave of Sorrows is beyond our reach, or else we'd have all the chains we wanted by now. Who amongst you has ever ventured there?"

Silence.

"You see? We can't trap the others. It's too dangerous. Go anywhere near there and you'll be blasted to shreds."

"What about the girl?"

"What *about* the girl?"

"I mean, what are we going to do with her?"

Contrapassi guffawed and hammered heavy fists on the table. Her fate was the biggest joke in history, apparently. She wondered who were *the others*?

Tyler slipped away to the end of her prison and clawed at the ground with the butt of her gun. Whatever the contrapassi had planned for her, it would not be pleasant. She had to escape. Now. Whatever the cost.

A meagre amount of rock and gravel came away. She worked again and soon excavated a small divot. She was amazed to find that the more she dug the softer the ground became and she broadened the hole knowing she would need to fit through it if she was to tunnel out.

But how long might that take? And how long do I have before they come for me?

Something gave. A gap appeared at the very bottom of the small pit where light glowed softly. Tyler checked behind her where the contrapassi bickered and feasted and howled. They were busy. She shoved a foot into the pit and kicked. A clump of rock broke away and the ground beneath her collapsed. She fell with tumbling rock and fire fog, hugging her wings close to her body for fear they would catch the wind and burst open to shred where they were damaged. She fell for such a long time that she wondered if she would ever stop.

Just a bad dream, she told herself. *I'll wake up soon and everything will be alright.* But even as she thought this, she knew it was untrue. The chasm was very real and she was really stuck in it. She impacted fire fog at great speed and climbed out of the resulting crater to look around. The cave was gone. Above her the *lake of fire* smouldered away, a perpetual sunset, although ruled by a huge, ashen moon. Alone, she stumbled into a patch of bone-like, blackened trees, their outer reaches catching, clawing at her as she walked. She recognised nothing in her surroundings, which shifted like desert sands, until a bank of mist dispelled to reveal the *Tower of Doom*. Fog was syrup around her legs as she strove towards it, fighting against the chasm's chaotic elements that hindered her. She fended off branches and grasping twigs. She called out, frustrated and exhausted.

"Albert? Zebedee?"

Nobody answered. A cruel wind caught her, blowing her backwards as she recalled Izabella's words once more.

Hope is your best weapon in the chasm.

Tyler hoped. Hoped she'd find Albert. Hoped she'd overcome the elements, the swirling, disorienting fire fog. She hoped she'd return to the world where gravity held sway over chaos. She wasn't sure if the wind caught her wings and blasted them open or if her hopefulness had caused them to spread but, either way, they unfurled at that moment and she was quickly free of the ground and soaring again, lifting over the tops of the hideous trees.

The pain was immense and she fought to remain conscious, but her wings held and the holes barely affected her flight. Nor did her wings tear. From the air she could see the tower more clearly. She rose, buffeted by winds and banks of fog, all the time inching closer.

And then she saw the birds, large and dark, ruling the sky around the tower like blackened, majestic eagles.

Below her, fire fog blazed and she tilted her wings to climb higher still and saw the tower was on an island, a vast disc, cut off from the rest of the chasm's morphing terrain by flowing rivers.

She noticed something else: The tower did not shift at the will of the chasm. It stood on its island, stationary. Tyler watched the ominous birds approaching. They had seen her. She dived away, unsure if they would be helpful, presuming they would be ferocious. She plummeted towards the tower's roof with its crumbling, unfinished edge and spread her wings only to slow her descent and to settle within the battlements, feeling ill-prepared for the danger ahead.

The Tower

Blocks inched into place and Tyler had to sit down to take it in. Tiny rivulets of dust-like mortar streamed in to cement stones together. One side was complete. Battlements stood proud and undamaged. The opposite side was in worse shape. It resembled an old ruin with ancient, shattered stones, but she saw it was growing. Previously unable to see detail from the air, she now watched with fascination as the tower, ever so slowly, grew. But did that show progress in her quest, or that of the contrap's wearer? She had no way of telling, or even knowing if Melissa or Lucy were wearing it.

The relatively stable stone structure was a relief to her reeling senses. For once, nothing around her dispersed or collapsed. *As long as I don't peer over the battlements*, she thought. She found a spiral stairwell and began descending, interested to know what was further down the building but, before she had taken five steps, one of the huge birds appeared over her and landed with remarkable agility on a jutting battlement. The bird, at least twice her size, cocked its head to one side to eye her suspiciously. Tyler froze. Watching. Waiting. The bird did nothing threatening.

"What? What do you want?"

The bird blinked its dark, glossy eyes and continued to watch. Tyler stepped down into the next level with a wary glance at the bird behind her. She entered a chamber and had to find the wall for support.

Food!

Good bread, and clear water in a crystal pitcher. A table laid and ready for guests. She steadied herself and stepped closer. There were cheeses and fruit; grapes and apples and pineapples, oranges and melons and cherries. She wanted to rush forward and stuff her mouth full, drain the pitcher in one swig, but a feeling stopped her and held her feet clamped to the floor.

Where's the host? Who's is the food? What new trap have I stumbled into?

She stood stock-still, waiting. The bird called raucously from the upper level.

Is the food poisoned? If I eat some will it trigger an army of contrapassi to erupt from the lower levels?

Tyler considered her options. The bird crowed again. She tentatively approached the table. Nothing happened. No trap. No army. She reached out and took an apple, panicked and replaced it quickly. Still nothing.

Perhaps it's safe after all!

She grabbed the apple again and sniffed it. It smelled sweet and ripe, and she craved its juicy, tangy flesh. All the same, she did not bite but instead skipped back up the stairs to the waiting bird. She stood facing the creature, now taking in its immensity and doubting her plan.

Will you devour me or the apple? She gave a soft whistle, hoping to charm. The great bird clucked and jabbered, jutting its head in short, swift movements. It fixed its eyes on her. Tyler offered the apple and took a small step closer. The bird flapped its giant wings and for a moment Tyler thought it would flee, but it left its battlement perch to hop down onto the rooftop before her. Raising its huge, hard beak level with Tyler's face, it crowed loudly. Tyler shook, presented the apple on her palm and closed her eyes. The apple's weight left her hand and when she looked again the bird was tossing it in its beak and chomping it apart.

"What kind of a *Hell bird* are you?" she asked.

The bird clacked and crowed, swallowed the shattered apple.

"More? Would you like more?" She backed away and returned to the room with the food. Seconds later she was back on the roof offering bread and fruits. The Hell bird ate and allowed her to stroke its sleek head. Other Hell birds descended until an entire expectant flock was gathered.

"So you want to be friends, do you? Hungry?" She returned time and time again until all the Hell birds had been fed.

Tyler took an apple for herself and ate. She did not know why the food was there, or whose it was, but she ate and for the first time in days felt sated. The water, too, was good, clear and clean. In fact, water had never tasted so good. She quenched her thirst and hoped she would not die an agonising death, but if the food or water was poisoned she could not tell. It tasted amazing. She found an ancient looking, carved chair - one of a pair - and swept away dust before sitting. There were other pieces of furniture on other levels of the tower. She had hoped for a large, comfortable bed but her search proved there was none. She did find old tapestries depicting cruel scenes from the chasm and these she tore down to use as blankets for later, and she fashioned one into a bag large enough to carry a supply of food from the table.

There seemed no shortage of water at the table and more than once she emptied pitchers only to return a while later to find them full again. She searched the upper levels looking for any kind of living being, not knowing what to expect and it was strange to her that she could not find the provider of the feast or the keeper of the tower. All the same, right now it did not matter. She used some of the water to cleanse the wounds on her wings and when all the Hell birds had left the roof and she was alone once more, she rested. She would have slept but fear for her friends prevented it. She rose from the feasting room and walked the battlements, grateful they were not crumbling around her. *No time to hang around.* The tower would begin to crumble if she stopped making progress, if indeed the tower was responding to *her* progress as it did in the world she'd come from. She planned to stay only as long as she needed. She would rest up, sleep through the night, take supplies and set out in the morning. Her wings were still painful when she stretched them so she did not wish to fly. Instead she toured the rooftop hoping to see some small sign of her friends. In the far distance a camp sent ash billowing into the darkening fire fog sky. She peered at it, shivering. Another camp caught her eye, and another.

How many death camps are there in here? This place is hideous!

She scanned great swathes of forest, rolling valleys and hills. Traced dark rivers for miles, wondering what kind of venom flowed there, and all the while she searched for her friends. She also looked for a cave. The *Cave of Sorrows* the contrapassi had called it. But what *was* the Cave of Sorrows? And *where* was it?

A movement close to the tower caught her attention. Someone was coming, cleaving the mist and fire fog of the island. Fear and hope swelled in her chest as she strained to see who it was, but the tiny figure was too far below to tell.

Tyler raced down the stairs, descending three levels before finding an arrow slit from which to peer. Hope sent waves throughout her weary body.

Is that Albert? Please let it be Albert!

She dashed down more stairs and looked from

another narrow window. This time she was sure.

"Albert!" She stuck an arm through the slot and waved frantically before hitting more stairs. The tower's door was massive, heavy and bolted in numerous places on the inside. She drew the bolts to release the door and tried to heave it open but it wouldn't budge.

"Albert! Albert, are you there?" she bellowed loudly.

Damn, it's rusted shut.

A muffled response came from the other side but she could not discern words. She hoped beyond hope that it really was Albert and not some kind of chasm illusion.

"Help me with the door!" she shouted. "Push!"

The door creaked before giving as rust broke away. She hauled on the large iron handle and the door swung open an inch. She could see him now, grinning on the other side of the crack. They slid fingers between and grasped each other.

"Missy, you alright?"

"Fine now you're here. Push! Let's get this open!" Tyler pulled and Albert shouldered the great door. It opened enough for him to squeeze through sideways and together they forced it shut again and closed the bolts. She hugged him tightly and they stood for a long while embracing.

"Are you okay?" she asked at last.

"I'm alright, I guess," shrugged Albert. She noticed blood dampening the clothes at his shoulder.

"You're hurt! Let me see." She removed his waistcoat and unbuttoned his tattered shirt to inspect the damage. "I have water. I can clean it. I have food." She abandoned the shirt, choosing to haul him upstairs by the hand instead. "Come see! Come and eat!" She told Albert what had happened to her as he ate ravenously.

"Hey, slow down or you'll be sick," she warned. She recounted the conversation she had overheard in the contrapassi cave and asked if he had news of the team.

"Them twins was caught I reckons, but I can't be sure. When I reached the ridge it looked like the contrapassi was on 'em. Kylie got away, I fink. Don't know what 'appened to Zebedee or Izabella, or Claudia."

Tyler shook her head and Albert took her hand.

"Goebbels and Bagshot?"

"Ain't a clue, Missy. They could be still there, tucked away under that old cart."

"We can't leave them there. The contrapassi could set them free of the chains if they find them."

"Right."

"We'll have to go back for them."

"Better find this cave first, don't ya fink, this Cave of Sorrows? Better get 'old o' them Mordecai chains before we do anyfink else."

"Yes, of course. You're right. We'll search for the cave in the morning. We also need to find a good place to leave the bound Nazis. Somewhere no one will ever find them." Albert nodded. "So you escaped the contrapassi in the woods?" Tyler asked.

"Aye. I did that. Stupid, great, lumbering idiots. I hid behind a tree soon as I cleared the ridge. They marched right past me. I been running ever since. I saw this tower and knew it from the contrap. Thought I might find you 'ere."

They huddled together in a lower chamber, cocooned in tapestry sheets as the temperature plummeted and the fire fog sky dulled to a glimmering, golden red, and Tyler slept a deep, peaceful sleep in Albert's arms.

*

When morning came she led Albert out onto the roof and whistled. She had something she wanted to show him. Hell birds soared in ever decreasing circles to perch on the battlements and Tyler tossed bread and fruit to them, to Albert's delight.

"What are they?" he asked.

"Who knows? I call them Hell birds, but they're

friendly enough if you feed them."

Albert cautiously approached the closest bird and offered his palm for it to sniff before running a hand down its flank.

"They'll come to me when I whistle 'cause they think they'll get fed."

"Brilliant!" said Albert admiring the feeding birds. "Will they carry us?"

"I'm not sure. They look like they could rip you to shreds if you put a foot wrong."

"Yeah."

Tyler took an apple and offered it, coaxed a Hell bird closer. It snatched the apple and lowered its head, chomped and swallowed.

"Let me try." Albert grabbed a bunch of grapes and dangled it in front of the bird. It stalked towards him and began stabbing at the grapes with its bill as he backed away to save himself from being lacerated. He dropped the bunch and the bird stooped to pluck them from the ground. As it fed, Albert crept round to its side and edged closer.

"Careful," whispered Tyler. "They're pretty wild."

Albert reached out to tentatively stroke the bird's flank. The bird continued to chomp and guzzle.

"Throw it some more," said Albert, seeing the grapes were almost gone. Tyler dropped a second bunch onto the floor. The bird crowed its delight and rolled its head as Albert soothed it by stroking the soft feathers of its neck, and it cooed. Albert grasped a handful of feathers on the bird's muscular neck and hauled himself up. The bird lurched and, shrieking objections, turned its head. The attack was swift and thorough. Albert recoiled with a shout as the huge beak raked his shoulder, tearing his shirt and waistcoat, and throwing him against the battlements. Tyler ran to him, swinging the bag of food at the bird's head wildly. The bird staggered and pecked at her but then backed away as she threatened to swing again. She grabbed an apple and tossed it away. The bird chased it, leaving her free to help Albert. He waved her off as he stood, assessing his wound.

"It's nothin'. I'm alright, Missy."

"You don't look alright. You look like you've been in a war."

Albert laughed but winced when it hurt.

"Let me get you downstairs. We'd better wash that and bandage it." She helped him down the stone steps and took care of him and all the while he complained that he didn't need looking after and maintained he was fine. Only when Tyler was satisfied that she had done all she could and that he truly was alright did she venture back out onto the rooftop. The birds had gone and were circling at a distance.

Just as well. We're better off without them.

"I'm going to go and search for the others and for the cave. Wait here and don't let anyone into the tower. I'll be back by nightfall." She climbed onto a parapet and spread her wings, testing them, allowing the slight breeze to fill them and take her weight. They did not hurt. She lifted away to rise up and glance back at the shrinking figure on the tower and realised with dread that the Hell birds were coming back to attack. She turned to dive for the battlements, already knowing she would be too late to help Albert. The leading bird, the one she fancied had raked Albert's shoulder, was almost on him. It dropped with wings folded back, harrier-like, and brought its huge talons forward to meet its target.

Tyler could not fly as fast as the birds and she was further away. She watched helplessly as the bird struck, but was surprised to see it did not land or attack. It gripped Albert by his shoulders and carried him from the tower to follow her. The bird brought Albert to her and flew beneath her as she turned again to resume her original course. It was carrying him. Not attacking. Not trying to kill or hurt, but transporting Albert for her.

They flew high, spiralling over the tower. Tyler stretched her own wings and whooped with delight as she broke away from the bird beneath her and looped to re-join its path. There came a strong hope, like the driving pulse of her heart, and she realised all the pain had left her. Her wings had healed and she knew that Albert's arrival at the tower and the food and the rest had done her good. Her hope was high and looking down she saw the *Tower of Doom's* battlements building. She checked the tapestry bag strung over her shoulder. It was holding well and crammed with food and a corked flask of water from the table. The machine gun, also strapped over her neck and shoulder, was another comfort. Beside her, Albert endured the Hell bird's clutch, baring gritted teeth to the wind, looking for Zebedee, the other ghosts, and the Cave of Sorrows.

Let the search begin!

Hell Birds

Lucy looked anxiously at the laptop screen over Melissa's shoulder.

23 Hours : 59 Minutes : 55 Seconds

"Well, there we go," said Lucy. "Less than a day left and she's still in the chasm."

Melissa stood and paced, clenching and unclenching her fists.

"I'll bring in my medical crew," said Chapman. "If she's not back by the deadline they might be able to buy her some more time. They can hook her up, keep her alive artificially..."

"Got to be worth a try," said Weaver.

"Alright, do it," said Melissa. "But I don't think it will work though. Not if she's late back. Izabella said she would die after seven days." Chapman nodded and made a call.

"Check again," suggested Lucy, chewing her lip.

"There's no sign of her. Really. I've been checking it every two minutes. All I can see is a big lake of fire."

"Oh. Guess it's time to start worrying," said Lucy.

"*You think?*" Melissa shot her a black look and stormed off to her bedroom.

*

Albert spotted her first, a tiny spec far below, moving slowly through fog and broiling terrain. The giants pursuing were more obvious.

"Over there!" he alerted Tyler and they both altered course to head down.

"It's Kylie!" shouted Tyler, closing in. She waved a handful of fruit in the air and whistled. Hell birds swooped in behind her and Albert. She tossed them bits of fruit which they snatched from the air and quickly turned their attention upon the movements below. On the ground three contrapassi lumbered after Kylie, cleaving fog. Behind them the forest sprawled. Tyler opened fire and the closest contrapasso dropped. She dived at the next one but pulled away when the bullets ran out and her target did not slow. She reeled about to attack again as Albert and his bird harried the third contrapasso. Tyler swung the gun like a club, struck her contrapasso a blow to the head that did little except enrage him. He lashed his whip and caught her midriff, but was overpowered the next moment as Hell birds hammered in, talons slashing, beaks ripping.

Tyler hit the ground and rolled, her side blistered with fire fog lash. She forced herself to her feet and ran to Kylie, who was doubled over, painfully breathless. Tyler summoned a Hell bird with another whistle and it collected Kylie in it talons, deciding to be helpful. The birds needed little encouragement to attack the contrapassi and they continued with their barrage as Kylie looked up fearfully at the bird towering over her.

"AWAY!" Tyler shouted and the bird launched with a

great flurry of wings and carried Kylie into the sky, beyond reach of the contrapassi. Tyler and Albert followed. Hell birds battled on the ground, clawing flesh as the two remaining contrapassi staggered, but the beasts were too strong for the birds to kill and Tyler knew this. She whistled again, trying to call them off and they peeled away one after the other, leaving the furious contrapassi to nurse their wounds.

Tyler had lost her gun in the fight but she didn't care. They had rescued Kylie. She dropped behind a Hell bird to slipstream, tired and in pain. A cliff top came into view beyond the forest. Tyler studied its barren platform.

"There!" she shouted above the wind. "We'll set down there. Rest a while."

The Hell birds cleared the forest and sped over fog, rolling valleys, dark rivers and crags. They descended to the cliff top, set their passengers down and landed to clack and crow. Tyler alighted, folded her wings away and took fruit and bread to Kylie, who couldn't believe her eyes.

"Where'd ya get this?"

"The tower," said Tyler. She explained about Albert's and her night at the *Tower of Doom*. "Maybe we should head back," she said to Albert when she had answered all Kylie's questions.

Albert was sitting on the rough ground with legs splayed, resting back on the palms of his hands and looking out over the chasm.

"Maybe. I dunno. What about the others? Shouldn't we carry on searching?"

"You're right," said Tyler. "We don't have time to rest." She thought again about her allotted seven days and wondered how she was doing for time. She realised with a shudder of fear that she had completely lost track of the days, and tried in vain to count them. *Four, maybe five days? I think I still have a little time left, but not much. Better push on. Find the cave, get the chains, summon Hitler, get the Hell out.*

She scattered a handful of grapes for the Hell birds.

"Better keep them happy. Some of them are injured." Approaching with caution, she did what she could for the birds using a little water from their supply to wash wounds.

Albert smiled.

"So are you."

What? Oh yes. Injured...

"I'm alright. So where next?" she asked, studying the view with concern. She couldn't see the *Tower of Doom* anywhere. Beyond the smouldering forest the landscape shifted menacingly, fire fog banking and swirling. A river twisted into the distance, its course changing as she watched. Kylie joined her near the cliff edge as Hell birds pecked the ground, seeking out the last few grapes.

"We need to find a cave, right?"

"Yeah. Not just any cave. *The* Cave of Sorrows," confirmed Tyler.

"Then we need to follow the river upstream."

"What? Why?"

"Geography," said Kylie. "Caves are carved out of the rock by underground rivers. Subterranean streams occur close to the source of the river where the water is flowing fast. Usually hills or mountains. If there are any caves nearby, that's where they'll be. Upstream."

"Of course! That's logical," said Tyler, wishing she'd thought of it. "Though I'm not entirely sure logic works in a place like this. Alright, we'll follow the river. Eat what you need. Drink what you want from the flask and rest. We leave in five, if the birds are feeling helpful."

*

Medics arrived. Trusted people this time, members of Chapman's team. Melissa and Lucy knew the head man, Dr Marshall. He had seen them and Tyler through countless medicals over the past few years. His crew hooked Tyler's body up to monitor her, unsurprised by their findings. Mellissa arrived in Tyler's bedroom.

"Don't do anything but monitor her until her time's up," she warned. "She's not in any danger right now. Not until around eleven forty tomorrow night. Keep tabs on her EEG. If you notice any negative changes after then, operate, but I don't think this is going to work." The team nodded their understanding. "If her spirit doesn't re-join her body before the end of the seven days, it will be too late. The bond will be broken."

*

The cliff dwindled into the distance behind them. Tyler led the way, ahead of the Hell birds bearing Albert and Kylie.

The slick river below skirted hills and rock outcrops. Everything smouldered. It divided in places to envelope small islands, narrowed between steep valley sides and threaded ravines and gullies. Off to her left, Tyler spied another of the cruel death camps sprawling out over the land and spewing ash and dust. She was glad when the river bent away from that place and they left it behind. The bag slung at her side was lighter now, around a quarter of the food already used. She had not seen the tower since before finding Kylie, which worried her. A part of her wanted to wheel about and return to the tower's relative safety and comfort, yet she knew time did not allow for such luxuries.

Around them the air was becoming thick and dark with fog and a distant flash of lightning was soon followed by a peal of thunder. The birds descended for better vision and flew on until Tyler spied another tiny figure, this one at the river's edge. She pointed it out and they dropped for a closer look. The figure, a man, had seen then coming. As they approached, he took off his top hat to wave it frantically.

"Zebedee! It's Zebedee!" Albert cried. The Hell birds soared down to the river bank in Tyler's wake, where they set down Albert and Kylie as lightning and thunder continued to erupt in the sky nearby.

Tyler ran into Zebedee's outstretched arms.

"Well, well! This is a turn up for the books. The team is all together again. Fancy that!" Zebedee replaced his hat and grinned. "I must say, it's good to see you."

Tyler broke away from the embrace.

"What do you mean *the team is all together again*? We're still missing Izabella, Marcus and the twins. And Claudia."

"I do beg your pardon, Miss May but, on the contrary; they are all safe and waiting in the cave."

"What? Safe? All of them? You found the cave? *The* Cave of Sorrows?"

"Yes, yes. It's here." Zebedee pointed away from the river towards a cleft in the mounting valley side. "It's a short stroll down there. Come, I'll show you."

Tyler took a step towards the gap but stopped.

"Wait. How do I know this isn't some kind of chasm trick? Are you *really* Zebedee Lieberman? And what were you doing here, down by the river?"

Zebedee looked astonished. He took the pipe from his mouth, something he only ever did in weightier moments.

"I am the one and only Zebedee Lieberman, as far as I can tell. I simply came down here to study the river. I'm not entirely sure what it's made of. It isn't water."

Tyler looked at the flowing river and was reminded of the Shivering Pool. The substance was dark and glassy. She shivered.

"Then how did you escape from the contrapassi in the forest? And what happened to the others?"

"All in good time, Miss May. All in good time. *That* is quite a story..."

"One more question. Who was your housekeeper when you lived on West Street in London?"

Zebedee frowned at her briefly and scratched his head with the tip of his pipe.

"My housekeeper was named Orealia Stephensen."

Tyler backed away, casting a wary glance at the Hell birds, wondering if they would come to her aid. *Too good to be true and the real Zebedee would have known where he had really lived in London.*

"But I never lived in West Street," he added at last, to Tyler's relief.

"It really *is* you!"

"Who did you think I was? Come, my girl. Come and see the others. They'll be thrilled to see you!"

Tyler, Albert and Kylie followed Zebedee between stone rises, down a narrow, rock-clad gully and under the dark mass of churning cloud where it rained. Tyler glanced back to see the Hell birds pecking at the ground. A slippery path deepened and entered the base of a tall cliff face where a small doorway had been chiselled out of the rock. To one side, a disk of stone nestled in an excised hollow in the rock and Tyler realised this was a seal to the mouth of the cave. If the stone was rolled one way the cave was open. Rolled the other way the stone would completely enclose the entrance.

"That's strange," said Tyler, stepping over the hollow, out of the deluge and into the dim dryness of the cave. "That's not normal for a cave."

"Oh, but it *is* a cave. You will see," said Zebedee. "However it was also a tomb. The Cave of *Sorrows*, you understand?"

"So are there bodies? Skeletons?"

"No, nothing like that. Come see!"

She trod deeper in to enter a low chamber carved out of the bedrock where the rest of her team waited. To one side a long platform was recessed into the wall, the size and shape of a narrow bed. The floor, also of rock, was littered with glimmering lengths of chain.

"Mordecai chains," said Izabella, standing with an arm around Marcus' shoulders. "More than we could ever need."

Tyler, Albert and Kylie gazed at the many chains and

were speechless. A moment later, Tyler came to her senses.

"I have food!" She opened the tapestry bag and let the others help themselves.

"No pies?" whined Claudia. "I really fancy a nice pie."

Tyler glared at her and told them what had happened to her while they ate. "Who are the *others*? The *others* the contrapassi talked about?"

"Oh, the others," sneered Claudia. "They think they're *so* special with their big wings and the light and everything." She waved her hands about descriptively. "It's all just a load of hype. If you ask me..."

"You will learn of the others when you die," Izabella interjected.

"They visit here from time to time," explained Zebedee. "But I doubt we'll be fortunate enough to glimpse one. They're very busy these days."

"How did you get here?" asked Tyler. The other ghosts were clearly not at liberty to talk freely about the *others*, whoever they were.

Zebedee cleared his throat for effect.

"Ah! You'd better make yourself comfortable and I shall tell you what happened. When the contrapassi attacked us in the woods, I was lucky enough to run headlong into a tree. I was fleeing with all haste, fearing for my life, you understand, and at the same time twisting my neck to see what the beasts were up to. I hit the trunk and was knocked out, cold."

Man, Zebedee really knows how to lay it on thick. Tyler smiled, feeling weary all of a sudden. She found a place to sit and hugged her knees as he continued.

"Turns out it was the best thing that could have happened! I must have fallen and rolled down the slope. The leaves and fog covered me and the ghastly contrapassi passed me by. Who'd have thought it? When I found my wits, the place was quiet and everyone had gone. I climbed to the ridge and saw movement through the trees, way off in the distant forest. I followed, of course, and soon learned that what I was seeing was a band of contrapassi. I could see they had captives, too. They were moving fast, but when they stopped to rest I crept in for a closer look and found that their captives were Izabella, Marcus and the girls. I couldn't believe my luck!"

Tyler stifled a yawn. *So tired...*

"I waited and followed again when they set off. There were six contrapassi in all. Big brutes, too. I wanted to run in there and punch the lot of them on their ugly noses, but I knew that would be useless. Of course, they were too big for me to take on, so I wondered what to do and was greatly vexed for some time. An idea came to me. If I could only distract the dumb creatures for long enough I would be able to free their prisoners and we might all escape."

Tyler failed to conceal a yawn.

"That was when I... Oh... You appear a little fatigued, my dear. Perhaps now is not the time after all."

"No, go on, Zebedee. I'm listening." Tyler said, but she closed her eyes through necessity and began to drift off.

"If you're sure. Well, to cut a long story short, I rescued them and we walked for miles. We came here."

"I'm sure I'd like to hear the details someday..." Tyler slept.

The Oasis

Tyler awoke to the gentle notes of Marcus' violin and found her friends had settled nearby to rest, Albert beside her.

"How long have I slept?" she asked with a sudden fear rising. She could not afford to sleep.

"An hour. No more."

"I need to get up. Get going. Is everyone else alright?" She sat up and tried to clear her head.

"Aye, we're alright. Ready when you are, Missy."

Tyler rose and walked to the small doorway to peer outside. Above, the brimstone sky was a mass of dark cloud and the rain continued to pelt.

Wonder if the Hell birds are still waiting. She returned to the team.

"Izabella, can you summon Hitler from here?"

"No, child. I would need to be somewhere high to use the summoning command. A mountaintop or perhaps the tower. Preferably somewhere stable, not shifting around like most of the chasm. There can be no disturbance. I must warn you I have not attempted this before in such a place. It may very well not work."

"Oh, that's great," said Claudia. "You drag us all this way, get us captured and starved, beaten and punished, and now it might not even work! What was the point?"

Tyler found herself agreeing, but fought the notion. This was not 'hope'.

"Haven't you learned anything? Do you think we would have come this far if we all thought like that? You need to find some hope. Now, if you want to help at all, pick up a chain, or feel free to find your own way home."

Claudia stared for a moment before hoisting up the nearest chain.

Tyler addressed them all. "I know it's safe here – the contrapassi are forbidden to come here – but we must go. We're leaving for the tower in a few minutes. Get ready. The chains are really heavy so no one is to carry more than one. That means we can only take nine chains but that will have to do. If we can summon the oppressor from the tower, we'll use a chain on him. We'll still have eight left for Himmler and the others."

They each took a chain, mostly hoisting them around their necks like beach towels. Tyler watched Marcus with concern but he had recovered strength enough to carry a chain without too much discomfort. She made sure he ate extra food before they headed back out into the storm. The gully was far more treacherous with the weight of the chains. Every foothold was slick, like ice. They navigated the narrow way and with relief spilled out onto the river bank beyond the rain where they had last seen the Hell birds, but the birds had gone and Tyler's whistling did not bring them back.

"Oh well. Looks like we're trudging again."

They headed downstream along the bank, away from the thunder clouds. Again the chasm looked different. While they had retreated to the cave, the world had shifted and places were not where they had previously been. Tyler groaned and wondered how they were ever to find the tower again. All the same, they had followed the river upstream, so she traced its serpentine route back, hoping it would lead them in roughly the right direction. After hours of dreary hiking they tired and she sought a safe place to rest, settling upon a sheltered spot along the river at the base of a waterfall that appeared peaceful enough. Lush with tropical plants and billowing smog from the falls, it invited. A tranquil pool extended from the drop, edged with beaches of small pebbles.

"This is more like it," said Claudia, tramping in behind Albert.

"We'll rest here," said Tyler, eyeing the pool with suspicion. She deposited her chain on the growing pile as others did likewise. "Don't do anything stupid and keep your eyes open."

She shared out the remaining supply from her bag with the team, saving a little to entice the birds' help, should they reappear. It was hot here. No sunlight but the constant simmering heat of the chasm. Fire fog boiled over the pool and Tyler would have given anything to strip, wade out into the waters to swim. Still, she knew she could not. It would be too dangerous and she didn't know what might be lurking beneath the surface. All the same, the notion was tempting and she rested on a beach with Albert and imagined Hawaii, Corfu, beaches she'd visited on family holidays. She didn't realise the rest of her team were suffering the same temptations, the same wants and wishes, as she closed her eyes to dream. She was unaware, as Claudia threw off her sandals and skipped closer to the waterline. Claudia dipped a toe.

"It's so beautiful here. Such a blissful oasis. Ah! So cool! So refreshing..." she muttered as she waded in to take a swim.

Tyler heard the words - the noise of the rippling water - and opened her eyes, the next moment bolting upright.

"NO! GET OUT OF THE WATER!"

Movement from beneath erupted as numerous

waterlogged corpses boiled to the surface. Claudia screamed and thrashed as she was dragged under.

"NO!" bellowed Tyler. The other ghosts gathered on the beach.

"I'll go in after her," said Albert, stripping off his waistcoat.

"No. Don't. It will take you too! The birds! I'll call the Hells birds!" Tyler waved fruit in the air and whistled in vain as the pool warped and massed.

Claudia surfaced briefly in the foam and waves before disappearing again.

"RUN!" The waters swelled and overran the beaches as the ghosts fled.

"Albert, NO!" Tyler spread her wings and launched into the air as Albert wheeled round, heading for the pool, ignoring her pleas.

"Grab her and drag her free. Get her away from the water," shouted Albert over the roar of the foaming pool.

Tyler had thought that a monstrous creature was beneath the surface, but she saw it was the water itself. With its own treacherous will, it writhed, coiled and twisted; a huge, expanding, amorphous mass of malicious fluid.

"It's like the Shivering Pool, only much worse!" she yelled. Albert edged into the fray of billowing liquid, seeking Claudia. The others fought to escape as the waters grabbed hungrily at feet, ankles and legs. The beaches overflowed and they battled for freedom, grasping at the crumbling fire fog ground around the pool. Izabella managed to break away with Zebedee's help. Zebedee tugged Kinga free and he and Danuta dragged her to safety as Marcus joined them.

Albert thrashed through lurching arms of froth, shaking off the water's attempts to take him. He turned, thigh-deep, and lunged for Claudia as she surfaced. He took her arm and hauled, but the water overpowered him and he vanished beneath waves along with her.

Tyler screamed and dashed after them but stopped

before hitting the water. They were gone, not even their shadows visible beneath the surface. *Leave him*, she thought. He would tell her to if he were with her now. She knew it. *Leave him and get the others to safety. Get the chains to the tower and get out of the chasm. Save those who can be saved.*

She joined the others beyond the water's reach as a thousand memories flooded her being. Meeting Albert for the first time and talking to him in the contrap. Him saving her on the car park rooftop in Whitechapel. Him watching over her, night after night, while she hunted down summoning artefacts. Him reveried in the graveyard in Berlin. Him beaten and crushed by ghosts of the Brazilian castle. Albert and her holding hands, ghost on ghost... There was no way she was leaving Albert behind. She shook herself. She couldn't leave him here.

Not ever.

"It has Albert. I'm going in."

"Wait," said Izabella, yanking her back by the arm. "If you go back there now it will take you too!"

Izabella was right and, yet, the small voice in Tyler's head murmured. *You are not a true ghost. It is not your appointed time. Only you can do what must be done.*

Tyler broke from Izabella's grip, turned and strode purposefully towards the pool, ignoring the pleas of her friends to 'stop!' Her stride became a sprint and finally she spread her wings to take off. She climbed and dived, screaming at the water.

"GIVE THEM BACK TO ME!"

Hitting the water at full pelt, she plunged through foam and surface swells. Beneath, it looked very different. Bodies floated, buoyed in surges, victims of the terrible water. Hundreds of them.

And somewhere among them were Albert and Claudia.

Tyler searched, wings folded, and heard a liquid, rushing voice from the mass of fluid around her.

"I will consume you," it roared. "I will swallow you

and all who come for you."

"You cannot take me." Tyler responded, the voice not spoken but little more than a thought echoing in her mind. "My body still lives and this is *not* my appointed time."

The fluid voice hissed and the waters pressed her but she searched on, checking the floating, jostling bodies, one after another. A great vortex dragged the bodies away as though the pool was taking them from her. She found Albert and Claudia amongst them and swam to them as they drifted into the spiral, reached them and grabbed them each with one hand. She hauled their limp bodies with all her might but before reaching the surface her strength gave in and Albert slipped from her fingers. She snatched at him with her other hand and held him tightly. Realised, too late, that in doing so she had let Claudia go. Tyler watched helplessly as Claudia spiralled away into the depths. *Where does the vortex go?* There was no way of telling. Tyler reluctantly left her in the water's grip and headed ashore, dragging Albert, and feeling a new burden.

Guilt.

"She's gone," she told the others as she collapsed beyond the bank at their feet. "And it's my fault. I can't search anymore, but it's no good anyway. The pool has her. It's taken her somewhere else. I know it."

The group gathered on higher ground a short way from the writhing pool that seemed angered by its denied feast, Albert having been saved from it. Albert was suffering its affects and looked asleep.

"The chains!" said Zebedee peering back at the water. "We've left them behind. The water has them."

"We have to go back for them," said Izabella. "Or else we'll truly have wasted our time."

Tyler rallied enough energy to launch again, sweeping in towards the expanding pool. The chains were submerging as Tyler closed on them.

"Claudia!" she shouted as she swooped, with a last,

lingering hope, but there was now no sign of any bodies in the water.

Tyler dived to snatch at a chain, and switched back to avoid a vast, looming arm of water that swept down to dash on the ground. Waters swelled and she returned repeatedly to salvage chains from the depleting pile. By the time she reached the last chain, the vortex was swirling the entire surface of the pool and even sucking in the fire fog banks and beaches at its edge.

"Well done, my girl!" said Zebedee. "We have all the chains."

Tyler scowled.

"We can't carry them all now that Claudia has gone," she said, stumbling to Albert who still appeared to be unconscious. "But eight will do."

"We better go," said Zebedee. "Before we're all sucked in."

"Zebedee, will he be alright?"

"Indeed! He's a ghost. Give him a moment. I'm sure he'll recover." Zebedee stooped to study Albert's face, turning it left and right. He gave Albert a single, firm slap. Albert blinked and looked about.

"See," said Zebedee. "He's better already."

"Thanks, Zebedee."

They rested a while, a safe distance from the spiralling pool, and Albert slowly recovered. Tyler gave him the last drop of drinkable water from the flask, unable to meet his gaze, and when he was feeling strong enough, broke the news that they had lost Claudia, and they set off once more in search of the tower. An hour or so later Kinga gave a shout.

"I see it!" She pointed and Tyler squinted into the wind. Ahead in the far distance, the *Tower of Doom* pierced the glowering rubble and heaving fog of the chasm.

At last!

Hell birds perched on battlements, waiting. Knowing instinctively the table would be freshly laid with fruit, cheese, bread and water, Tyler flew the rest of the way and let the others into the tower.

Is this the contrap showing a kindness to its owner?

They climbed stairs and gazed in awe at the table.

"The birds want food, too," said Tyler. "They're waiting on the roof."

Danuta, Kinga and Kylie collected food and ate as they climbed. They tossed plump grapes, apples and melons to the hungry birds, and tore grainy loaves into chunks for them. Zebedee and Albert descended the tower to explore as the others continued to graze, revelling in the choice delights of the strange table.

"So who owns this place?" asked Izabella, before taking a bite of bread.

"I don't know," said Tyler. "I looked around for somebody when I first came here, but I couldn't find anyone. The table somehow magics the food out of nowhere. I thought *you* might be able to explain it."

Izabella peered at Tyler, shrugged her rounded shoulders and swallowed.

"I haven't a clue, girl. I don't know everything."

"But you know how to summon a ghost from here."

"Eat. When we are finished at the table we will try."

A shudder of excitement traversed Tyler's spine.

Finally!

When they had all eaten their fill and emptied each of the pitchers several times over, they headed back to the roof but Albert and Zebedee clambered up the stairs from below before they could leave the feasting room.

"We found just the place," said Albert.

"The place for what?" asked Izabella, turning with irritation.

"The place to put Goebbels and the others," said Zebedee. "A place they'll never be found. Deep in the bowls of the tower there's a dungeon."

"An' in that there dungeon there's an oubliette."

"What's an oubliette?" asked Tyler.

"It's a deep pit that's impossible to escape. It's where

they used to put prisoners who they wanted to forget about. An inescapable place of death by slow starvation."

"That's nice," muttered Kylie.

"Come up with us," said Tyler to Albert and Zebedee. "Izabella's going to try the spell."

"You must come, Albert," said Izabella, knowingly. "You are needed."

The Spell

The sky had darkened while they were inside. Tyler knew the biting cold would soon descend. Izabella stood on the tower's roof, dead centre and raised her arms. She seemed to be in a trance as Tyler watched, wondering what she was doing. Albert was way off in the fog, still on the island but no longer in the safety of the tower. Tyler feared for him.

Get a move on! The sooner you get this done, the sooner Albert can come back inside. Albert was waiting to be summoned, having been carried out by an obliging Hell bird, beyond the black trees, to land and dismount in the cloudy heat of the evening.

Izabella began to chant with little more than a murmur at first.

"Fero tuli latum, phasmatis licentia hac." She closed her eyes and repeated the phrase, casting her arms open to the sky. She turned on the spot, chanting over and over before bringing her arms down and resting her hands on Tyler's head. Finally she ended the chant with a name.

"Fero tuli latum, phasmatis licentia hac, Albert Christopher Goodwin."

Those gathered waited in hushed silence. Izabella opened her eyes and looked around, saw that Albert had not appeared and closed them again. She shouted the line loudly and the words echoed across the landscape as lightning flashed. Billowing fire fog clouds stirred overhead.

"Fero tuli latum, phasmatis licentia hac, Albert Christopher Goodwin!"

Tyler was blown sideways as Albert's form materialised in her place.

"By God. It worked!" chirped Zebedee. "She did it. She summoned Albert!"

Albert grinned and looked down to be sure he was all there.

"Try Hitler now," said Tyler, rising and dusting herself down. She fetched a chain and stood at the ready, brandishing it. Izabella beckoned for Kylie to step forward.

"You were bound to the oppressor once," said Izabella. "You have the perfect association to help with the summoning. Step forward, child." Kylie took position before Izabella as she began chanting again.

*

Knives hammered into the board and Lucy tugged them free. She had always been the cool one, the one who didn't get flustered, but now she was losing it too.

"Come on, Tyler. Come on Tyler. Come on Tyler." She let fly at the target again and the three blades massed around the centre, driven deeper than before. "How long now?" she asked Melissa, who was unable to take her eyes from the laptop screen. Melissa read the clock aloud.

"Seventeen hours, thirty-four minutes, forty-two seconds and counting. Not long enough."

"She can still make it."

"We haven't heard from her in days. What if something bad's happened?"

Chapman's phone rang. He listened and ended the call without speaking.

"Sorry, girls. I have to go. Nothing to worry about. I'll be back in the morning along with the medics. Hang in there. Get some sleep. Oh, by the way, I'm keeping two men on the doorway downstairs until it's fixed. Not that you girls aren't capable of defending yourselves. When Tyler's back, we'll relocate you three asap." He gathered his coat, gave them a nod and left.

"Wonder what that was all about?" said Melissa.

"Nothing to worry about. Guess he has to go home sometime. He said don't worry, so *don't worry*."

"Easy for you to say."

Lucy considered taking his advice and going to bed but returned to her knife throwing.

"Come on Tyler..."

*

With eyes closed, Izabella echoed the spell. She opened her arms to the blackening sky as before and turned about, chanting. When she had addressed all corners of the chasm and called out in every direction, she rested her hands on Kylie's head to utter the final command as lightning cracked the darkness into red all around the tower. Dense cloud obscured the moon. Thunder rumbled.

"Fero tuli latum, phasmatis licentia hac, Adolf Hitler." As before, Izabella opened her bulging eyes to see if the spell had worked. Hitler was not there. She shook her head and tried again. She cried to the tumultuous heavens.

"Fero tuli latum, phasmatis licentia hac, Adolf Hitler!"

Nothing. Not a sound, except the distant groaning

of the chasm as her words echoed and died on the wind. The storm clouds quietened and dispelled and an orange glow shone over the tower casting long shadows from the battlements. She tried again, clearly frustrated.

"Fero tuli latum, phasmatis licentia hac, spirit of the oppressor!" When these words failed to bring Hitler, she looked at Tyler with resignation and shook her head.

"I am sorry, child. He does not appear to be in the chasm."

"Then the contrap was right," said Tyler. "If he's not in the *Ghost Portal* and not in the chasm, he must have found a way to return to the world. Hitler is still *at large*." She sat on the roof, crushed by disappointment.

After all this effort. All this time.

"Try for Himmler," she said. "Lucy put him in the contrap too. He had a lot to do with the concentration camps where the twins died. You can use them to help the summoning."

Izabella tried the spell once again but Himmler did not appear.

"It's no use. They're not in the chasm," she concluded. Albert joined Tyler, hugging an arm around her.

"It'll be alright, Missy. You'll see. It'll be alright. We'll find a way to stop 'im. At least we proved they ain't in the chasm."

Zebedee approached, refilling his pipe and lighting it.

"If I might interrupt – we still have the others to deal with - the other two we left in the woods under the cart. We should recover them and put them in the dungeon before we return to the portal. Tyler's time is limited, though we have no way of knowing how long she has left – we really shouldn't tarry unless we have a very good reason."

"He's right," said Tyler. "We'll get Goebbels and Bagshot, bring them back here. Then we leave for good."

"*If* you can find the forest," said Kylie.

"Well then, what are we waiting for?" asked Zebedee with an unaccountably merry tone.

"We don't *all* need to go," said Tyler, thinking it through. "We'd best leave a few here. If the party doesn't return, the others can launch a rescue. They will have the birds and the supplies."

"Agreed," said Zebedee. "So who's going?"

"Not me," said Kylie. "I'd like to stay here, if that's alright."

"Zebedee and I will go," said Albert. "Two of us should be enough. No point riskin' more. An' Tyler should stay 'ere. She could get really killed out there. Killed for good, I means."

"No," said Tyler.

"Agreed," said Zebedee. "We'll take two extra birds to carry the Nazis, if they'll oblige. We'll be back before morning. I promise."

Tyler met Albert's eyes imploringly.

"Can't someone else go? Why does it always have to be you? How are you going to find the forest in this darkness?"

"We'll manage. We'll be back soon, Missy. You'll see."

"If it has to be you, at least eat something before you go. And take the bag with supplies in case anything happens and you're delayed."

"Alright, alright. Now we'd really best get ready. Zebedee's getting all flustered like..." Albert ate from the table and drank as much water as he could, hoping to placate Tyler. They filled a bag with a good selection of fresh fruit, bread and cheese, and Tyler whistled for the birds, salting the battlements with fruit to entice them down.

She planted a kiss on Albert's forehead. "Come back quickly. Be careful Albert. Don't take any unnecessary risks. Come back to me soon."

"I will, Missy. I promise."

The unpredictable birds seemed to know what was

required of them and with a little encouragement and bribery, took hold of Zebedee and Albert by the shoulders.

"Fare thee well, Tyler May!" called Zebedee as they launched and swooped away from the tower into the night.

*

They had been gone for ages. Tyler paced the floor and could eat nothing, the irony of the loaded table before her a mocking irritation. She tried briefly to sleep but soon gave up on that. She was far too worried. She walked the battlements and noticed they were almost complete.

Must be doing better than I thought.

Hours passed. Tired of studying the night for a small sign of Zebedee and Albert's return, she descended the spiralling, stone steps to the depths of the tower to examine the dungeon and, in the very base, the small hole in the floor that was the entrance to the oubliette. It was a grim place. The Nazis would certainly be safe in there. Never to return. With the tower's mighty door firmly bolted, no one would even be able to get in, even if they knew the ghosts were there. She didn't know what the contrapassi would make of the Nazi ghosts, but the giants didn't seem to come close to the tower in any case. She'd never seen one on the island. She took one last look at the oubliette and shuddered before heading back up to the roof. She took a tapestry and huddled inside it against a parapet, waiting. Kylie joined her for company as the others found places to huddle and try to sleep in the more sheltered levels below.

"Thanks for sending the money, by the way," said Kylie. "I'm sure Mum and Dad appreciated it."

"You know about that?"

"You know lots of things when you die."

"Yeah. I heard. Anyway, it seemed the least I could do. I'm really sorry I couldn't save you. I still feel bad, you know."

"You shouldn't. It wasn't your fault and I don't blame you. I blame Hitler. We *will* find him. *You* will find him."

Tyler nodded. A stirring in the air made her look up. Silhouettes approached in the brooding sky. Four Hell birds carrying figures in their talons coasted in a vast arc around the tower before coming to land. Tyler ran to Albert as his bird deposited him and settled, awaiting reward. She saw the bound Nazis carried by other birds and hugged Albert tightly.

"You did it!" she said. Albert grinned and then it was Zebedee's turn to be hugged.

"Oh, my dear, it was nothing," he said.

"Any trouble?" she asked.

"No. The hardest part were finding 'em in the forest," said Albert.

"We thought we'd never locate them. Then, all of a sudden, there it was, the upturned cart. And they were waiting beneath. Come on Albert. Time we put these twerps into the dungeon and then we can all get out of the chasm."

Tyler fed the birds, gratefully.

Albert took Goebbels as Zebedee dragged Bagshot and they hauled the Nazis down the stairs. In the dungeon the whole team gathered to see the two imprisoned. Between them, Albert and Zebedee lowered the bound ghosts into the oubliette with grim determination. Tyler took out her list and, surprised to find it had not been erased, ticked off the last two items before adding a new item.

Check the Room of Faces √
Search the Shivering Pool √
Find Hitler
Find Goebbels √
Find Himmler
Put all Nazi ghosts into the chasm

Find somewhere safe to leave Goebbels and Bagshot
in the chasm   √
Locate and secure Mordecai chains   √
Get out of the chasm!

"Will they stay here forever?" asked Tyler looking down into the hole at the two prisoners.

"That's not for us to say," said Izabella.

"Time to go," said Zebedee. "Everyone back to the rooftop, quickly!"

They climbed stairs, Izabella puffing away and complaining at every step, and emptied into the cold of the night once more, to peer out over the rolling chasm nightscape.

"Now," said Izabella as the others gathered round, each bearing a chain. "As long as Tyler is still the owner of the contrap, she should be able to call herself out and then us. You simply say *phasmatis lientia* followed by your own name. Once you are out of the chasm you can do the same for us."

"My word, I hope she's right!" muttered Zebedee.

"Okay," said Tyler as a Hell bird hopped over, talons clicking against stone. "Goodbye. You probably won't see me again, but I'll be watching for you. Thank you for all your help." She scattered food for the birds one last time.

"Here goes," said Tyler. "See you in a minute.

"Phasmatis licentia, Tyler May." Tyler uttered the words and was immediately lifted. A moment later she was tearing up into the fire fog of the night and dashing through cloud and simmering brimstone. She found herself in a darkened room looking down at a stationary figure on a bed surrounded by medical monitors that flashed with green and yellow lights. *Her* bed. *Her* figure. The contrap lay on the chest of her body, the lens emitting a fluctuating, orange glow. She studied a hand. She was fully translucent once more, a ghost without substance. She looked around at her bedroom and wondered what the time was. Wondered where Melissa and Lucy were. She remembered the others awaiting her call and listed them off as quickly as she could, starting with Albert, leaving Izabella until last.

"Phasmatis licentia, Izabella Kremensky."

The other ghosts spewed from the contrap's lens and formed from lightning-like streaks around her, filling her room.

"Alright?" she asked. "Everyone here?" They looked at each other and nodded.

"All present and correct, Miss May," said Zebedee as Lucy and Melissa appeared in the doorway wearing nightshirts.

"Sorry to wake you," said Tyler.

"You're back!"

"You made it!"

Tyler went to embraced them but remembered she was a ghost and stopped.

"You got the chains, then," said Melissa gazing at the Mordecai chain that glimmered as it hung from Tyler's shoulders.

"Yes, but it's not over yet. I have to go back into the *Ghost Portal*. Hitler isn't in the chasm, which means he's not in the contrap at all. He's on the loose somewhere. Himmler is still in the *Ghost Portal*. I have to go back in and find him."

"Can't Izabella summon him out?" asked Kylie. Everyone looked at Kylie and then at Izabella.

"I could summon him from out here if I had a strong enough artefact."

"What about the twins? You used them in the chasm."

"Yes, but that was different. Different realm. Different rules," growled Izabella. "Out here, or even in the portal, I would need a very powerful artefact. The association with the twins would not be anyway near strong enough. Do we have such an artefact to hand?"

"Yes!" said Tyler. "We have finger bones. The girls each have a finger bone taken from Himmler's remains.

Don't you?"

Melissa looked at Lucy and then back to Tyler.

"I threw mine in the trash. I thought we'd got him. I didn't know we'd need it again."

Tyler looked imploringly to Lucy.

"Sorry. Flushed it."

Tyler's hopes dwindled. *Will this never end?*

"You can't go back in," said Melissa. "You don't have enough time."

"How much time *do* I have?"

Melissa ran to the lounge to check the laptop.

"About ten hours. Like I said, you can't possibly consider..." Tyler cut her off.

"I'm going back into the portal."

Foolish Girl

Melissa closed the Brimstone Chasm.

"Vorago termino."

The wavering light diminished until the crystal was dark and smoky again. She released the lever and watched it rotate with a soft clicking back into its original position, turned the contrap over and set the switch to the spiral symbol.

"Better stand back," she warned Lucy, aiming the lens at the other ghosts and drawing the lever clockwise around the contrap's edge. "Just for the record, I think this is a really bad idea."

"Do it," said Tyler. "I'll be quick."

Melissa gave the command.

"Phasmatis Licentia."

The ghosts morphed into spinning tendrils of blue light and, the next moment, spiralled into the contrap with a rush of wind. Melissa sat on the edge of Tyler's bed and looked up at Lucy.

"What have I done?"

*

"Himmler will, no doubt, be somewhere in the city," Zebedee said as they gathered themselves. "But where?" He drew his pocket watch from his waistcoat and began tinkering with it. "It's a difficult place to search by its very nature but we'll do it more quickly if we split up into pairs. Marcus, do you feel up to this?" Marcus nodded assuredly. "Good. If you others find Himmler, trap him with your chain and bring him out. He must be put into the chasm with the others."

"How will we know if he's been found?" asked Kinga.

"You won't," said Zebedee, shaking the pocket watch by his ear. "You know, we could really do with a clock of some description. Does anyone have a small screwdriver about their person?"

"It's useless, Zebedee," said Izabella. "Markers of time simply do not work here. You cannot fix it."

"How do we know when we've searched the whole city?"

"We won't. It moves about too much." Zebedee tucked his watch away and puffed on his pipe.

"Where will we meet once we've searched? Where do we take him if we find him?" asked Kylie.

"We'll meet back here at the portal window. It won't be easy, but do your best and then return here."

The ghosts trudged wearily, glad to be out of the chasm. Tyler felt the familiar tug on her spirit but it was nothing like the draining, constant fear and uneasiness of the previous realm. Rather, it was a relief. When she had first entered the *Ghost Portal* it was frightening and strange. Now its familiar, roving fog and the enormous, black orb - watching over them from above - were benign as she walked towards the turbulent mass on the horizon: Memoria Gravitas.

They reached the sprawling edge of the city, exhausted from bearing the weighty chains, and chose partners.

"Danuta and Kinga, you should probably stick together," said Zebedee. "I'll keep an eye on Marcus." Kylie took one look at Tyler and Albert.

"Guess I'm with Izabella. *Hurray*."

The teams split, each aiming for their allotted quarter of the city. Tyler and Albert walked treacherous streets haphazardly lined with mismatched dwellings from differing eras. They searched every building in their path, ignoring the objections from disgruntled occupants, ducking when an old Viking woman launched several soapstone cooking pots in their direction. The pots dispelled like sand before ever smashing.

"Oy! Watch it, Missus!" Albert retaliated.

"Maybe we should knock," said Tyler.

Tyler tried in vain to keep an awareness of the passing hours. The only real way to mark the time was to laboriously count seconds. This quickly became so irritating that she gave up to focus more upon the search. A massive, grey block came into view several streets away, ladders and doorways punctuating its hulking, slipstreaming sides.

"See that?" asked Albert, pointing over rooftops. "Should take a while for that to shift. We'll aim for that. Search everyfin' between."

"Okay. It'll give us a bearing for a while at least. I wonder how the others are getting on."

"Lord knows." Albert squinted down the road at dwellings dwindling away into the massing city. "This'd be faster if we each takes one side of the street. Don't ya fink?"

"Alright. I'll take this side." Tyler headed over to search a picturesque medieval manor house with vast wooden gables and a thatched roof.

"Just holler if ya needs me," said Albert, turning to his side, where a gothic castle was busy rearranging itself in a whirl of memory mist. Tyler skipped sideways to avoid a small collapse of the road and jumped into the manor house porch. She tested the door and opened it enough to squeeze inside. The place was dim, strewn with cobwebs, sagging wall hangings and burned-down candles. A long, dusty table divided the main hall into two and nobody seemed to be at home. She watched as a gust of mist swept through, rearranging substance as it went. In its wake tapestries became bright with colour and sagged no more. Candles lengthened and took points of flame. The table was swept clean and laid with roasted swans and boar, sizable pies and carafes of drink. She wondered what would happen if she tried some of the food - though she wasn't hungry – and decided there wasn't time for fooling around. She slipped down the side to search servants' quarters and kitchens. All empty. Wooden rungs led her up to a second level where a lord and lady watched her intrusion intently.

"Oh! Excuse me," said Tyler. She left the bed chamber promptly.

She searched house after house, gradually drawing closer to the large block and she noticed it was rearranging too. Huge cubic sections rose like towers. Ladders, stairs and entrances expanded and collapsed. By the time they reached the building, it looked more like a complex that might house several hundred ghosts, an intricate honeycomb of walkways and stairs that reminded her of an optical illusion she'd once seen, in which stairways swapped vertices impossibly. She stood with Albert, wondering where to begin. Once again they each chose a doorway and parted.

Tyler instantly regretted the decision as a feeling returned to her. That feeling of being watched. It unnerved her as she crept up concrete stairs towards an arch where a junction offered other routes. She peered around the corner of the arch, thought she heard footsteps and ducked back. Why? She didn't know. She backtracked, hoping to find Albert, wanting to rearrange the plan. They would stick together, hunt as a team and watch each other's backs, but Albert had gone. Had disappeared into the complex. Tyler shook herself. *Pull yourself together. So you heard footsteps. So what?*

She returned to the arch and skirted the corner into a covered walkway. At one end, some way off, the path was melting into mist. She turned and headed in the other direction down a long passage with adjoining walkways, stairs and doors. A sound startled her. *Definitely footsteps, and quite close.* She wanted to find the source, see the ghost who was making the noise before it saw her. She followed the sound, edging through a doorway and across an open veranda. A scuttling close by. She turned, searching, but the place looked empty. *Ghost rats?*

Leaving the balcony she entered a room where wind brushed substance from a broad window and, sitting there, gun in hand, was the ghost of a soldier and she knew at once she was in trouble. She'd seen the Nazi before. He was one of two ghosts she'd captured in the Museum of World War II, Massachusetts.

Tyler backed out of the room but he'd seen her and, before she could turn to run, a second soldier blocked her way, his ghost breath in her face.

"Albert!" she screamed, and tried to launch the chain, but they were on her, the closest wrapping arms around her and pinning her to his chest while the one from the room approached to lift the chain from her neck. Albert did not come. She sobbed and struggled, the little energy she could muster wasted against overpowering odds. To her surprise they didn't use the chain on her but took it and marvelled at it as a curiosity.

"Well, well, well. Look what we have here. It's the famous Tyler May. The Reichsführer will be pleased to see you." Her captor laughed.

They don't know what it is! Perhaps I can still get out of this somehow. Calling for Albert was no longer an option. The ghost holding her had a hand clamped over her mouth. She struggled but he was too strong. The other draped the chain over the back of the chair and returned to cuff her hands.

"Didn't expect to see you here," he mused.

Tyler struggled against the cuffs.

Albert, I need you!

*

The room was devoid of décor. Four concrete walls showing no sign of degrading to the ethereal winds. A sturdy ceiling and floor. Tyler sat, fastened to a chair with ropes, gagged, hands still cuffed at her back. An empty chair stood next to hers. They had guessed she was not alone and were searching for other ghosts. Her two captors had been gone a while, leaving her to fantasize about Albert turning up heroically to release her and steal her away, but when he arrived it was under very different circumstances. The two Nazis kicked him into the room, bound and gagged and strapped him tightly to the spare chair. Tyler sobbed mutedly beneath her gag as the soldiers left again. She looked at Albert helplessly, distressed and losing hope but his gaze offered something solid. He couldn't talk but his eyes spoke. *It will be alright. You'll see. What can they do to us?*

She calmed, moderately consoled by his company. *At least I'm not alone.*

She drifted in a haze of fatigue. Slept uncomfortably for a time until the door to their dismal chamber cracked again with the soldiers' return. Himmler strode in after them and made a tour of the room, inspecting his prisoners with small, dark eyes through circular glasses. Last time she had seen him he was wearing civvies but now, pure ghost, he was in full Nazi uniform with a peaked cap. His rounded, small-chinned face came close to hers. Too close. She could see each hair of his thin moustache, each line on his stubbly ghost skin.

"Welcome, Fräulein May. I'm glad you could join us. Do I detect a hint of defeat about you? You wear it like a robe, yet it suits you well, I must say. You appear to be rather, well, dead... An unexpected pleasure. You have brought something of interest." Himmler paused to loosen and remove Tyler's gag. "Never one to disappoint, are you? You will tell me about these chains." He gestured to the chains that the guards were now wearing over their necks, one taken from her, the other from Albert.

Albert's eyes widened and he shook his head, holding Tyler's gaze intently. *Don't tell 'im nuffink!*

"Never," said Tyler.

"I see. You think you are untouchable now that you're dead. Is that it? May I remind you, your friend here knows otherwise? It is possible for us to inflict palpable damage to a ghost if we really set our minds to it."

"The chains are just chains we found. They're nothing special. You can keep them. Consider them a gift."

"Ah, but you are wrong. There *is* something special about them. Or else why would they sparkle so. They are not merely *ghost*, like everything else in this wretched place. They are different. So tell me. What are they?" Himmler motioned for the others to join him and commanded them. "Beat him until he loses all recollection of what he was."

Tyler fought against her bonds but achieved little more than a wriggle as the soldiers prepared to torture Albert. They took the chains from their necks and approached, and Tyler could stand it no more. *Whatever happens, whatever they do, I can't watch them disfigure him.*

"They're Mordecai chains!" she blurted.

"Mor-de-cai chains?" Himmler sounded out the words slowly in wonder as he paced. "And what are *Mordecai chains*? What do they do?"

"They bind ghosts. There is a command. You say the command and throw the chains and they bind ghosts."

Himmler paused.

"We have ropes and cuffs, as you well know. We can already bind ghosts if we so choose. What is so special about these chains?"

Tyler watched Albert shake his head. *Don't tell 'im no more!*

"I'm sorry, Albert. I can't watch them hurting you. Whatever the cost." Albert battled with his ropes frantically.

"What is so special about these chains?" Himmler repeated, turning on her impatiently.

"No one else can release the ghost who is bound by one of these chains. Not unless they know the command. The bound ghost cannot escape. They can't even talk once they're bound."

"The commands, Fräulein?"

Tyler hesitated until Himmler waved on the soldiers to lash Albert with the chains.

"Wait, wait! I'll tell you." The soldiers backed off with a small gesture from their leader. "To make the chains bind, the command is *Mordecai obligo*. To release the chains you touch the chain and say *Mordecai resolvo*."

Himmler tested a chain, taking it from an obliging soldier and hurling it at him.

"Mordecai obligo!" he bellowed and the chain lurched speedily to ensnare the soldier, who stood statue-like, struck dumb and only able to watch helplessly. Himmler approached. "Escape!" he commanded, but the soldier was still. "I command you to answer me!" he shouted in the soldier's face.

"He can't," said Tyler. "The chain has him."

Himmler wheeled on Tyler.

"Foolish girl. You have sealed your own fate." He gave another command and reached out to touch the chain. "Mordecai resolvo." The chain fell to the ground as the freed soldier staggered and stepped away from it. Himmler reclaimed the chain. "Untie them," he ordered the guards. "We have better bonds to use on these two.

And then the Shivering Pool will take care of the rest."

Foolish Man

Himmler did not have the energy for speeches, having exerted himself on his enthusiastic march out to the pool. He waved for his guards to bring the captives closer to the banks. Tyler watched silently, acting frozen. It was all she could do to remain quiet as the two soldiers swung Albert's bound form, like a log, and launched him into the silvery, dark waters of forgetfulness. The pool shivered eagerly. It was her turn. She plunged into the gloom and sank, instantly searching for Albert, knowing she was safe below the surface. The pool was almost impossible to see into from the bank, but she could see out. She watched distorted figures leave the bank, and she uttered the command.

"Mordecai resolvo." The chain fell slack and sank. She swam to Albert, now on the bed among the other ghost weed, his feet already entrenched with grasping miasma.

"Mordecai resolvo." Albert's eyes widened as he was released and he gasped, staring at Tyler, mystified. She helped him fight free of the pool's grip and they headed up.

"How did you?" he spluttered when they broke the surface. "What's..."

She realised she had never told him about her experience with the chain in the contrapassi cave. "The chains don't work properly on me. Don't ask me why, but I'm guessing it has something to do with me not being a true ghost. My body still lives. Anyway, no time to discuss. We need to follow them and find out where they're staying. Then we can get Zebedee and the others and we'll use the chains to trap Himmler. The chains!" Tyler ducked back beneath the surface. Albert followed. They reclaimed the sunken chains, hauled them to the bank and dragged themselves out of the pool. Himmler and the two soldiers were small figures in the mid-distance, heading back to the city.

"We mustn't let them see us," said Tyler. "Give them a little more time. We can follow more closely once they're in the city. We'll have places to hide as we move."

"Right you are, Missy." Albert surprised her by pulling her into a close embrace. "Old 'immler were wrong about you. You ain't no fool!" He kissed her, a long, soft kiss and, when it was over, no words needed to be said. She had heard his thoughts as her own, and he knew hers just as intimately.

They waited until they thought it safe to venture out and followed, tramping over memory mist like hikers do a moor. Their one fear was that they might lose Himmler and his guards at the city's edge before getting close enough to track them through the jumble of buildings, caves and hovels, but they found the three easily enough and shadowed them all the way back to the hulking, grey block.

"That's where they're stayin'," said Albert as he and Tyler peered from the cover of a courtyard wall further down the street. They snuck closer to head up stairs towards the arch where Tyler had first heard footsteps.

She turned to Albert.

"This is far enough. They're in one of the rooms around here. We should get the others."

"Agreed." They left the block and headed back out of the city in search of their friends.

They found Zebedee and Marcus almost immediately and a thrill of excitement coursed through Tyler's core. *Four ghosts and four chains against three unsuspecting fools. I like the odds.* She wanted to get on with it immediately, but Zebedee had other ideas.

"I think I saw Kylie and Izabella a while back," he said, once Tyler and Albert had explained what had happened. "Over that way. We should take a look for them. The more we have on our side when we launch the attack, the better."

"Okay," Tyler conceded. "But if we don't find them quickly, I'm coming back here to do the job, with or without you."

"We'll find them," chirped Zebedee. "Don't you worry."

They set off, being careful to conceal themselves from the block's temporary windows and doorways, behind sheds, fences, houses and the never-ending, odd assortment of buildings.

Zebedee was right. A short trek across town they found the girls busily working their way down a steep street, torn by a savage crosswind as they searched dwellings. Albert called to them over the blast of the gale.

"We found 'im. We found 'immler. We needs your 'elp. We're gonna trap 'im."

"This will be enough," said Tyler as they regrouped in the shelter of a cave entrance. The Neanderthal trying to light his fire appeared oblivious to their presence. Zebedee took pity and helped him out with a lucifer.

"Alright," said Zebedee. "Let's do it." They battled the squall and the slope to wind their way towards the block, still visible from this distance as a tall shape, and

Tyler wondered at it. *Is it something remembered collectively from the three Nazis? Is Himmler trying to recall one of his huge houses or castles? Or perhaps he is, even now, trying to create some kind of power base from which to launch a new Reich, with an army of three?*

Tyler spearheaded the assault. She edged up the stairway and into the passage, her back to the wall, chain held at the ready. Footsteps echoed. She froze, startled, waiting watching, trying to ascertain the location of the walker. She decided the sound was coming from further in the complex beyond an arch that opened onto a broad hallway, lined with doors. She put a finger to her lips and held a palm out to the others at her back.

Wait here. I'll check this out.

She skirted the edge to glance through the open exit at the other end and spied a figure standing on a balcony, smoking a cigarette. One of the guards. Her feet were feather-light on remembered concrete, her movements swift and sure. The chain left her hands and the soldier turned, surprise warping his face.

"Mordecai obligo." She whispered the words so as not to warn the others.

One down.

She dragged him into the shadows at the balcony edge and left him to collect later. She turned back to find the others. At the end of the hallway another shadow darkened the doorway. Himmler stepped out before her. He stopped with a jolt, drop-jawed, as he reached for his sidearm.

*

Lucy was surprised by the knock at the door. Chapman had gone out again and wasn't expected for another hour or so.

"Who's that?" No response. Melissa was talking with Freddy in her bedroom. Lucy answered the door. Her phone clattered to the floor as she raised her hand to her mouth in surprise at the figure staring back at her.

*

"But..." Himmler began.

Tyler had used her chain. She thought desperately. *Where are the others?* A chain appeared behind him, twisting and purring through the air. She heard a London accent from the other end of the hallway.

"Modecai obligo."

The chain engulfed Himmler and he toppled. Albert appeared at the other end of the hall and shot her a wink, followed closely by Zebedee and the others.

"Let's dispatch this one, too, shall we?"

"There's another out there on the balcony."

"Already on the way, Missy."

"What about the third one?" Kylie asked. They looked at each other uncertainly.

"I think we'd best get Miss May back home, now. Don't you?" said Zebedee.

"Alright. We have the one we came for. I can live with that. Let's go." Tyler helped drag the guard and between them they took the two captives out of the block and headed out of the city. They caused a stir in the streets. Ghosts of all ages came out from their doorways to watch and a murmur of what was going on passed around to all, but they weren't talking about Tyler.

"It's that girl. The one Hitler killed with the bomb."

"They've caught Himmler. They're taking him away."

Soon hundreds of holocaust ghosts arrived to line the streets. Izabella, Kinga and Danuta joined the team to help transport the prisoners. They led a growing procession to the edge of the city where Kylie pointed into the distance.

"What's that?" The others looked out beyond the city at a faint, fiery glow. Tyler recognised it at once.

"It's a benign, temporal failure of the plural curtain,"

she said.

"Huh?"

"It's a tear," said Albert. "It leads into the chasm."

"Perfect," said Tyler. "I wish we could put him in the oubliette with the others, but this'll have to do." They headed for the tear and the glowing brightened as they left the city behind. They soon arrived at the tear and thousands of ghosts gathered around, watching the seething light issue from the vast rip that began beneath the ground layer of memory mist and extended high above them in the invisible mantle of the portal's side. Tyler shoved Himmler towards the void and his eyes widened in terror. She paused, him teetering at the very edge. A moment of doubt flashed in her mind. Was she being cruel? Was it really right to put Himmler into the chasm? It felt like a merciless action. She corrected herself. It was merciful for all those souls who would suffer if she didn't remove him.

"You know, someone once said *the foolish man built his house upon the sand*," she mused. "*And it all came tumbling...*"

"Down!" said Kylie, giving Himmler an almighty shove. He toppled into the chasm and they watched the bound ghost turning in descent. Zebedee and Albert helped the other Nazi into the chasm. The gathered ghosts did not cheer or clap in celebration of Himmler's fate. They bowed their heads in solemn acknowledgement.

Tyler and her team left the council and headed back to the portal. She expected to feel a sense of accomplishment, a degree of self-satisfaction. Instead she felt hollow and tired.

I shouldn't be doing this. This should not be necessary. People shouldn't need to chase evil and battle it into a corner. Condemn ghosts to the chasm or the pool – or even the Ghost Portal. Do horrible things to others. Then again, somebody had to stand up for the innocents. Tyler looked ahead. The portal lens was still some way off. She didn't know how long she had left. She hardly cared in any case. Himmler was in the chasm and she now knew, without doubt, that the ghost of Hitler, the oppressor – whatever you want to call him – was not in the contrap. He was in the world and planning. With renewed vigour she strode towards the portal. Shook off the portal's weariness that had previously waylaid her. Ignored the numbness she'd received from her dip in the Shivering Pool. She marched with increasing pace to her goal and would pause for no one. She needed to get out and re-join her waiting body. Needed to be whole and well enough to seek out the oppressor in the world. To find him. To hunt him down. To destroy him for the sake of those who did not know he was coming for them. She reached the portal lens and called out.

"Melissa? Lucy?"

Nobody responded. She waited, watching for a face at the crystal. She called again. A shadow passed.

"Finally."

Tyler recoiled when a face appeared. Not Melissa. Not Lucy. But Silvia Bates, looking smug.

And the portal closed.

PART
THREE

Possession

Melissa puffed her way down the busy street, her mobile clamped to her ear. Somewhere ahead in the crowd, Bates was fleeing. She scanned faces, searching for the green coat. Chapman finally picked up.

"Hello, Melissa."

"Sir, they're dead. Bates has the contrap. I'm in pursuit. Just left the apartment..."

"What?"

"Bates has the contrap. Lucy's down. I've left the apartment."

"Slow down, Melissa. You're not making sense," said Chapman. Melissa couldn't slow down. She was running flat out in pursuit of an insane murderer while making a call and her friends lay dead or dying. Her brain whirred at a million miles per hour. The blood pounded in her head. She clocked Bates up ahead and calmed a little. There was still hope. She tried to explain again. Tried to take things slower.

"Lucy must have answered the door to her. I was in

my bedroom with..." She hesitated while a memory flashed.

She tried the bedroom door again. Repeated herself.

"It won't open. Like I said." Freddy came over.

"Give it a good shove. It's just sticking. Here, let me try." Freddy shoved but the door didn't move. "That's odd. Oh well." He turned to Melissa with a suggestive smile. "You know, there are pros and cons to every situation..." He shrugged his brows and grabbed her around the waist, pulling her close. Melissa giggled.

"Mmmm. You smell like toffee."

"Just promise you won't chew me up and spit me out," said Freddy.

A yelp and a thud from one of the other rooms stopped them.

"What was that?"

"Lucy?" called Freddy, releasing his hold.

No response.

"Very funny, Mojo," shouted Melissa. "You can let us out now."

Silence.

"Something's not right. She's not mucking about. Break it down."

"What, me?" Freddy looked at the door and then down at his slight frame.

"Oh never mind," said Melissa, backing up from the door. She charged, stamped the door open with a splintering of wood. They stumbled out into the lounge to find Lucy flat on her back, unmoving. They dashed to Tyler's room, Melissa breathing a sigh of relief when she found Tyler's body still there. Then it hit her.

"The contrap's gone!"

Melissa reordered her thoughts and continued to explain what had happened to Chapman.

"Bates showed up. She took out Lucy and trapped me in the bedroom. When I got out, we found the medics butchered and the contrap was gone. Bates must have thought Tyler was dead and she took it. Freddy and I heard someone on the stairs. We saw her. Freddy stayed to help Lucy and guard Tyler. I'm not sure there's anything he can do for the medics – blood everywhere. Dr Marshall's okay. He went out to get something before she came. Guess he'll be back soon. I'm following Bates."

Chapman was silent for a brief moment, digesting the news.

"Stick with Bates. Don't lose her whatever you do. Tyler's life depends upon it..."

You think?

"Follow her. Do you understand? Nothing more. Don't try anything alone. Bates is too dangerous. In the meantime I'll send someone over to help the others. Stay in touch." Chapman hung up.

Thanks. Big help, you are.

Melissa stuffed her mobile in a pocket and threaded her way through a sea of people. Bates was moving quickly, making small, agile adjustments to her path. She turned a corner and Melissa feared she had lost her, that, when she finally reached the corner, she would learn of yet another of Bates' disappearing tricks. She forced herself to move faster, turned the corner and found the green coat easily but needed to pause for breath.

She shadowed Bates firstly onto a bus and then a train at East Dulwich, to exit at London Bridge. Bates took the Northern Line to Euston and finally ended up on an outward bound train heading for Watford. *What is she doing?* Familiar landscapes fled past carriage windows. *Does Bates know I'm following her?* Tailing was not Melissa's strong point and she wished she could swap places with Lucy.

Lucy... Is she...?

Bates seemed less desperate now, but then what could she do on a train, anyway? They sat at opposite ends of a carriage, Melissa trying to look inconspicuous, Bates gazing blankly out of a window as the train hurtled closer to Watford.

Melissa's phone rang, startling her and she rushed to take the call and silence it.

"Sir?"

"You okay? Any news?"

"Yes, Sir. Fine. We're on a train bound for Watford."

"Yes, I see. Looks like she's taking you back home to where it all began."

"That's what I'm thinking."

"Right, well keep on it. You're doing fine."

"How's Lucy?"

"She's alive. Seems Bates head-butted her at the door. She has an impressive lump and she's mad as Hell, but she'll live. She's lucky really. Bates didn't stop to carve her up. You must have disturbed her."

"She must have wedged something under my door handle before murdering the team and taking the contrap. I'm sorry about the others."

"No time for that. There's something else. Lucy says the lead box is also missing. Bates must have taken that too."

"Right. I could use some back-up, Sir."

The reply was unintelligible as the signal waned and died.

"Sir?"

Static on the line.

Fantastic...

Melissa tucked her phone away and tried to stay awake as the train jostled. The recent days had been highly stressful and she was exhausted. She took a packet of mints from a pocket and popped one into her mouth. At each stop, nerves mounted as the carriage flowed with bodies and she struggled to keep eyes on her mark, but it wasn't until Watford Junction that Bates rose to leave. Melissa navigated newly-boarding passengers to exit via the closest door and step down onto the platform. Bates led her out of the station and into Watford town centre. Melissa didn't bother calling Chapman to tell him. He was tracking the signal from her mobile and if that failed he could always find her using the tracer implanted in her left arm. In the meantime no word from her meant nothing had changed. She was in pursuit.

She'd left her gun back in the apartment having left in a hurry. She didn't like guns anyway. Didn't like what they did to people, even though she knew Chapman and Lucy would berate her for her stupidity.

Bates wandered through the town, glancing at her wrist from time to time.

Late for something, are we?

Bates ducked into a newsagent's at the edge of town. Melissa waited across the road, but when she had been there five minutes and Bates had not reappeared, Melissa tentatively crossed the road to investigate. She peered in through a cluttered shop window. The place looked deserted. She pushed open the door, jangling the small bell overhead and entered to find it was not completely empty. A young, blonde with a pinched nose and narrow eyes waited behind the till, watching with interest while chewing gum. Melissa pretended to be searching for something on the shelves of sweets, newspapers and magazines. In the end she pulled a copy of Cosmopolitan from the rack and slapped it on the counter.

Bates definitely came in here. She's here somewhere. Out the back? What is this place? What's going on here, exactly?

The blonde didn't take her eyes from Melissa. Didn't even glance at the magazine.

"You're not really here for that, are you?" she asked.

Melissa cocked her head to one side with a frown.

"Sorry?"

"Oh." The blonde seemed taken aback. "It's just... I thought you were here for the meeting. Sorry. My mistake. That's five fifty-two, please."

"Oh, yes," said Melissa, quickly. "Of course. I *am* here for the meeting, but I also want the magazine." The blonde nodded and took the money, rang it into the till with a *tring*.

"You'd better hurry through, then, my love. I think they started already."

Melissa smiled and headed out back, passing the till and a darkened doorway, not knowing where she was going and without any semblance of a plan. She rolled up the magazine and shoved it into her coat pocket. The hallway ahead was unlit but a strip of light at the bottom of a door gave away an occupied room. Muffled voices reached her. She didn't want to go in. Couldn't go in. They would know at once that she was an imposter, whatever the meeting was. Instead, she gently turned the door knob and let the door slowly drift open an inch. She heard them instantly. Glimpsed a circle of seated figures. Bates was in mid rant.

"...and I told you I would return to you, more powerful than ever before and you clearly didn't believe me. Well, guess what? I'm back."

"You've been gone for so long!"

"We thought you had forgotten about us. Left us."

"We thought you were... Well, we all saw the reports."

"You've been busy while you were away."

"I have indeed. I've been seeking the device I told you about and now I have it. I shall be your High Witch; the Priestess of the coven; a queen amongst witches. And you will bow to me!"

One of those gathered sniggered cynically. Melissa inched forward to see better what was going on in the room. She spied Bates holding the contrap.

"But we needed a leader in your absence, oh *Queen*," said the cynical witch. "And I was chosen. You can't just waltz back in here and reassume your position. That's a ridiculous notion..."

Bates turned calmly to address her critic.

"Of course. You are quite correct." She adjusted the contrap and took aim as her face contorted. The expression was that of Violet Corpe. Bates had somehow mastered the Tudor ghost but allowed her to surface when it suited. "Do it!" The coaxing, scratchy voice was not Bates', but Violet's. "Do it now! Phasmatis licentia!"

Melissa tensed, preparing to invade the meeting, but she was already too late to stop the killing. Besides, Chapman had ordered her not to try anything. She watched the new head of the coven wince, neon light spooling from her body. Her ghost bolted into the *Ghost Portal* with a shriek and her body collapsed to roll from her chair, dead. The witnesses gasped as Bates scanned faces.

"Any more usurpers who fancy their chances?" Bates, herself again, nonchalantly eyed her way round the circle. "No? I didn't think so. We'll meet on the hill at midnight for an official ceremony of ordination. You will crown me your queen and swear your undying fealty." She made another small adjustment to the contrap and let it hang from her neck. "Now it's time to leave and think about what happened here. You, you and you," Bates pointed. "Dispose of the body."

People began moving around the room and Melissa decided it was time for her to get out before she was discovered. She left the door and headed back out through the shop front, waving to the blonde on her way past.

"Thanks."

"You're welcome."

The doorbell jingled. Outside, she ditched the magazine in a bin and found a seat at a nearby bus shelter to watch for Bates. She could not afford to let her slip away. She had to find a way to retrieve the contrap as soon as possible. She did not wait long. Bates left the shop, fully composed, and the other witches exited in ones and twos. Melissa gave them a few minutes to disperse before following. Bates strode away quickly, black boots scissoring along the street and disappearing at the next corner. She caught another bus and left Melissa stranded. Melissa walked out in front of a silver

Audi and requisitioned the car with a flash of her badge. The balding businessman shimmied across into the leather passenger seat, barely able to take his eyes from Melissa's curves.

"This is the most exciting thing that's happened to me in ten years," he announced as Melissa took off in pursuit of the bus. She had memory flashes of bombs detonating in Westminster Abbey, Hitler's blue-tinged face, Nazi ghosts in the Museum of World War II, and of herself wrestling with the contrap as it tried to suck Lucy into the chasm.

"Wish I could say the same." She drove, keeping five cars' distance before the bus stopped. She pulled in to the curb and followed on foot, familiar with the area. Now they really were in her old stomping ground. Her old school was a mere two minutes' walk away.

Why are we back in Northwood? What are you up to?

Bates walked briskly, leading Melissa down roads and pathways and over a rail line that came out onto Rickmansworth Road where she had to wait for a gap in traffic. Bates crossed to a path edged with a long, wooden fence too high to see over. She climbed the fence with ease and vanished into the trees on the other side.

What's she doing in Haste Hill Golf Course?

Melissa crossed and scrambled inelegantly over the fence, wondering if this would be a good place to jump Bates and take back the contrap. She landed in the shade of a small wood in time to see Bates assessing the way ahead before slipping out onto the edge of the green. No one was around. Bates had a choice of four bunkers close to hand. She walked to the nearest - a circular sand pit - and stooped to dig. Melissa watched with interest as Bates lifted the contrap from around her neck and began refilling. Melissa couldn't see exactly what was going on, for the bunker slumped away into the middle and Bates' coat also blocked her view, but she was pretty sure she'd just witnessed Bates bury the contrap. Melissa padded away into the deeper shadows and hid behind a tree as

Bates returned, heading back towards the fence. Melissa checked. No sign of the contrap or its chain around Bates' neck. Bates heaved herself up and over and then was gone.

Thank you very much, Bates. Couldn't have made it easier.

Buried

Melissa ran out from the treeline to the bunker and dug frantically in the sand. The bunker was easily large enough to make her wonder if she would ever dig in exactly the right spot, but what choice did she have? She'd seen Bates bury the contrap here. Hadn't she? She cast handfuls of sand aside, clawing her way down. *Nothing here.* She stood. Reassessed her position. Bates had been dead centre. She was sure of it. Melissa began a new hole and was rewarded a few moments later with a glint of metal. She excavated with short quick movements, forcing fingers down the sides, and lifted out the lead box.

I have it!

She took out her phone to call in the news. She opened the box only to find it empty. She turned at a sound behind her but never saw what hit her.

*

Tyler listened to Marcus' sweet, sweeping melody, admiring his dexterous fingers play across narrow frets. The tune was sad and conveyed his empathy effortlessly. Tyler felt *that* as strongly as she heard the music. He was crying for her. With her. They all were. Zebedee put a comforting arm around her but could find no words. What could he say? Where was hope now? Gone were her wings. Gone were her living friends, trapped at the other, unreachable side of the portal's lens.

Albert had taken himself away, unable to deal with it. She saw him a short way off, standing in the mist. Looking out at a vast nothingness.

She wondered what the time was. Wondered if her time had already run out and if she was already a permanent ghost. She didn't feel any different. She wondered if she would know, when it happened, if she would feel something, or instantly receive the full knowledge. Would that be the sign?

Izabella came over and opened her mouth to speak but she didn't seem able to find any words either. No lectures about hanging on to hope now. No defiant, rallying talks. Only an inert sadness. Izabella turned away.

Tyler took out her list and pen. She began a new list because the old one had vanished again, but gave up half way through the first line. What was the point? Her lists were about things she intended to do.

What would I write? If I'm dead, I can't do anything.

*

Water dripped like a pulse close to her pounding temple. She heard it, was aware of its steady, small vibration. She opened her eyes and blinked them shut again. It hurt. Too much light. The image she'd seen was an unfamiliar bathroom. Melissa was wet and cold. Bath water covered most of her body and her neck, stopping only at her chin. She looked again. She was fully clothed and her feet

223

bound together at the ankles at the head end of the tub. She tried to move, wanted to get herself out, but her wrists were tied behind her back and wouldn't budge. She adjusted her position to ease the pressure on the bruise at the back of her head. She screamed into the cloth gag that bit into the sides of her mouth. The muffled noise brought Bates to the door.

"Oh, she awakes. Good." She sauntered to the side of the bath and bent to tighten the dripping tap. Melissa watched her, helplessly. "I do hope you appreciate the trouble I've gone to, to get you here. It took three of my associates to carry you over that fence and bundle you into the back of a car. Anyway, you're here now, and that's what matters."

Melissa tried to ask "Why *am* I here?" But her words were unintelligible.

"All in good time," said Bates. "I'll allow you to talk when I'm ready. For now, why don't you just have a nice soak in the tub?" She left, locking the door behind her.

Melissa studied the bathroom again. Lavish, marble tiles, white ceramic fixtures. Pristine. *A hotel? Surely not Bates' house.* Bates wouldn't take her home. Better to do her dirty work elsewhere. Not that MI5 had succeeded in tracking down a property actually owned by her. Bates was an enigma. A fleeting wind. Here one moment, gone the next. Melissa wriggled and twisted her wrists, trying to loosen her bonds but whatever Bates had used dug into her flesh and, when she gave up, she had only succeeded in causing herself more discomfort and proving the futility of her situation. She was utterly at Bates' mercy, which was something she was not expecting to experience.

A turn of a key announced Bates' return. Her welcoming smile turned Melissa's stomach.

"Alright?" asked Bates, meeting Melissa's fiery gaze as she placed a chair by the bath. "Good. I have a few questions for you, as you can imagine. With your friend already dead, I figured *you* will have to do. You probably know just as much about the device anyway. So, it's time to talk and this is how it is going to work: You will answer my questions; I will keep it simple; You will blink once for *yes* and twice for *no*; If you're a good girl I may even let you use your tongue, but you should remember I have several quick and easy ways to silence you if you prove troublesome. Do you understand?"

Melissa blinked once.

"Okay. Do you know what all of the symbols are for?"

Two blinks.

"Do you know nine of the symbols?"

Melissa thought. *Don't pretend to be too ignorant or you'll lose all value. It's information she wants.*

One blink.

"Oh! Interesting." Bates chewed on a knuckle briefly before bringing the contrap close to Melissa's face, almost too close to focus. She tapped each of the symbols on the rear of the contrap in turn. "Is this the one you do not know?"

The skull. *No.* The tower. *No.* Melissa noticed a tattoo on the inside of Bates' wrist. A strange mixture of symbols. She tried to get a better view but Bates was moving and the tattoo was partially covered by her shirt sleeve. At length Bates tapped a glossy, green fingernail against the heart symbol.

One blink. Bates replaced the contrap chain around her neck and sat back.

"Well. There's a thing. You just bought yourself some time. I do hope you aren't lying, for your own sake."

Melissa blinked twice. *No, I'm not lying, you mad cow.* Bates left the bathroom, returning a few moments later with a glass in her hand. She sipped honey toned liquor while studying Melissa. She put the glass down on the basin and approached.

"I'm going to let you speak now. Shout or scream and you'll die before anyone can come running."

Melissa believed her.

"Thanks," she surprised herself by saying once the cloth was removed.

"My pleasure," said Bates, sickeningly. "Now, about these symbols... What does the fire symbol do? I think I have a pretty good idea about most of the others, you see. But the fire symbol, well, that's a bit of a mystery..."

"I don't know *exactly* how it works," said Melissa. *I'm not telling you anything.* "But it seems to be some kind of flame-thrower. You have to know the magic words, of course, but you aim the crystal, say the words and the person you don't like very much is toast."

"A flame-thrower? Are you serious?" Bates seemed honestly disappointed. She considered the new information, perplexed. She paced, becoming increasingly unhappy with the answer and muttering to herself. "It doesn't make sense. Why? What would be the point? If I want someone dead, I kill them. I don't need a flame-thrower. I suppose in medieval times it could come in handy, but really? Nobody needs a flame-thrower. Do they?"

"She lies!" hissed Violet Corpe from Bates' lips. "Hurt her! Damage her! Kill her! Let me do it!" Bates calmed as she took control again.

"I don't know. What if she tells the truth? But, a flame-thrower? Really?"

"Of course she's lying! It's preposterous! Don't let her fool you. Kill her!"

Bates' controlled self turned back to Melissa. "You're lying to me, girl." She grabbed Melissa's feet and hauled them up so that her head was dragged beneath the water line. Melissa snatched a breath and thrashed. She tried to raise her face out of the water but it was hopeless. Bates let her feet down and she gasped great lungfuls of air.

"Tell me the true meaning of the symbol!"

"I told you." She was under again, panicking, watching Bates through a turmoil of water as she struggled. A third time Melissa surfaced and refused to change her answer. Bates replaced the gag, ensuring it was tight, as Melissa shook her head and pleaded. Bates fetched the heavy iron base of a standard lamp from another room and heaved it onto Melissa's chest. She set the cold water tap running and left the room with a royal wave. Melissa screamed into the gag and thrashed. A little water splashed out of the tub and she calmed. *Perhaps I can get enough out to stop it filling up!* She thrashed some more and was rewarded with several spays of water flung out, but it was not enough. Bates had left the tap fully open and water was gushing in to raise the level fast. Eyes bulging with fear, she gasped and gasped to get as much oxygen into her system as possible, watching the level reach the sides of her face and then ebb over her mouth. She closed her throat and breathed through her nose, feeling cold water creep up her face and invade her mouth. She held her breath as water enveloped her nostrils and knew she had breathed her last. This was it. Bates had won.

A figure appeared in the room. Melissa tried to focus as water washed over her eyes.

Forgot your rum, Bates?

She heard a voice and recognised it as Freddy's, even through waterlogged ears.

"She's in here!" Hands reached in to remove the lamp base and raise her head from the water. Her vision cleared and she gasped for air through watery nostrils.

Freddy!

"Sorry we didn't get here sooner," he said. He held her face, checking her eyes, and removed the gag.

"Freddy. Thank God." She let her head rest against his.

"We tracked your mobile to a golf course. Found it abandoned and figured you were in trouble. We'd have lost you altogether if you didn't have the tracer implant."

Weaver appeared in the doorway, looking every bit the dashing, young, capable agent that he was.

"How is she?" he asked.

"She'll be fine." Freddy unfolded a lock knife and cut the cable tie binding Melissa's hands. He helped her out of the bath. "Good job we got here when we did, though."

"Bates just left," said Melissa. "Seconds ago. You didn't get her?"

"She must have slipped past us, but we have others after her. Don't worry. We'll find her," said Weaver.

Melissa saw the bathroom window and the darkness beyond its glass. She checked her watch. Smashed and waterlogged.

"What's the time?" she asked. Freddy glanced at his watch.

"Five to ten."

"We have one hour and forty-five minutes to get the contrap and get it to Tyler's body or she'll die for real. Permanently."

"Relax," said Weaver. "I said we have other agents on it."

Freddy held her by the shoulders.

"Right now you need to get checked out. There're medics waiting downstairs." He wrapped a large hotel towel around her.

Melissa rubbed at her hair with a second towel as she headed downstairs in the lift, dripping water wherever she went. She left the hotel and stood watching as medics in the back of an ambulance attended Tyler's body. Chapman and Lucy greeted her.

"Well done, Melissa. You made it. We brought Tyler with us. Figured if we couldn't bring the contrap to her, we'd get her as close as we could to the contrap."

Lucy hugged her.

"We still don't have Bates or the contrap," said Melissa. "And we're running out of time."

"Get checked over and into some dry clothes. We're not done yet." Chapman walked down the side of the ambulance to make a call. Two medics attended Melissa, leading her to the back doors of the ambulance, making her sit on the edge while they checked eyesight, reflexes and pulse.

"There's a shop. Did you check the shop?" she asked, leaving the medics and the ambulance crew and ignoring their objections. Lucy shook her head but beckoned to Chapman to re-join them.

"What shop?"

"The newsagent's where the coven met. I followed Bates there and she went into a meeting out the back with her old coven. What was it called? Blue Solstice. Tyler and I looked her up on Facebook years ago. We should go back to the shop where they met earlier today. I'm not sure what else to suggest."

"Everything else is being covered. We have multiple teams out on the street and CCTV Control are on the lookout. The green coat should be a giveaway. I'm sure we'll find her."

*

The newsagent's was locked up with lights out in the shop front when they arrived. Chapman raised the occupants from the upper floor and showed his badge while Weaver headed around the back of the property. Lucy and Melissa hung back by the MI5 mobile unit that looked little different than any other silver-grey van.

"We need to ask you some questions regarding a meeting that took place at this residence earlier today," began Chapman. "May we come in? We don't have much time." He walked in without waiting for a response. The others followed, hearing the back door close and a shout from outside the back of the house. Weaver escorted a slender brunet back into the building and into the kitchen where he pushed her down onto a kitchen chair. The others gathered round, Chapman following the husband in from the front door. The thirties-something woman was attractive, with tanned skin, a strong, aquiline face and shabby-chic attire. She sat eyeing them with distrust as her husband, bearded and wearing beads and a hippy neck scarf, took a seat on the opposite side of the table. He gave his wife a hapless shrug that seemed to say *told you so*.

"Bates. Where is she?" asked Melissa, addressing the woman.

"Who? I don't know no Silvia Bates," the woman replied.

Lucy laughed. "Oh, you're a bright one, you are."

"Really? And I suppose you're also not part of Blue Solstice. Her coven. And you weren't present in the meeting in the back room today when she killed a woman."

Recognition flashed in hard eyes but the woman denied this also.

"What are your names?" asked Chapman.

"Ian Johnston and she's Margaret, my wife," said Ian.

"Know anything about a murder that took place here this afternoon?"

The couple exchanged glances. Ian shrugged.

"Gutless idiot," sniped Margaret. She turned to Chapman. "Are we being arrested?"

"No. Not yet, but you will be if you don't give us your full cooperation. So, you're going to tell us right now, where is Silvia Bates?"

"Silvia Bates?"

"Wanted for murder and other violent crimes. If you help locate her we'll give you police protection until she's incarcerated. If you withhold evidence, I can't guarantee... Well, put it this way, you'll regret it. Do you understand?"

The couple nodded.

"Can't help you, though. I don't know nothing," sneered Margaret, throwing her hands up. "Don't know no Silvia Bates. Don't know nothing about no murders."

Melissa noticed it then, the small tattoo on the inside of Margaret's wrist.

Tattoos

Melissa studied the mark until Margaret noticed and yanked her hand back. Margaret glanced at the wall clock at the end of the room.

"I've seen that tattoo before," Melissa told the others. "Bates has one just the same."

"Leave me alone. I have rights, you know," said Margaret. The police arrived with an explosion of flashing red and blue beyond the lace-curtained window.

"For God's sake. I said no lights!" Chapman stormed out.

"Let's see it," said Melissa. Margaret shook her head and protectively held her arm close to her body. Lucy gave Weaver and Freddy a nod and they restrained Margaret while she fought the tattooed arm out into the open so they could see.

"Get off me, you fascist pigs!"

"What *is* it?" asked Lucy.

"I don't know," said Melissa. "I was trying to work that out when I saw the one on Bates. There's this humped thing at the top. Some kind of animal? Then these crossing lines and what looks like a quarter moon."

"Blue Solstice? It's the coven symbol, isn't it?" asked Lucy. Margaret stared furiously

"That's it. That's what it is. Their symbol. And look, the animal at the top is a boar. A stylised boar. I've seen similar images used by the Celts."

"But why use a hog?" asked Lucy. "Seems a peculiar choice."

"The boar was a symbol of strength and virility in the Bronze Age and the Iron Age amongst the North-European Celtic peoples. Nothing to do with witchcraft to my knowledge."

Margaret laughed derisively.

"What would you know about witchcraft?"

"Shut your face and tell us where Bates is," said Lucy.

"Make up your mind, lover. I can't do both, can I?"

"Forget her," said Melissa. "She's not going to help. I bet she doesn't know where Bates is anyway. The police can have her." The boys released Margaret, who glared at them.

"That's a violation of my rights, that is." She rubbed at her arms where the boys had clamped her and looked at the clock on the wall again. Melissa wondered why.

"You want to know about violation of human rights? I work for a department that can make you disappear for good! Get rid of her."

Chapman and the police were audible from the back room as SOCO set to work. Melissa recounted the coven meeting. She remembered peering through the gap in the door. Remembered the witches talking as an argument about who was in charge broke. That was when Bates had killed the new leader with the contrap and then...

"Wait a minute. Bates arranged another meeting for tonight. Her *grand ordination*. It's happening at midnight but I don't know where. That's why she keeps looking at the clock. She's wondering if we're going to let her go in time for her to make it."

"Then I don't suppose it matters where the meeting is. It will be too late by then anyway. For Tyler, I mean. Her time runs out at eleven forty. That's in fifteen minutes, by the way."

Melissa checked the clock and swore.

"But the medics are going to try keeping her alive," she said. "We can't give up."

"Alright. So we need to know where this ordination is happening."

Melissa was already working on this. A distant word, some small, intangible thing was hiding in her mind and she couldn't quite pin it down.

"What did you call it?" she asked. "Something you said..."

"This ordination?"

"No, not that. What did you call the animal? The boar?"

"Oh, that. I'm not sure. A hog, I think."

"That's it. It's a hog. The meeting is happening at Hogs Back. At *the hill*. That's what she said. That's why they use it in their coven symbol. It's where they meet for sacred rituals."

"And Bates will be there tonight at midnight, but Hogs Back is a big space. We'd better get over there now and stake it out."

Margaret shot from the chair, making for the door.

"Stop her!" Lucy fell over a chair in her hurry to pursue. Weaver and Freddy reached the door as Margaret bolted through.

"Stop her! She's going to warn Bates," shouted Melissa as the boys gave chase. They all spilled out onto the road after Margaret but Melissa grabbed Lucy and stopped her from following.

"Let them take care of it. They've a head start and we need to get over to Hogs Back right away." The girls ran back inside to update Chapman.

"Okay. We'll go. Bates has vanished, lost us after the hotel somehow. I'll say this for her; she's slippery."

They climbed into the mobile unit, issued orders and sped away down the dark street. Melissa shared more about her bath tub experience that she thought might be pertinent.

"She knows a lot about the contrap. She asked about the fire symbol and I tried to mislead her, but I think she knows about the flight symbol. Probably knows how to use it. Thought I should say. It could have a bearing on how this thing goes. She'll be difficult to catch if she suddenly takes off into the night."

"Understood." Chapman gave a nod and made a call. When he finished with his phone he looked at Lucy.

"Just how fast is that bike of yours?"

*

Chapman closed the briefing.

"Good luck."

Agents checked over gear, collected radios from charger packs in the mobile unit and studied a map of the area. Melissa headed out to find her position, nerves churning her gut.

Lucy raced her Aprilia down the road to rein it in, roaring eagerly, at the side of the van. She tossed Chapman her spare helmet.

"Better hold on tight."

Chapman donned the helmet, swung his leg over and clung to Lucy as she throttled away. The Aprilia bolted with a squeal of tyres, Chapman's suit tails flagging wildly.

*

The black and yellow G-GMPX Explorer idled as Chapman led the way out from the hanger, buffeted by the whirling blades' windstorm. Lucy kept pace, hair flailing, as Chapman strode. Wind stung her face.

"You have your side arm?"

"Yes, Sir." Lucy patted her shoulder holster through her jacket.

"Good." In his right hand Chapman carried a black case. Lucy knew it housed a loaded LM7 sharp shooter's rifle with a powerful scope, her weapon of choice. She'd used one on the range and was a crack shot.

They reached the helicopter and he indicated for her to climb in the back. She boarded through the sliding door as Chapman climbed into the front and took a seat next to the pilot.

"Andrew, Lucy. Lucy, Andrew." With introductions done, Chapman gave a nod and Andrew handled controls, winding the blades up with an increasing roar. The craft danced briefly on the pad before tilting, nose down, and lifting off.

*

Hogs Back seemed larger now, at night, than it did in Melissa's memory of the place. She recalled playing here as a child, chasing friends beneath the trees on balmy summer afternoons and fighting away wasps crazed by the jam and Coke of family picnics. In her head Hogs Back was a friendly place. A fun place. But as she entered, alone and in the dark, squeezing past the green painted, metal swing-gate and the public footpath sign, the wooded knoll ahead emanated an altogether more sinister character. A slight wind rustled leaves and she flinched at every small noise of the night as deep shadows under the trees cloaked all manner of evils.

Others were also staking out the place, taking up their positions, concealing themselves in hiding places around the perimeter, but she couldn't see any of them. She checked the new watch Chapman had supplied: 11.42pm.

She tried to swallow a lump in her throat. *Has Tyler just died?*

She hoped Weaver and Freddy had taken out the

woman from the shop. If Bates received warning of their interest she would never show and all hope was lost even if the medics were keeping Tyler's body alive artificially. They still needed the contrap and they couldn't keep her hooked up to machines forever. Bates would disappear into the night like the nearby hidden agents and Tyler would be a ghost forever.

They had ditched phones and gone to radios and *in-ears* for the operation, but when she had tried to raise Lucy all she'd received was a rowdy mash of background noise, though she was sure she'd heard a voice in there somewhere.

She edged closer to the wooded zone. Chapman had given her a strategically important position, close to one of the few entrances. The rest of Hogs Back was hemmed in by houses and gardens, except for an expanse on the western edge where a hedge skirted to meet the gate. Most of the gathering witches would likely come by this route, including Bates. The thought sent a flotilla of wicked butterflies through Melissa's gut.

She looked behind at the gate, the hedge and the street beyond, where she could see one end of the primary school. No movement except the slight shimmer of the wind in the bushes.

She shivered and stepped into the shadows of the trees, heading for a dense mass of foliage on her left side at the very edge of the area. Here she found a tree trunk to lean upon, chewing her lip and making a quick study of her surroundings. It seemed as good a place as any. She waited and watched. Glanced at her watch again: 11.45 pm.

Fifteen minutes and counting.

She drew the Taser gun she had selected from the mobile unit, checked it over and counted out the charges. Enough to take down Bates and half the coven.

She tried to reach Lucy again but received the same din. Chapman's reply was just as garbled and noise-filled. Were they in the same place? Minutes ticked by. Finally

Freddy's voice hit her ear.

"We got her. Over."

"Fre..." Melissa caught herself. No real names over radio - only codes. "Pratt, glad to hear your voice. You have the queen bee? Confirm. Over."

"No, sorry to disappoint. Not the queen, just the worker who fled. Over."

It was still good news. Freddy and Weaver had taken Margaret out of the picture.

"Did she warn the queen? Over." Melissa whispered, keeping an eye on the approach to the trees through leaves, twigs and branches.

"We don't think so. She was on the run the whole chase. No time to make a call, but we're not a hundred percent on that. Over."

Silence on the line.

"Wish you were here. Lonely and exposed. Over."

"We have to deal with the worker, but hope to be there soon. Over."

"Great. Out."

No one mentioned Tyler. No one wanted to admit what may have just happened.

I wasn't even with her when she died.

*

Lucy looked down at the sprawling city far below. Street lamps and lights from windows peppered Watford's dark streets. The Explorer had more than enough fuel for their expected mission, so Chapman had ordered the pilot to hover less than half a mile away from Hogs Back until they had a confirmed sighting of Bates from sources on the ground.

Lucy scoped out the area through the police helicopter's thermal imaging camera. Smudges of light showed her agents concealed about the park, even from this distance. She watched as other figures, radiating a more obvious light, closed on the meeting point.

The witches were gathering.

Lucy shifted her view, zeroing in on a stationary ambulance only two streets from the park. She felt sick. Tyler was in there, wired up to machines that tested her vital signs. More machines at the ready to bellow air into her stagnating lungs and pump blood around her body. *Are they operating now?* Lucy looked away, focusing back on the park where blurred heat signatures drew close to enter the perimeter.

*

Footsteps startled Melissa. A figure passed the gate and walked across grass only feet from her position. She wondered briefly if she had picked a hiding place too close to the gate but the moment of panic passed when the figure continued into the woods without noticing her. A couple of women were next to pass her, talking in whispers too low to hear. More came in and Melissa scrutinised each one, seeking only Bates. She counted, but didn't really care how many came. If Bates wasn't among them, what did it matter?

Thirteen, fourteen, fifteen. Surely they are all here. She tried to recall how many she'd seen in the back of the newsagent's, but really had no idea how many had been present, or how many she had seen leaving. The gap in the door had shown her the smallest sliver of the room. In any case, Bates was not among them.

12:04 a.m.

If Bates is coming, she's late to the party.

The slow stream of visitors had stopped and Melissa was alone in an abandoned end of a dark park again. Her radio was silent. Others were watching and waiting for Bates too, not wanting to give away their positions by even the softest of whispers. *But where is Bates?* Melissa couldn't stand it any longer. She had to know if any others were heading down the road to the park and she risked a jaunt out to the gate and peered around the hedge. The street was empty. She retreated, wanting to know what was happening further in. *Are the witches all gathered? Where are they? What are they doing? Has Bates arrived via a different route?* There were areas of hedge not as dense as others. It would certainly be possible for Bates to have slipped through somewhere. Melissa had to know. She left her hiding place and wormed her way deeper into the park.

*

Lucy watched them assemble, wondering if comms were down. No word of a sighting of Bates and yet all who were due had apparently arrived. A clear circle of human shaped signatures was clear, even through the partial covering of trees. She felt hopeless. Bates wasn't coming. Margaret had somehow managed to warn her. She and the team were now only wasting their time. Bates was gone, along with the contrap.

And so was Tyler.

The Queen

Melissa negotiated trees and shrubs, edging the outskirts of the park. At her back, gardens and homes were in shadow. No lights, barring the occasional bathroom or bedroom window. Traffic on the encompassing roads had also quelled. Before her, trees blocked her view and it was all she could do to creep without tripping or making her presence obvious. She stopped in her tracks when she glimpsed movement through branches. *The coven...* She crept closer and found a vantage point behind dense foliage from where she could look out and watch. The circle was complete and witches talked in whispers. Clearly nothing official had begun. They were waiting for something.

But what?

12:09 a.m.

A murmur fired the circle animatedly. *Something's happening out there!* She saw several witches pointing up into the night and tried to see why, but trees were in the way. She was considering moving to a better spot when

Bates made her entrance, descending to the centre of the coven circle from the sky, to the amazement of all. Melissa pressed the talk button and whispered into her mouthpiece.

"Bates just flew in. No broomstick required." There followed some confusion as, she guessed, every other agent with a reasonable line of sight had tried to radio similar news. Chapman responded over background noise.

"Hold positions. We have visual. We're heading over."

Melissa wondered at the delay.

"Your queen has arrived," announced Bates with sickening glee, turning on the spot as awed whispers evolved into applause of admiration from the coven.

Deluded or what?

"Let the ceremony begin!" Bates sat cross-legged at the centre as the others marked symbols and rings in the grass with stones. Candles were lit and placed at intervals and the coven members took places at the edge of the outer circle, knelt and began to chant. Melissa tried to distinguish the words that were being uttered but a distant throbbing grew louder and drowned out all other sound as a helicopter approached.

Bates came out of a trance and looked up. She realised the helicopter was not passing by but was homing in on her.

"Run!" she cried, getting to her feet and grabbing the contrap from her shirt. She worked the small controls and lifted off the ground.

Chapman's voice crackled over the radio.

"Green light! Green light!"

Melissa didn't notice. She had already broken cover, dashing out and fumbling with her Tazer gun, trying to grab Bates before she climbed beyond reach. Vaguely aware of other agents doing the same, she ran and leapt but was too late. She came down with a jarring thump, sprawled on the grass, where she watched in fury as Bates escaped. She shot off two darts but missed, the second one falling short of Bates' increasing climb. *Why did Chapman wait so long? What was he thinking? We had her! We bloody well had her!*

"The queen has flown. Repeat, the queen has flown. Over," an agent nearby radioed in.

"Roger that. In pursuit," said Chapman through Melissa's earpiece.

*

Lucy slid the door open for a better look. She had seen Bates leave the ground in the infrared camera but had quickly lost her when she shot off-screen. Now she trained the scope sights of the LM7 on the green-coated target. Bates was clearing rooftops, moving quickly through the night sky, but so was the Explorer as the pilot tracked her trajectory with practised skill. Lucy relaxed into the shot. Held her breath, held the gun snuggly. Not too tight. Not too loose. Just as her training had taught her. She felt the pressure on the trigger rising for the kill.

No. Not this way. If the contrap smashes to pieces on a road, Tyler will be trapped forever in the realm of the Ghost Portal. She shoved the gun aside and yelled at the pilot.

"GET RIGHT ON TOP OF HER. CLOSE AS YOU CAN."

Andrew gave an affirmative nod and the Explorer lurched forwards, churning air. Lucy ditched her headset, gripped the edge of the door and waited, buffeted by the wind, watching as they closed on Bates. Chapman noticed Lucy had ditched her weapon and frowned, removed his headset to shout.

"Don't even think about it!"

Lucy didn't take her eyes off Bates. *A little closer. Just a little closer.*

She leapt from the helicopter to free fall, spreading arms and angling her body to steer towards Bates. For the first time, she considered the consequences of failing to hit home and feared a messy death. *Oh well, at least it will be quick.* She pushed the thought from her mind and locked onto the green coat, plummeting at a rate that outdid the contrap's powers and hit Bates like a lead eagle from on high. They grappled, fighting for possession of the contrap. It would not carry both their weights. Lucy remembered the occasion Tyler had tried and failed to carry passengers. Bates clawed at Lucy's face. Bit her hand. The contrap remained clamped in Bates' fist as they dropped, tumbling, all power from the flight symbol lost. They smashed into the branches of a tree and hit the ground with bone-splintering force, Bates first. Lucy, cushioned by Bates' hapless body, rolled away in agony, grabbing her left leg. It felt like it had been blown in half. She checked it through a silent scream and only then took the time to swear. It was broken at the thigh and she couldn't walk. Could barely move. Still, she was in much better shape than Bates. Lucy dragged herself over to Bates' crushed body and wriggled the contrap's chain free. Bates' curled fingers gave it up easily, her glassy eyes gazing through Lucy.

"What goes up..." Lucy told her, putting the chain over her own head and tucking the contrap safely into her shirt. She hauled herself into a more comfortable position, wincing at every movement, to make a better assessment of her damaged leg. She'd had all the training. Knew the risks of a broken thigh. Internal bleeding. Infection. And so on. Judging by the angle of her leg, the break was well below the femoral artery. That was good; less danger of her bleeding to death through blood pooling in internal cavities caused by ruptured bone. She lay back and waited in the strangely quiet night, the distant drone of the helicopter approaching the only sound. She looked around, wondering where she had landed and saw a large house nearby and, opposite, the blue shimmer of a swimming pool. She was in someone's garden. The helicopter hovered when it arrived directly overhead and a searchlight illuminated her in a blinding circle on the ground. The pain was excruciating. She rummaged in her jacket. Found and popped several painkillers, gulping them down dry.

She checked herself over as best she could, felt blood in her hair, and examined her left elbow to find that, too, was bleeding. She didn't need a doctor to point out her insides were deeply bruised, and by the pain in her chest she presumed she'd cracked, if not shattered, at least one rib.

Two minutes later, Melissa arrived, breathless, but relieved to find Lucy alive.

"Hi."

"Thought you were a gonner." Melissa removed her coat, rolled it up and placed it behind Lucy's head for a pillow. "Don't get *too* comfy. There's an ambulance five minutes away. They'll be here for you soon."

"Thanks," said Lucy, letting her head back. "Take the contrap to Tyler."

Melissa stooped to lift the chain from Lucy's head.

"You'll be alright here?"

"Go! Quickly! Maybe it's still not too late."

"Right. Hey, you did okay, Mojo." Melissa grasped the contrap firmly in her fist and ran. She knew the location of Tyler's ambulance, two roads from Hogs Back. She sprinted as never before, only hoping her heart wouldn't give up before finishing. She left the garden and the big house behind and dashed down the first road, not caring when she inconvenienced night-time drivers. They would see her. They would slow. Let her pass. She turned a corner, preparing to speed on the straight, but a man blocked her path a few steps in front. She slowed, meaning to dodge past and continue but he side stepped into her line and she looked up to his face, puzzled.

"Good evening," said Johnathan Hatherow. "You know? It's been quite entertaining – watching this little game unfold. Very... enlightening, I'd say."

No! Not now. Not when I'm so close!

Melissa took a step back and felt for her Tazer.

"Oh, I see I've surprised you!" He smiled. "You really thought old Hatherow was a creeping cripple, hobbling with a stick." He mimicked an old man staggering with his walking stick before straightening and unsheathing the long, slim blade concealed within. He levelled the tip at Melissa's throat across the space between them and nonchalantly discarded the sheath. "It's not the first time my little ruse has proved useful."

Melissa reached for her Taser but stopped when he lurched forward, his point stopping an inch from her skin.

"Uh-uh. Don't be silly, my dear. Just hand it over and I'll be on my way."

Melissa turned and fled back towards Lucy.

"You'll have to catch me first," she shouted. She pulled her Taser and loaded a fresh cartridge on the move, shouldered her arm round to aim at Hatherow, but he was close behind and lashed out with his sword, catching her hand before she could fire. The blade opened her flesh with a searing pain and her Taser clattered across the road. Now unarmed, she knew her only chance was to outrun him or he would kill her and take the contrap. She wondered if she would survive the night and seriously doubted it. She rounded the corner and almost ran into another figure coming her way.

Thank God!

She bolted into Freddy's arms as he pulled a gun on Hatherow. Hatherow slowed to a stop.

"Drop it," said Freddy, holding out the P99 and aiming for the chest a meagre two metres before him. Hatherow took a step forward, testing his opponent's resolve. Freddy shuffled back, taking Melissa with him.

"Where's Weaver?" whispered Melissa.

"I thought he was right with me," said Freddy, eyes fixed upon Hatherow.

Hatherow edged closer.

"Why don't you just shoot me?" he asked. "I'm not going to leave without the device. I've come too close for that."

Freddy's gun hand shook visibly.

"He'll do it. He'll blow you away," warned Melissa, hoping Hatherow would back down, but he kept coming as she and Freddy backed away.

"Stop, or I'll shoot," said Freddy loudly, but Hatherow seemed to doubt it.

"Really? You'll shoot a man in cold blood? Out here in the street? You know, we're being watched by some of the best curtain-twitchers in town."

"Don't listen to him," said Melissa. "It's self-defence. And it's your job." Freddy squeezed the trigger tightly, bracing himself for recoil but couldn't shoot. Hatherow was right.

Footsteps brought their talk to a halt as Weaver approached from further down the road. Weaver's gunshot echoed in the barren street. Freddy stared at the cold end of his gun as Hatherow buckled, dropped the sword and crumpled to the ground grasping a shattered knee.

"Go!" Weaver said to Melissa, jutting his chin and holstering his gun. "Tyler's waiting."

Melissa turned and ran.

Separation

A streetlamp blinked. Lights glowed yellow from ambulance windows. Melissa hammered a fist against the closed back doors, breath heaving and hands shaking.

"Let me in! Let me in! I have it."

The doors burst open and Marshall helped her up inside where machines beeped and lights flashed and medics monitored Tyler's cerebral activity.

"Am I too late? Did anything change?"

"No change as far as we can tell," said Marshall. "We haven't operated."

She took the contrap and set it to the *Ghost Portal*, jittering hands making manipulation of the small switch a challenge. She turned the contrap, pulled its lever, and peered into the lens, trying all the while to steady herself.

Inside the contrap, Zebedee saw it first.

"The portal! It's opening!" He pointed.

"At last," said Tyler watching as the portal brightened and she ran to it. She looked up through the lens and was relieved to see Melissa's desperate face.

"Tyler! You okay?"

"Never better. Do it!"

"Phasmatis licentia," Melissa gasped out the words. Pearlescent blue light glimmered from the crystal and dashed out, filling the ambulance's small space with dazzling tendrils and folds. *"Corpus resurrectio!"* It disappeared just as quickly, flashing into Tyler's chest as a second entity left the portal, coalescing at Tyler's side to astound the medics.

"Wotcher, Mel."

"Hi, Albert." Melissa closed the portal, set the switch to the *Safeguarding Skull* and hung the contrap around Tyler's neck.

Tyler felt the release, like drawing breath after holding it for a year. Like a burning iron plunging into iced water, she quenched into her physical form. Her entire body racked and shook on the ambulance gurney as she overcompensated, hyperventilating increasingly. Her hands and feet were numb and cold. She could barely feel them at all and a shrill tone shrieked hideously inside her head. She opened her eyes and fixed upon the first person she saw.

Melissa.

She calmed, feeling Melissa's hands seeking hers. Drawing the warmth. Clasping her tightly.

"It will be alright," said Melissa, her own fears gradually subsiding. Tyler calmed. Breathed. Tried to rise, until medics eased her back down.

"Woh there. Not so fast. All in good time. We need to check you over first. And we have to unhook you. Watch the wires."

"You've been flat on your back for a week," said Melissa. "Better take things steady."

Tyler nodded. She rested, taking in the apparatus surrounding her and attached to her by various cables. She felt a shaved patch of scalp near one temple and she noticed someone had changed her clothes. She wore a surgical gown. A hint of irritation passed. She had a list in the pocket of those jeans.

"Thanks Mel."

Melissa fell on her and hugged her, ignoring the protesting medics.

"You made it."

Tyler battled to breathe through the bear hug.

"Yeah. Yeah, I made it," she managed to squeeze out hoarsely.

"Oh, sorry." Melissa loosened her hold. "It's just that, well, I thought you were gone for good that time."

"Yeah. Me too. Where am I? Where's Mojo? What's going on?"

"We're in Watford. Lucy took out Bates mid-air by jumping from a helicopter. You should have seen her. It was amazing! Bates is dead. Lucy's broken a leg. An ambulance should be with her by now, though. How do you feel?"

"Kind of hazy," said Tyler, looking round at the ambulance interior. "I feel different somehow. I'm hungry."

"Probably just shock," said Melissa. "You cold? You feel cold."

"Freezing. What's a girl got to do to get a blanket around here?"

Medics tripped over themselves to find blankets and Melissa helped her wrap up.

"We have hot tea if you fancy it," said the driver from up front. They passed steaming tea back to Tyler and she sat up with some help, and sipped gratefully. The tea tasted amazing.

"Oh yeah," she sighed cupping her hand around the plastic mug. "That's good." She felt solid. Felt alive. Felt human.

A doctor settled at her side.

"If you're feeling strong enough to get up, we'll unplug you."

"Yes, of course. Just one minute." Tyler turned to Melissa. "Pen and paper?" Melissa produced both.

Tyler began a new list. One that wouldn't evaporate by the time she returned to it.

Meet with friends for hot chocolate
Take some time out
Walk on a beach eating ice-cream
Buy and eat anything I want
Get warm. Stay warm
Visit family
Sleep in
Do nothing
Holiday

Inevitably, her mind turned back to her cause and with resignation she added three new items.

Work out how Hitler escaped the Ghost Portal
Find and destroy Hitler and the three remaining gloves
Find a man and start an outward bounds centre in the county

She smiled to herself as she folded the list and handed it to Melissa.

"Keep this safe for me, will you?"

"I'm so glad we got the time wrong."

"You did what?"

*

The hospital ward was stuffy with an ever-present smell of disinfectant and heat from the many machines punctuating the bays. Tyler and Melissa gathered round Lucy's bed and doodled on her cast with marker pens, much to Lucy's annoyance.

"It doesn't matter anyway. I'm painting it black as soon as I get out of here."

"Does it hurt?" asked Melissa.

"Not as much as learning your friends, who you trusted with your life, dropped the ball and forgot to make a note of the time," jibed Tyler. "It's nice to know a text from Freddy Carter is more important than my life."

"You'll have to drop it at some point," said Melissa, giving Tyler a forbearing look before turning back to Lucy. "When do you get out?"

"Soon, I hope. Maybe in a day or two. They just want to be sure there're no complications."

"Weaver been in?"

"Just once. He doesn't like hospitals."

"Man, there's some ghosts in here," said Tyler, looking around. "Don't you feel it?" Melissa and Lucy exchanged looks.

"No," they said in unison.

"What are you talking about?" asked Melissa.

"I don't know. It's just a feeling. It's like I feel them here. I know where they are."

"Shall I fetch a nurse?" asked Lucy. "I have a call button."

"Seriously?" asked Melissa.

"Seriously. You don't feel it?"

"Not so much."

"Uh-uh." Lucy shook her head.

"Oh. It's just me then."

"You feeling alright?"

"Well, you know I said I felt strange when I finally got back – in the ambulance – remember? The feeling hasn't ever really gone away and, everywhere I go, I can sense them."

"Sense who?"

"Ghosts. I can sense ghosts. I just seem to know when they're close by. Maybe something's changed. Maybe the chasm affected me somehow, or maybe it's because I came so close to being dead – you know – almost died, but didn't. Maybe the separation went on too long. Albert's here," she said, brightening. "Did you know?"

"No. He's not visible," said Lucy. "Can you see him?"

"Not exactly," said Tyler. "But I know he's here. He's standing right beside Mel. They can hide themselves from us if they choose, remember?"

Melissa recoiled with a shiver.

"Stop it. That's creepy!" she objected.

Tyler laughed.

"Sorry. Didn't mean to freak you out."

"Well you *are* freaking me out. No offence, Albert." Melissa chomped a grape and took another from the bunch. "Well, whatever the reason, I guess that could come in handy."

"No kidding. That's awesome," agreed Lucy, eyeing the white, plastic TV set on the drop down arm over her bed. "Wait a minute. Here it is." She unplugged earphones from the unit, turned up the volume and swivelled the screen so they could all watch the news report.

"Further protests today as supporters of the latest activist group surface on London's streets. TAAN, known otherwise as The Activists Against Nazism, have this morning staged a march through London massing at the Houses of Parliament with chants and placards." The reporter continued as video of the march filled the screen. "A spokesman for the underground movement at today's protest gave a statement, requesting anonymity." The video cut to a blacked-out and blurred shot of a head and shoulders.

"TAAN is a peaceful organisation with one goal: To oust Nazism from our streets and our communities. It's creeping in everywhere. People just don't see it because it's actually moving under the cover of political correctness. Extremist groups, who easily get the sympathy vote and the protection of so-called *political correctness* on religious grounds, or even because of ethnic minority, are infiltrating, and being infiltrated with, Nazi philosophies. We need to look more closely at these so called religious groups. They don't call

themselves Nazis, of course, but they're just the same."
The shot returned to the march where placards read
NAZIS OUT! and *T.A.A.N. - KEEP BRITAIN CLEAN!* The
reporter continued.

"An anonymous letter to the press containing
allegations of governmental infiltration by Nazi
organisations on a global scale has also been claimed as
the work of TAAN."

Lucy grinned.

"And the cat is out. Thank you TAAN."

"Chapman's gonna freak!"

The Start

Steam fogged glass and the scent of freshly brewed coffee permeated the air. Tyler sipped hot chocolate and stared at Lucy's cast, which protruded hazardously beyond their table. Adolf's was quiet. Tyler and her friends were the only customers, so they talked freely when the café staff were busy away from their corner.

"That's the scary thing," said Weaver. "What the spokesman of TAAN said on the news is true and we know it. This is just the start. There's going to be a war because of this and it's time we pulled our heads from the sand."

"The spirit of the oppressor," mumbled Tyler. She knew it was safe to talk. Sensed that Albert was the only ghost in the room.

"The oppressor, Hitler, Nazism, whatever you call it, it's here and it's happening. It's really happening."

"Alright, Weaver. We get it," groaned Freddy. "And we're gonna fight it, but right now we're trying to enjoy a quiet coffee. Okay? Anyway, nowt we can do about it at the moment. Not now Chapman's sending us all back into training."

"Well, I'm just saying," said Weaver. "It's only until Lucy's leg's better. Meantime, others are on the NVF network case, INCI, and it's proving bigger than anyone ever dreamt. We've found money linking London, Berlin, New York, Brazil, Syria, Russia, Iraq, Libya, Zimbabwe, South Africa, Palestine and Pakistan - the list goes on. It's frightening, but you'll soon be back out there. Chapman wants you girls working as a team. Says it's the only reason you've survived this long. He thinks you work well together because you cover each other's backs."

"Guess he's right," said Lucy. She supped hot, bitter, black coffee.

"I never really thanked you, did I?" said Tyler. "Thanks for taking the fall for me, Mojo."

"'S'okay," said Lucy. "You'd do the same for me."

"So when's the cast coming off?" asked Melissa.

"Another four weeks. The doctors reckon after that, at least four months before I'll be using it again. Then I'll have some serious rehabilitation to get into shape. It sucks."

"Hatherow has some rehab too," said Weaver. "But he'll be doing most of that behind bars. His trial starts tomorrow and he was refused bail."

"Not that he can *run* anywhere," sniggered Freddy. Melissa turned to Tyler.

"So, you searched the Shivering Pool and the chasm, and no Hitler?" Tyler nodded.

"He's not in there. He's not in the contrap at all."

"I don't understand," said Freddy. "I thought you said you put him in there."

"I did, but he's not there anymore. He's escaped. I'm not sure how."

"You really certain he's not in there somewhere?" asked Freddy indicating the contrap partially protruding from Tyler's neckline.

"I'm sure. I just risked my life checking."

"So where is he, then?"

"He's out there somewhere. He's busily working away, planning, plotting, building armies, stirring trouble. Did any of those names ring bells? Syria, Russia, Iraq, Libya, Zimbabwe, Palestine and Pakistan? He's out there working on his master plan: World War Three. He's stirring up nation against nation through racial hatred, prejudice and greed. That much I know. The big question is *How did he get out?* Ever since I put him in the *Ghost Portal*, I've had the contrap. It's been bothering me. I can't figure it out. Who let him out of the contrap?"

"Wait a minute," said Melissa. "You didn't always have it since Hitler went in. For a few minutes Bagshot had it, that is, until he lost it on Westminster Bridge."

"That's right," said Lucy. "And then Mengele fetched it out of the Thames. You saw him. That's when you took it back. So Mengele also had the contrap for a few minutes, though, granted, he was under water for most of that time."

They looked at one another, thinking, and sipping cooling drinks.

"When you have eliminated the impossible, whatever remains, however improbable, must be the truth," said Freddy.

They all looked at him.

"Sherlock Holmes."

"He's right," said Melissa. "Think about it."

"Well, it wasn't Bagshot. I watched him the whole time he had the contrap. I followed him through the city onto the bridge and he had the contrap in his pocket for the duration. The only time he took it out was when he paused on the bridge and that was when Travis tricked him into the portal."

"So, following Freddy's, sorry, Sherlock's logic, it can only have been Josef Mengele who helped Hitler escape the portal."

They looked at Lucy as though she was mad.

"It must have been. There was no other time that the contrap was in someone else's hands. Mengele did it while he was still underwater."

Tyler's mind was a-buzz.

"And what a coincidence. Who appeared to be their new Führer when we were trying to escape the castle, in Brazil?"

"Josef Mengele," said Lucy and Melissa together.

"The gloved ghost of Josef Mengele. The gloved ghost that could not be summoned out. Not even with the most powerful artefact that exists – the human remains." Tyler looked around at her friends in turn. "Do you get it?" She recalled occasions when she had witnessed strange mood swings in Mengele. "Do you remember me saying there was something weird about Mengele? It was like two people trapped in the same body. One minute he was smiling and was his normal, *charming* self, the next he was like a raging animal."

"But... No..."

"It can't be. Can it?" wondered Lucy.

"Mengele must have had a strong summoning artefact with him to be able to call out Hitler's ghost from the portal, but it's possible," said Tyler.

"It's more than possible. It's the only explanation left. That's exactly what he did. He had an artefact already. Something small tucked away in his pocket: a medal, a badge or a cufflink. He waited on the bank of the Thames until it was safe for him to go in without drawing too much attention. He swam out to the contrap, knowing exactly where it was because he could sense it. He dived for it and engaged the *Safeguarding Skull* while he took out the artefact. He switched to the *Ghost Portal* and quickly used the artefact to call out Hitler's ghost and rescued him from the Room of Faces."

"But you didn't see Hitler's ghost with Mengele when he came out of the river, did you?" asked Freddy.

"Don't you get it?" asked Lucy. "Hitler's ghost joined Mengele. They're in the same body."

"The body of some poor kid."

"Yeah."

"I'll have to check, of course," said Tyler.

"Check?"

"Check what?" asked Freddy.

"With the contrap. Go back to the Thames and make a dive with the contrap. Use the *Past Eye* to watch exactly what happened under the water."

"Good idea," said Lucy. "All we really have is a theory. It would be good to know for sure what we're dealing with."

"I don't like it, but I agree," said Melissa. "Check. If we're right it'll explain why we couldn't summon Mengele's glove. Perhaps we need an artefact for Hilter's ghost too, before either of them can be summoned."

Freddy gawped around, slack-jawed at the gathering.

"This is *totally* bonkers."

Nobody disagreed.

*

Albert had been withdrawn since Tyler's return to her normal state. She felt his sorrow. In a way it was like mourning a close friend's death. In the portal and the chasm they had been able to touch, to know each other on a deeper level. Now she was removed, untouchable and unreachable again and Tyler bore the same grief, her only compensation the unnatural chill that flashed through her each time he came near.

She turned over in her bed, in her new bedroom, in their new apartment and watched him secretly. He stood by the window vigilantly peering into the night, watching for ghosts and the blue shimmer of the gloves in the London streets below. One day, one night, they would come for the contrap but Albert would be ready. The contrap was back in its lead box on her bedside table.

"They're out there somewhere, aren't they, Albert?"

"For sure, Missy. They're there, somewhere. Don't

you fret, though. We'll get 'em. Maybe we'll get 'em before they finds us. Go to sleep, Missy. I'll watch through the night."

She slipped from the covers to join him at the window, missing his touch.

"I can't sleep anyway. I'm glad you're here, Albert."

Below, in the road, late night drivers navigated lamp lit uncertainty and sidewalks bustled with dark figures. Albert reached for her but stopped.

"We'll be alright, Missy. You'll see."

Acknowledgements

My thanks go to Matt Cooper for help researching into an appropriate motorcycle for Lucy.

My thanks also to Anne West for assistance with research into Auschwitz and other death camps (for which the chasm is a metaphor).

The Brimstone Chasm was edited by Edward Field.

4981887R00157

Printed in Great Britain
by Amazon.co.uk, Ltd.,
Marston Gate.